Octavia's Journey

A tale of the glass singers of Albermarle

By Lynette Hill

Copyright © 2015 Lynette Hill

All rights reserved.

ISBN: 1519540159
ISBN-13: 978-1519540157

DEDICATION

Once again, to Ruth.
Thank you for everything.

And to everyone who loves dragons: Enjoy!

Acknowledgements

Dan Webb for his wonderful cover art and illustrations;

Miriam Selwyn, Louise Burnham, Sara Brook, Sara Jane Errington, Jenn Fay and Mary Tanzer, among many others, for their unflagging encouragement and support;
The Cat Vacuuming Society Writers Group in Arlington, Virginia (USA) for their insights into the character of Octavia;

Milton Keynes Art Centre (UK) for good company and space to write. Finally, I would like to thank the Smithsonian Institution of Washington D.C. for holding a most amazing festival in 2002 celebrating the traditional arts of the people who live along the fabled Silk Road. This is where I first encountered Tibetan throat singing and became inspired to write the Glass Singers series.

CONTENTS

Alive and well
Knowing
Aftermath

Sandrigal teases the birds
Are you worried about something?
The healing gift fades

We sing the songs of dragons
Bad news travels slowly
No more impossible choices

Who's fault?
Water reflects, but not the monster
One last try

On the balcony
Singing with Mama
An argument overheard

Did someone call me?
Dragon tales
The apprentice challenge

A cleansing
A spy reports
Kitchen boy

On the river
A busy night
Are you Khelani?

Why Robbie persists
Deep in the forest
Bottling

If
A visit from the guard sergeant
New friends

Time to create the next piece?
Oleny
The Queen prepares her trap

Private tutoring
Hope
The Liar's Revenge

Hammered
At the library
The River Rat and the Glass Princess

A curse on this house
The Lochsa Rapids
Tested

Peacock tile in the east
In the presence of the Queen
Inside the looking glass

Sandrigal
Release the monster
Trapped

Author's note
About the author

Octavia's Journey   *by Lynette Hill*

Alive and well

    Octavia pulled her mass of dark braids into a tight bun with quick, practiced hands. She glanced at the mirror to make sure all was in order. Her eyes flinched instantly away from the round glass's silver surface. Taking a calming breath, she forced herself to look back at her reflection. She kept looking at it until her heart's pounding slowed to normal. Only the undisturbed image of her own black eyes returned her determined gaze.

    "I am Octavia Breydon, a glass singer of Verre House." Alone in her own room in the early morning no one else would hear. "I survived the monstrous mirror. Perhaps not by my own voice, but still. I survive." She took another breath. "And as a result, I have a new gift to share."

    Octavia smiled. Her double smiled back.

    See, her image seemed to tell her, *all is well. All will be well.*

    "Octavia?" Sylvia called. "Are you awake?"

    Halfnote, youngest apprentice of Verre House of Glass Singing, put the heavy tray down on the table outside her grandparents' door. Both Grand Master and Madame Verre had recently recovered from the plague and so chose to breakfast in their own chambers.

    Halfnote raised a hand to knock. She paused at the sound of voices inside. Of course she shouldn't listen. Of course she couldn't help overhearing anyway.

    "Fortis, you look nearly as ill as when you suffered from plague. Shall we ask Octavia in to diagnose this new ailment?" Grandma asked. Halfnote could not make out the words in Grandpa's rumbling response.

    "Honestly, Fortis. Must you worry? Surely this new ability of Octavia's is a blessing and not a curse. She is well. Thanks to her we are all alive and well."

    "This apparent gift ... I'm afraid it means that the tainted mirror's influence continues," Grandpa said.

    Halfnote sucked in her breath. From the sound of it, so did

Octavia's Journey   *by Lynette Hill*

Grandma. "Will Octavia become *mortolo* after all?"

"Not a monster, no. I believe that danger is past, dragons be praised." Halfnote let out a relieved breath.

"But ..." Halfnote strained to hear the answer.

"I don't know," Grandpa admitted. "I just don't know what will happen next. *That* is what concerns me. I have read every scroll in our library. I am writing to all of the most learned scholars. As far I can find out, no one else has ever survived the monstrous glass. That's why I asked Physician Cornelius to observe Octavia as she makes her diagnoses. If anything unusual happens perhaps he will know what to do. And you may be right. I may worry unnecessarily."

"But," Grandma prompted again. "You must have some reason for your concern."

"There are rumors, ancient stories of glass walkers; those who deliberately entered the living glass and returned."

"Alive?"

"Ye...es, though not always unchanged."

"Octavia appears ... better for her experience."

"I hope so. But she will now certainly be of interest to anyone who dabbles in the dark arts. I have already received some enquiries which concern me. If anyone is still foolish enough to try creating living glass, they will most certainly have an interest in Octavia."

Halfnote considered her own encounter with the mirror. Would it affect her as well? She didn't feel any different. She wanted to ask Grandpa but now certainly didn't seem like the right time.

"Sandrigal, I do not understand. Explain what is happening in Albermarle. How could anyone survive the *mortolo*?" Bhima Suresha Niliya Anula, Queen Mother of Samoya, demanded. She stood in an outer room of her tower chambers, peering out the great window at the clear morning sky. Queen's Companion Clara stood straight-backed beside the curtain, hands clasped, attentive to whatever her mistress might require.

"I do beg your pardon, Brightest Star," Sandrigal, the Queen's Scryer, replied. Daylight reflected off the intricately intertwined red and silver dragons decorating the giant looking glass's frame. "I can add little to what you already know. As far as I can tell, your great-grandson's report was correct in every detail."

"So this Singer Octavia was taken by the unformed mirror?"

"Indeed, my Queen. Grand Master Verre was already stricken with plague when they attempted to make the healing mirror. He fainted at a critical point. The singer naturally moved to protect her grandfather. She saved him but was devoured herself."

"Yet she survived even though the mirror was destroyed."

"As the Intan reported."

"Was the *mortolo* truly destroyed?"

"Yes, Illumined One. Completely destroyed."

"And yet, Verre House discovered and disseminated the cure to a plague no one else could stop. What of this Octavia? My agents say she now diagnoses the sick. Apparently she brought back remedies for all other ailments as well."

"It does appear that the singer absorbed the unformed mirror's healing properties. She spends her hours observing the ill and providing remedies, as a mirror would."

"A human *Hygeia potencia*," Queen Anula murmured. "In all your days, Sandrigal, have you ever heard of such a thing?"

"No, Great Lady. There is no precedent that I am aware of."

"Has she become a true creature of the glass? I wonder ... I have heard stories of others who walked through living mirrors. Not *mortolo*, of course, but formed and settled mirrors such as yourself. Having entered a mirror and returned once, do you think this Octavia could do so again?"

A moment passed. "It seems likely."

"Yes. Excellent. You will bring her to me. You *can* bring her to me, can't you, Sandrigal?"

His silver surface rippled. Clara thought the looking glass seemed agitated, if that was possible of a solid object.

"Sandrigal. Answer. Can you bring her to me?"

"My Gracious Queen ... the matter is complex. Much depends on Melampus. Perhaps ... at the peak of the full moon ... and we do not yet know if she has changed ..."

"How can we know that?"

"Further observations ..."

"Pah. The time for watching is done. Now is the time to act. If we wait too long someone else will take her. We will know for certain if she can do what I require when she enters the mirror."

"Apologies, Beautiful Majesty, but I must recommend caution. If she has not been changed, Octavia might still be brought to us by Melampus; however, once she enters the mirror she will not leave it. To destroy such a talent ..."

"Once inside the mirror, changed or not, will the glass singer do as I require?"

"If she survives the entry, Bright Star, I believe so. However, I do not believe she could live through such a thing unless she has undergone a true metamorphosis."

"Surely this healing ability she now manifests is a sign of transformation."

"Not ... necessarily."

"Enough, Sandrigal. You grow as cautious as the girl's cowardly grandfather. It is time to put theory into practice. Clara, call Melampus. Our preparations begin."

It looked almost like a normal day at Verre House, Halfnote thought as she joined the breakfast table. She sat with Robbie and cook Alma at the end closest to the kitchen. The rest of the apprentices sat next to them. The older staff, those with the hard-earned rank of singer, argued noisily about the uses of melody at the other end.

Octavia and their grandparents were the only usual occupants missing. No visitors remained. The now healthy Samoyan royal party and their shrill-voiced crown prince, the Intan Negarawan, left as soon as the quarantine was lifted. Even new master Lorraine and her husband Geoffrey had returned to their own home.

Halfnote sighed. Mama and Papa were also gone. They left the day after the Samoyans, eager to collect baby Cadie and cousin Mischa from the northern village of Haverley. They would return in a few days, but she always missed them when they were away.

Alma, Verre House's portly cook, surprised everyone with the announcement of a trip to the market.

"Can I go?" Marissa, the oldest apprentice, asked eagerly. "I'm desperate for some fresh air."

"Oh me too," the other apprentices echoed. Halfnote and Robbie just grinned at each other. As the youngest apprentices they *had* to go to the market with Alma.

"Settle down. I can't take everyone. Dan, Galliard, you'll stay and do the washing up."

Galliard, the oldest boy apprentice stopped whistling his scales long enough to nod. Dan, the next oldest boy, scowled and dropped his fork onto his plate with a loud clatter. Alma ignored him.

"When you've finished the dishes, go see Master Verre. He needs to send some messages to the aviary, to let your families know that you are well."

Galliard whistled cheerful agreement. Dan's scowl deepened.

"Is the aviary even open?" Frank, the oldest singer, asked. He blinked at Alma through thick spectacles.

"I think so. They always send the first flight of pigeons out about dawn. Didn't you hear them this morning? All that fluttering and cooing just after first light?"

"But what about the market? The quarantine only ended a couple of days ago. Will the farmers know they can come back?"

The cook shrugged. "Somehow word always gets around. I have to think that at least the closest farmers will come in. People still need to eat; and to earn a living. We can't be the only household in Albermarle running out of just about everything. Robbie, Halfnote, when you're finished eating, grab the shopping bags. Marissa, when *you're* done, go hail us a carriage. Frank, what do you need on the business side?"

"As you say, Alma, we're out of just about everything. Dan and Galliard can help me do an inventory after they get back from the aviary. If you could check who's open, that would help."

The cook nodded. "We're also in desperate need of ordinary bowls and plates and cutlery. The Samoyans cleared us out."

Octavia's Journey   *by Lynette Hill*

"What did they want with our dishes?" perennially cranky Phyllis asked. The singer's spindly fingers tugged on the buttons of her blouse the way they always did when she was nervous.

"Well, they all wanted their souvenir of Verre House, didn't they?" Alma laughed. "We are the founding house of glass singing, after all. This is the place where dragon and human made their amazing pact of cooperation. Even the Samoyans are impressed by that. And our glass is famous for not breaking, among other things. After everything that happened I could hardly begrudge them a few plates and spoons. If one of you singers could organize the making of a full set I'd appreciate it. I've made a list of what we need. Add the supplies for that to your inventory, Frank."

Phyllis scowled again but Martin, another singer, spoke up before she could break into a fresh complaint. "I'll lead the making." He ran a hand across his bare head. Most glass singers, male and female alike, kept their uncut hair in thick braids.

Halfnote knew Martin considered braiding too much trouble, so opted for a clean shave instead. "Can the twins help me get started after breakfast?"

Annie and Alice, apprentices a year and a half older than Halfnote, nodded. Annie smiled.

"Oh, and while you're at it, I could use a mirror," the cook added. "I gave mine to Healer Argana."

The table fell silent until Frank cleared his throat. "All right Alma." He blinked furiously behind his spectacles. "I'll see to the mirror. I'd rather make just about anything than scrub another floor."

Halfnote's eyes lingered on the empty chair next to Sylvia. Octavia had left at dawn to speak to the city physicians and to continue her diagnoses of the sick. It wouldn't really be a normal day at Verre House until her sister returned to singing the glass.

Octavia's Journey   by Lynette Hill

Knowing

"Initially, it came to me as a knowing. After returning from the monstrous mirror I knew what to do about the plague without knowing why I knew."

Octavia had been told it would be a small group; an intimate panel of the city's leading physicians. In fact, the early morning gathering was much larger. They met in a large conference room just off the grand council chambers of Albermarle's city hall. A pair of bailiffs stood at the door to ensure their privacy. Even so, physicians and their assistants, council members and others Octavia didn't recognize filled the room. Thick woolen wall hangings muffled the audience's murmurings.

Not all of the faces were friendly. Falchion, the leader of the Metal Workers Union, entered in the wake of a younger healer. A grey-haired bailiff stepped forward to stop him, then realized who he was up against. The bailiff turned pale and quickly stepped aside. The master metal worker took a seat. Octavia, sitting in front of the restless audience, sighed but said nothing. Falchion would attack the glass singers, or not, regardless of what she said now. She knew, as he did, that his entire family owed their lives to the cure she'd provided.

As she waited for the crowd to settle down, she counted the glass pieces in the room. A giant timepiece graced the back wall. Probably half of the audience wore spectacles or some kind of eyepiece. Many wore jewelry with glass settings. These flashed and glittered in the light of the 300-candle chandeliers, of course also glass. Octavia took a breath to settle her stomach, not sure why she felt so nauseous. She would not show fear in this place, not with that hypocrite Falchion leering at her. She would not.

"As I sat beside my grandfather in the sick room," Octavia continued after the disruption, "I understood just from looking at him that his veins had begun to close up. I realized in that instant that he must drink Hawthorn tea daily to open them. The healing inspiration comes to me as a sense of what is wrong followed by the knowledge of what to do about it. The first few times it happened, this knowledge

Octavia's Journey   *by Lynette Hill*

came as a complete surprise. In a little while, after I became aware of Intan Negarawan's asthma, Healer Argana's cold and the arthritis in Sgt. Chevalier's left knee, I began to understand the process.

"When I look at a person, I go very still as I do when about to sing. Then I know. With understanding comes need. Especially in the first week, I needed to help the next person and the next. Not diagnosing physically hurt."

The physicians, still intent on her words, murmured among themselves. She found herself caught by the sight of small glass diamonds woven into a woman's robe. What was it about those tiny pieces that she found so compelling? The room's spreading silence called her back to her task.

Focus, Octavia.

"As soon as the quarantine was lifted, those of us who could be spared rushed out to share the cure. The others pounded on doors, called out the recipe and hurried on. I could not leave a place, however, until I had seen all within and diagnosed all of their ailments."

Some of the doctors shifted uncomfortably. At the first sign of the plague, every professional healer in the city fled. Not one stayed behind. Octavia could hardly blame them; the Samoyans reported that their own physicians were among the first to die when the sickness struck there.

Still ... Octavia pushed those thoughts aside. *Today is what matters. The past is done.*

"When I sing the glass, I act. I plan. I choose. I determine and visualize what piece to make. I decide what notes best suit the task. This healing gift is just the opposite. I do not act. I simply know.

"Now, in this second week, the diagnoses come in a much more measured pace. Each day it takes longer for the awareness to arrive. Each day the *need* to heal lessens. I begin to believe that this gift may only be temporary."

Octavia's Journey *by Lynette Hill*

Aftermath

As happy as Halfnote felt about getting out of the house, she almost regretted going to market. The palpable sense of grief and loss there reminded her strongly of the days just after the great flood. This time there was no damage to buildings but everywhere people's faces bore the same marks of grief and loss. There were clear gaps in various family and work groups. Here a number of people huddled together, openly weeping. Over there others loudly celebrated the discovery that they all survived. Almost unaware that she did it, Halfnote took hold of Robbie's hand. He accepted it with a light squeeze. He understood.

Many stalls stood empty. Some held dust-covered merchandise, as if a neglectful owner had just stepped away. Extra city guards stood about but no one looked interested in stealing from the newly dead. Still, as Alma predicted, the market was coming back to life. They returned home with full bags.

"Go see if Master Verre wants any tea," Alma told Halfnote. The apprentice obediently hurried off. *Making* vibrations trembled out of the creation rooms. Someone was working on Alma's dishes, by the feel of it. Life really was getting back to normal.

Halfnote came to a quick stop when she reached the reception hall. Someone shouted in Grandpa's office. She listened carefully and sighed in relief when she was sure that it wasn't Papa.

As she stood trying to decide whether to wait or return to the kitchen, the office door flew open. Junior master Geoffrey stalked out. His bushy black eyebrows bunched together like storm clouds over a face bright red with fury. Halfnote faded back into the shadows before he saw her. A moment later Mistress Lorraine, Geoffrey's wife, hurried out as well. The diminutive blonde hunched over as if in great pain and brushed tears from her eyes.

Grandpa came to the door and watched them go, his expression as angry and upset as Halfnote had ever seen. She turned to make her way back to the kitchen too late.

"Halfnote," Grandpa called. "Tell everyone they must meet in my chambers immediately. Everyone must attend, including Alma."

"Yes Master Verre." Halfnote even remembered to curtsy. She turned to leave and found Ted, a singer, standing behind her. His face was white with shock.

"Did you hear ..."

"Yes I did. I'll go get Frank and Martin." Lanky Ted turned on his heel and ran before she could say anything else.

"This is an announcement I deeply regret," Master Verre told them. "And I know many of you will find it upsetting. Junior Master Geoffrey has been dismissed. This is because he accepted bribes from the Samoyans and knowingly acted against my specific instructions. From this moment forward he is not welcome in Verre House. Mistress Lorraine has chosen to leave as well, in support of her husband. She is still welcome here, however."

"I'll miss Lorraine but I won't miss Geoff," fat Marissa was telling the twins Annie and Alice when Halfnote hurried into the apprentice girls' room that night. "He was always such a bully. But at least it was one day that didn't revolve around Octavia."

Alice hissed at Marissa. Halfnote turned her back on the others and started changing into her nightdress as if she hadn't heard.

"Did he really take bribes?" Annie asked.

Halfnote didn't hear the answer or bother to join in the discussion. In fact, she'd seen Geoffrey take the coins from Chancellor Razak's hand. But who else knew?

The Samoyans left as soon as the quarantine was lifted. She'd only told Papa. And *he* agreed with Geoffrey. She doubted that he said anything to Grandpa. Besides, Papa and Mama hadn't yet returned from Haverley village. Halfnote climbed into the large double bed she shared with Marissa and pulled the sheet over her head, determined to ignore the others.

An unknown amount of time later, a familiar footstep outside the door woke her. Halfnote slipped out, careful to avoid disturbing the snoring Marissa.

Apprentices weren't allowed in singers' quarters as Madame

Verre and Phyllis often reminded Halfnote. Even so, Octavia gestured her up the stairs.

"Come on. Just make sure that nobody sees you."

They traded stories while Octavia got ready for bed. Halfnote was angry that iron monger Falchion forced his way into the meeting. Octavia was even more upset about Lorraine's abrupt departure.

"Who told?"

Halfnote shrugged. "I only told Papa. He's not even here at the moment. I don't think he told anyone else."

"Well, Father told me. But only because he thought we should make the mirror. I can't imagine he would ever tell Grandfather. Hmmm. As you say, the Samoyans left last week and I doubt that they would have said anything anyway. Oh, this is just not right. Lorraine was already preparing to open her own studio, but what a horrible way to leave Verre House. I do hope we stay friends."

"Even after Grandpa fired her husband?"

"Grandfather fired him. We didn't."

"Do you like Geoffrey?"

"Not really, but that's not the point. Lorraine loves him. She is my friend. I honor her love for him, regardless. Halfnote, it's late. I need my rest and so do you."

Halfnote got up to leave. "Octavia, are you afraid to look into your mirror?"

"What? Why? Are you afraid of your mirror?"

"No, but you keep avoiding yours. Even when you washed your face you wouldn't really look into it."

"Go to bed, Sweetie. We're both tired. Now you're starting to imagine things."

But once Halfnote left Octavia sat on the edge of her bed and stared at the floor. The truth was she did have a problem with mirrors. Every now and again, when she glanced into one, it seemed that she saw something looking back. Something that was not a reflection of the scene before it. The truth was ... the truth was that she needed to get some sleep.

The next morning Robbie and Halfnote joined Sylvia in the smaller making room to sing up more cutlery.

"This will be good practice of your rolling and flattening skills," the soft-eyed singer told them. "Once the basic shape is in place I'll add the fork tines and spoon bowls and so forth. If things go well perhaps you can start adding the edges to the knives."

But things didn't go that well. Robbie's voice kept cracking at just the wrong moment. The fluid tableware would bend or warp in response. Halfnote did what she could to help, but there was no predicting when he'd lose pitch or wobble. Sylvia finally told Robbie to just maintain the fire and collect the finished pieces. Even with this change they only managed to fill one cooling rack with completed pieces by noon. On their way to lunch they ran into Dan handing out messages.

"Master Verre paid for replies, so everyone has one from their family," Dan said. "Oh, except you, Robbie. But then you don't have a family, do you?"

"Dan, that was unkind," Sylvia snapped. Robbie shrugged.

As it turned out, no messages arrived for Sylvia or Laiertes either. Sylvia's dark eyes looked worried, but red-headed Laiertes seemed less concerned.

"Canton's pretty far away. It always takes an extra day or two for the birds to get there and back again," the apprentice said.

"True enough," Alma agreed as she ladled soup into his bowl. "At that distance and with the mountains in-between, Canton may have avoided the plague altogether."

Sylvia's village was right on the river, Halfnote remembered. Likely her family hadn't avoided the illness. Frank gave Sylvia's hand a sympathetic squeeze.

Sandrigal teases the birds

Perhaps, Sandrigal thought, *the old wives are right.*
With age comes wisdom; even patience. He could not choose his view but he could choose to enjoy it. As days and nights passed he savored the ever-changing light of sun and stars that poured in through his window. He ruminated on the subtle shades of grey and black in passing storm clouds.

He teased birds that perched on the balcony railing into preening themselves in his mirror. They hopped through the window and tip-toed ever closer, their heads bobbing with curiosity. Then Queen's Companion Clara would come into the room and chase them out again. She considered a bird inside unlucky. Sandrigal just smiled at this.

The facts as he knew them were thus: the glass singers' attempt to make a new mirror of power had failed.

Miraculously, the girl survived. Her situation was less than ideal but at least she still lived.

Where there's life there's hope.

Low clouds covered the sky, diminishing his light. Sandrigal napped. He dreamed. Lightning woke him.

He had convinced the Queen to bring the girl here.

What if, somehow, he actually managed to protect the child from the Queen's plots? Could he take her into his own care? Could he then teach her how to survive her most unusual predicament? Under his protection, how long would she last? Could he perhaps even train her up into a usable instrument?

And just how would he do that?

Patience. Wisdom. *Enjoy the view you have.* Wait for the right opportunity. Already he had exceeded his own expectations. He had convinced the Queen to bring the child here. What else might he accomplish, if he could be patient and cunning enough?

Octavia's Journey *by Lynette Hill*

Are you worried about something?

The next morning Robbie and Halfnote found Alma in the kitchen planting a cutting in a clay pot. This surprised them as she usually had apprentices like them do the gardening. She put the plant under a glass cloche in the brightest corner of the kitchen window.

"Are you doing magic?" Robbie asked Alma.

She smiled at him in surprise. "I didn't realize that I'd taught you so much."

"What's it for?" Halfnote asked.

"Well, give us a guess. What do you think?"

"A new start, new beginnings?" Robbie said.

"Mmmm, close. Do you know what the plant is?"

"Snapdragon? No, it's a Lady's Sigil," Halfnote guessed.

"Well spotted. And the spell?"

"Protection?" Robbie asked. "Keeping out evil spirits?" He frowned. "Cleansing? Are you worried about something? I thought … the *mortolo's* gone, isn't it?"

"My, but you have been paying attention. Oh dear, is that the bread I smell? Check the oven, will you?"

For whatever reason, Alma's new mirror still hadn't been made. When Frank asked for a volunteer to help with it at breakfast everyone just stared at their plates.

"All right." Halfnote rolled her eyes. "I'll do it."

"Um, I need someone who can swirl," Frank said.

"I can swirl."

"I'll b..be your d...dragon," Robbie added.

Frank wiped his spectacles on his shirt. "All right."

The healing gift fades

It happened in the Physician Cornelius' offices. Octavia arrived in the city's medical district just after dawn as she did every day that

Octavia's Journey   *by Lynette Hill*

week. The line of people waiting to see her stretched down the main road nearly to the edge of the market. Some had clearly slept the night in their places. Shouting hawkers sold food and other goods. Yawning city guards stood here and there to keep order, though the crowd seemed peaceable enough.

    Sgt. Chevalier guarded the physician's back door with two others. He nodded a greeting and opened the door.

    "Alma sent you these." Octavia handed him a cloth covered basket. "I didn't peek, but they certainly smell delicious." Sgt. Chevalier and the other guards all smiled in hungry appreciation. It was the last cheerful moment Octavia experienced that morning.

    One sufferer after another pushed through the doctor's front door, all desperate for her help. The spark of knowing arrived more and more slowly. The morning light outside the physician's windows turned from gray to bright to the full strength of noon.

    How many people have I seen today?

    Octavia felt hollowed out; tired in a way that had nothing to do with physical exhaustion. Glass objects, both useful and decorative, dotted the office. These bothered her. At times they unexpectedly caught the corner of her eye. They drew her attention away from the job at hand. It almost seemed as if something moved in the glass.

    She pushed this thought way impatiently. She had a job to do. She straightened her spine and forced herself focus on those who sought her help.

    The next patient arrived. A heavy-set woman wearing vibrant blue silk and an unhappy expression wheeled in a heavy wooden pushchair that at first glance looked almost empty. The tiny passenger was buried under several shawls despite the summer heat. She peered up at Octavia through cloudy eyes and smiled.

    Octavia smiled back and waited for the spark of knowing.

    It didn't come.

    Octavia thought the thick gray bun atop her patient's head looked far too heavy for such a frail woman to support. She counted the age spots that kissed the elderly woman's sagging cheeks. One twisted hand trembled as the patient tried to shift to a more comfortable position

Octavia's Journey   *by Lynette Hill*

in the cushioned chair.

After diagnosing hundreds or perhaps thousands of people, Octavia could guess at what was needed. This tea for breathing, that herb for cataracts, and well, a warm, restful place to nap until the end. Death was not far off. Even her healing gift could not push away that outcome forever.

Octavia waited. And then she knew. The time for diagnosing was done. She would not be able to pronounce a cure for anyone again. The spark was gone.

Octavia's heart twisted. Her patient's attendant, possibly a daughter from the age and facial resemblance, blew out an impatient breath. The old crone patted her companion's hand affectionately.

"I'm sorry," Octavia began.

"That's all right, dear," the woman in the push chair rasped in a creaking voice. "I knew before we came here that you wouldn't be able to help me. Death comes for us all. I know that my time is at hand."

"Mother! No!" the heavy-set helper gasped.

"Don't fret yourself, Deloris. At least I go knowing that my children and their children are well. Thanks to you my dear," the smiling old woman told Octavia. "That's the real reason I came today; to thank you for bringing us the cure to the plague. You saved so many lives. Thank you."

Octavia blinked, astonished to find tears in her eyes. She was hardly the emotional type. She barely knew if it was the woman's open-hearted gratitude or her own sorrow at reaching the end of the healing gift that sparked her tears. She brushed them away.

"What's this? What happened?" Physician Cornelius hurried forward, only now realizing he'd missed something important.

Octavia waved him away and bid the old woman and her daughter farewell.

"I need to rest," Octavia told the doctor. She hurried out the back way before anyone could stop her. She heard Cornelius urging her to take a companion but she ignored him. She needed urgently to be alone with her thoughts.

Octavia's Journey   *by Lynette Hill*

We sing the songs of dragons

They used the main creation room to make the mirror, a fact that seemed to disturb the rest of the staff even more. Halfnote told Robbie to ignore the others as they gathered their supplies.

Dan pulled a face and moaned, "I'm the *mortolo*, coming to get you." He stumbled after Robbie with his arms outstretched like a monster from a story. Alma grabbed Dan by the back of the neck and marched him into the kitchen for a day's worth of washing.

In the end, to Frank's apparent surprise, the mirror took shape without incident. Robbie, acting as dragon, handled the fire perfectly as Halfnote knew he would. It was a simple matter to melt and spin the correct ingredients into a flat, circular form. Frank demonstrated the tones for Halfnote, who picked them up without concern. She kept the flattened orb spinning while Frank added the silvering for the face. The finished piece dropped into the bath with a satisfying sizzle.

Robbie collected it with a net and placed it carefully on the curing rack. Frank examined himself in the new mirror. "I need a shave." He rubbed stubbled cheeks. "And well done, you two. Especially you, Halfnote."

She smiled. She thoroughly enjoyed the making. Something about the music spoke to her in a way it hadn't before. Perhaps if she made twenty mirrors a day the way they made bottles and cutlery it would also become boring. Still, she felt real satisfaction in learning a new technique. She liked the sound of a well-made piece hitting the cooling bath. She was beginning to understand Octavia's passion.

At first Octavia was too caught up in her own feelings to pay much attention to her surroundings. She came to herself in a damp alley that made a shortcut back to the main road. She was not alone. A boy and two girls, all about her own age or a little younger, trailed along with her. By their clothes and lack of guild signs she thought they must be two carpenter's helpers and an apprentice cook.

Her hand reached up to her dragon's head pendant, sign that she was a singer or journeywoman of the glass singers' guild. As a singer she wore her guild sign on a chain of clear glass beads. Other guilds used silver chains to indicate the rank of journeyman. Masters of all guilds wore their pendants on chains of gold.

The trio giggled together in embarrassment when they realized they'd caught her eye. She saw, with a fresh jolt of loss, that the healing gift was truly gone. She saw only a boy and two girls before her, with no arising sense about the state of their health.

"Hello," Octavia said cautiously. The last time she found herself in this alley she'd been fleeing a mob stirred up by an angry carpenter. The three looked surprised to be addressed, but the female carpenter's helper stepped forward with a mischievous look.

"So is it true? Are you that singer, Octavia?"

"I am."

Octavia surveyed the scene, hoping her panic wasn't obvious. Where were the city guard? She and her challengers stood alone in the alley, hemmed in on two sides by stone walls. Traffic hummed at the far end; Octavia doubted that she could outrun all three before reaching the busy main road.

"Well, go on," the blonde female carpenter's helper said. "Show us. Sing up some glass."

"What? Here and now? Can you conjure up a chair without wood and nails? I need sand and fire and the other tools of my trade, as anyone would."

"How does it work?" the assistant cook, a dark-haired girl taller than the others, asked. "Glass singing, I mean?"

"It's magic," the boy hissed. "Sorcery."

"Of course it's not magic!" Octavia snapped, stung by the insult out of fear into anger. "We sing the songs the dragons taught our ancestors. We simply apply the principles of acoustic science using the human voice."

"What?" the boy's smirk dissolved into confusion.

"Clap your hands." He shrugged at the girls and did so.

"Every noise makes a disturbance in the air. Your clapping created sound waves that your ears are specially designed to capture. That's why you can hear them. Glass singers focus the sound waves created by our voices. For reasons no one really understands, glass is particularly sensitive to dragon song. That's why glass singers wear the dragon's head as our symbol."

She showed them her pendant.

"Wow," the female carpenter's helper said. "Think I'll stick to making furniture."

And I, Octavia thought firmly after bidding the trio goodbye, *am going to stick to glass singing.*

As much as she enjoyed helping people, her meeting with the dying woman had truly unsettled her. New tears trembled just at the corners of her eyes.

Now really. When did I get so emotional? I know who I am. I am Octavia Breydon, a singer of Verre House. My ancestors learned the songs of dragons. Even if I cannot diagnose illness any more I will continue to sing the glass, because that is what I know how to do.

Halfnote retrieved the now cured and usable mirror for Alma that afternoon. She found Master Verre and Martin in intense conversation in the corridor.

"What have you got there, Halfnote?"

"A mirror for Alma, G... Master Verre. She needed a new one because she gave her old one to Healer Argana."

"Who made it?" Master Verre couldn't quite conceal the concern in his voice.

"Frank and I. Oh, and Robbie was the dragon." Halfnote handed him the piece. He stared into the face for a moment with a deep frown, then looked it over as if merely checking the quality.

"This is well made," he said. "Not a single distortion. I see Frank did the silvering but the main piece, is this entirely your work, Halfnote? You did the whole base?"

Halfnote flushed. "Frank said I needed the practice."

"Indeed, but well done." Martin, his bald head gleaming, gave her a cheerful nod as well. Halfnote couldn't help feeling they were both a bit distracted. Master Verre handed back the piece and she scampered off to Alma. Perhaps it was just her imagination, but it seemed that the cook also gave the mirror an extra look before thanking her for it.

"Excellent," Alma held the mirror up to show Galliard, Ted and Marissa. "See, Verre House can still make an ordinary mirror."

Galliard whistled his appreciation. Lanky Ted smiled at her nervously. Marissa just rolled her eyes.

Bad news travels slowly

"Is it true?" Galliard asked Halfnote that afternoon. "Laiertes says Octavia can't diagnose illnesses anymore."

Halfnote nodded. She, Galliard and Laiertes were out in the back garden, weeding Alma's vegetables. As they worked, Galliard entertained them by whistling and otherwise imitating the local birds. Halfnote had been happy to find herself with the laid-back Galliard instead of bad tempered Dan. Of course Laiertes was with them. Despite the difference in their ages and origins, Galliard and red-headed Laiertes had become fast friends over their time in Verre House. Where you found one, Halfnote knew, you generally found the other.

"She told me the … the *knowing* that she felt before just faded away." Halfnote said.

"So what will she do now?" Laiertes asked.

"She'll go back to glass singing. What else?"

"Isn't Octavia upset?" Galliard asked.

Halfnote shrugged. "She says she feels relieved. She's happy to be just another glass singer again. She's looking forward to things returning to normal."

Galliard and Laiertes exchanged a glance. "*Can* she go back?" Laiertes asked. "I mean, will the *mortolo* let her?"

"What are you talking about? The *mortolo* doesn't exist anymore. Lorraine and the others destroyed it."

"Do you really believe that?"

"Of course I do. How else did Octavia survive?"

I saw it happen, she wanted to add, but doubted they would believe her. Galliard and Laiertes knew she had been down in the tunnels with Papa and Robbie.

"Some people think, they think Octavia is the *mortolo*." Fair-skinned Laiertes flushed as red as his hair when he said it.

"Who says that? Octavia's not a monster. She's helping people, not devouring them. The *mortolo* was destroyed. Ask Frank, ask Ted or Martin. Ask Sylvia. They were there. They destroyed it. Ask them what it felt like when the *mortolo* called to them. Do they feel the same way around Octavia? I don't."

"Yeah," Galliard nodded. "That's what Frank said."

"So who said Octavia is a *mortolo*? Was it Phyllis?"

The boys suddenly became quite interested in their weeding. Galliard filled several moments of uncomfortable silence by whistling a new tune. Finally, Halfnote asked Laiertes, "Have you heard from your family yet?"

Laiertes smiled. "Alma was right. They didn't have any plague in Canton. Everyone's fine. And now they have the cure, just in case."

Word of Octavia's healing gift had spread like wildfire. News of that ability's loss took a lot longer to circulate.

Despite public announcements that she could no longer offer cures, the sick and curious still came to Verre House. It was near dawn five days later and already a line of hopeful-looking people filled the street. The crowd did look smaller than yesterday, Octavia thought. Perhaps the news was beginning to make the rounds after all.

"I'm so very sorry." Octavia projected her voice so that even those in the back could hear. Her stomach cramped. She could think of nothing worse than having to tell sick people that she couldn't help them. "My ability to see cures has ended. I cannot help anymore. The physicians will assist all who seek their aid."

The smiles and expectant expressions faded into disappointment and even anger. She should have asked Frank and Ted to come out with her. They were both tall enough to look intimidating.

"But we've come from Aethelstan," someone shouted.

"My brother is on death's door," a woman gasped. "You must

help him. You're Singer Octavia, aren't you? They said you would help anyone. We can't afford the physicians."

"I am very sorry." Octavia edged back towards the gate. "For a few days I could help, but that power faded. I know no more than you do about healing sickness. Please, the medical quarter is nearby."

The tramp of heavy boots echoed off the stone walls lining the street. Sgt. Chevalier himself led the squad. Just the sight of the city guards quelled most of the crowd.

"You heard the lady," Chevalier bellowed as his guards clustered around Octavia. "She can't help you anymore. My people will show you the way to the healers."

"Sorry we're late," he told her. "We were delayed in the market by a disagreement between a pair of rival fishmongers. You should have waited for us."

"The crowd was restless. It seemed cruel to make them wait when I can't help anyway."

"You are too kindhearted, Singer." The sergeant turned to send off some more persistent petitioners. Octavia hurried to the gate. She didn't get there fast enough.

"Singer Octavia?" A townsman smelling too strongly of rose water and dressed in a fashionably striped yellow tunic caught her arm. "I understand if you need to ... conserve your strength. But surely we can come to some mutually profitable arrangement?" He held out a heavy leather purse.

Octavia pushed the purse away. "I'm sorry, but no. I simply can't help anyone anymore. The ability has faded. Chevalier?"

The sergeant turned and reddened at the sight of the merchant. "Here, you ..."

Octavia left them to it.

"Singer Octavia?" another male voice called. She shook her head irritably and all but ran to the gate. Why didn't people believe her when she said she couldn't help them? Why would she lie about something like that?

"Singer Octavia, please wait," the new voice insisted. "I have a message from Chief Astronomer Rafique."

She turned to see a tall, vaguely familiar-looking man in the black robes of the astronomer's guild. The silver telescope he wore as a pendant on a silver chain marked him as a journeyman. Of course; Hipparchus. He attended her singer's celebration.

"I'm so sorry," she began.

"It's all right." He handed her a wax-sealed piece of parchment. "We're ordering another lens. There are new wonders in the heavens and we all want our chance to look upon them."

That same morning, just as everyone else was getting up from breakfast, a clattering on the stairs surprised them. It was Phyllis, dragging down several heavy bags.

"I've had enough of this house," she announced in reverberating tones. "I cannot bear to stay a moment longer. I'm joining Lorraine and Geoff at their new studio."

"Sure we can't talk you out of it?" Alma asked. Halfnote glanced at the cook in surprise. She didn't usually resort to sarcasm. Red-headed Laiertes caught Halfnote's eye and bit back a smile.

"As long as you've given Master Verre your formal written notice." Alma turned away with a frown. "Martin, help the singer with her bags. Ted, run get a carriage, won't you? We don't want Phyllis to think us rude."

"Oh Phyllis," Sylvia sighed. "Must you really?"

"My mind's made up. Don't try to talk me out of it."

"We won't," Marissa muttered.

No more impossible choices

Octavia ducked into the main creation room, grateful to have a chance to *make* something.

What a blessing to make beautiful things again. Even to make ordinary things like wine bottles and spoons. No more illness. No more life and death decisions. No more impossible choices.

Octavia's Journey   *by Lynette Hill*

She dumped sand into the melting box and scraped it flat. She expertly caught the extra grains with the scoop and dropped them back into the barrow.

Waste not, want not. Memories of her last desperate *making* in this room reverberated off the walls. She thrust them away as sharply as the bits of extra sand.

There are no dark corners in this rounded space.

The white-painted stone walls gleamed brightly. Sunlight streamed in through the ceiling windows. She sang out the cleansing tones, the music used to purify molten glass. Her joyous notes filled the chamber. Octavia's pulse and spirits rose.

I am Octavia Breydon, a singer of Verre House. My ancestors learned their songs from the dragons. I out sang the alarm tones during my singer's test to win my place here. I am the only person to ever survive a Hygeia mortolo…

Sounding self-conscious, the scrying mirror cleared his throat. Clara, dozing in a nearby chair, snapped awake.

"The event Queen Anula anticipated is about to begin," Sandrigal announced. "Octavia prepares to sing glass."

"Thank you Sandrigal."

The Queen's Companion ran to alert her mistress.

"Octavia?"

She squeaked and dropped her flint.

"Sorry. I didn't mean to scare you." Frank peered in through the door. Light from the ceiling sunports glinted off his spectacles. "Are you doing anything important?"

"The astronomers ordered a lens. I was about to make it."

"By yourself?" He hurried into the room.

"It's not hard. It's a small one, with a single focus."

"Not hard for *you,* you mean. Can I help anyway?" Hope fueled Frank's wide grin. "I'll happily get supplies or tend the fire or anything you need. If I don't find something useful to do Alma will have me cleaning floors or washing sheets or dragons only know what. My hands are already raw from lye soap and scrubbing. Please, please, let me help you *make* something."

Octavia laughed, glad of the company. *Just an ordinary day at Verre House. Please, Mother Piasa, let it be so.* She'd never complain of boredom again.

"Everything's set. Take over as dragon, if you like."

Octavia left him to deal with the fire and hurried up onto the platform. She reviewed the astronomers' note. They wanted one clear lens of a particular dimension with a strong curvature.

Just a glass to look through and not a mirror, thank you, Mother Dragon.

She ignored the sudden twinge of her stomach. She'd have to make a mirror next, just to put that fear to rest. It was definitely time to get back to work. There was nothing frightening or sorcerous about a bit of clear glass, no matter how it curved. She imagined the astronomers under their shelter on Piasa's Perch staring through the telescopes on a clear night; constellation upon constellation spread across the heavens, telling story after story. The astronomers would use this bit of glass to catch the starlight, to bring it just that bit closer so that they could … what? *What did astronomers do with their captive starlight?*

Why not admire the sky with their eyes, like everyone else?

"Um, Octavia?" Frank called. "The fire's ready."

Really, when had she gotten so distracted?

"Thanks, Frank. Just a second …"

Queen Anula slept on her back under a light linen sheet atop three down-filled mattresses. Imported wool drapes heavy enough to resist both sunlight and the day's breezes covered the sleeping chamber's large windows. Her heavy snores reverberated off the thick wood paneling.

"Oh Illustrious One, the mirror …"

Queen Anula sat up. She stepped quickly into furred house slippers and strode through the door to the antechamber where Sandrigal waited. Clara hurried after. She deftly placed a silk house coat around her mistress's shoulders just as the Queen halted before the mirror.

Octavia's Journey   *by Lynette Hill*

"Show me Singer Octavia," the Queen commanded.

The silver surface of the mirror rippled like a pond brushed by a breeze. The undulations vanished as the image of a slender girl with a mass of braided black hair came into view. The girl, nearly a woman, stood on a black marble platform in the center of an underground chamber. Light from a trio of sunports directly above the platform illuminated Octavia and her activities. Something about the texture of the light made Clara think it must be a bright sunny day in the far off city of Albermarle.

She glanced out the window. In this outer chamber the silk drapes had been pulled back to let in the breeze and the light that Sandrigal craved. Outside, the overcast sky promised rain for the capital of Samoya, and soon.

"She doesn't look like a glass singer, Sandrigal. I thought Octavia was Fortis Verre's granddaughter."

"She is, Illustrious One, and I assure you that this is indeed Singer Octavia. Her father is Khelani."

"Interesting. I'm surprised Verre allowed it."

"He had little choice. His daughter Melodia eloped with her lover after Prince Alfonso of Kenifra proposed marriage."

"Explain."

"Prior to his assassination, the last prince of Kenifra sought to create strong ties with the glass singers' guild. He hoped this would strengthen his city's economy and thus his own hold on power. He believed that marrying Melodia would help create these ties."

"That sounds wise; surprising given Alfonso's reputation."

"Indeed, my Queen. The plan was sound but poorly executed. Alfonso courted the father, but neglected the daughter. Fortis Verre found the idea attractive but the prospective bride did not."

"And why should he court the daughter? A child marries to enhance the family position, not for personal satisfaction."

"Among the northern peoples, individuals customarily choose their own mates."

"Barbaric. They are nearly as bad as the so-called Birdmen."

"As you say, Great Lady. Even in the north, Melodia's rejection of the prince was quite a scandal at the time. They still sing of her marriage to the Khelani trader in the public houses. Their story is considered romantic by some."

"Huh. And how long did that little love match last?"

"In fact, their marriage continues to this day. To all appearances they have made a great success of it. Melodia travels the Khelana River on a traditional raft with her husband Paul, a trader of Clan Breydon. They have three daughters. The second, Arpeggia, known by the nickname Halfnote, is an apprentice in Verre House. The third daughter, Cadenza, is still a toddler and remains on the river with her parents."

"How very interesting," Queen Anula said in a tone that suggested just the opposite. "And this girl is truly acclaimed as the greatest voice in three generations?"

"Yes, my Queen, and deservedly so."

"Well, Sandrigal, you would know. How fares Melampus? When will you bring her to me? I grow weary of this delay."

"The ceremony will take great power, Oh Gracious Monarch. Why not simply invite Octavia for a visit? Say that it is out of gratitude for saving the crown prince."

"Her grandfather declined our invitations."

"Ah."

"Sandrigal, this quibbling is unlike you. Why do you resist this course of action?"

Several moments passed in silence.

"Sandrigal! Answer!"

"Brightest Star ... I must humbly beg your forgiveness. Everything I know tells me that she should be able to make the journey. But the truth is, until Octavia takes that first step into the mirror I cannot know for certain. I could be wrong. The entry might be as fatal for her as for any other. To destroy such a voice ..."

"Enough. Melampus prepares even as we speak. You will give him every assistance. You will see to it that he succeeds. On your life, you will bring the girl to me."

"All shall be as you require, Great Lady."

Clara frowned at the ornate mirror for a moment as if suspicious of something. Still, if the Queen's Companion had a concern, she did not voice it.

Octavia rechecked her measure. It was exactly level with the top of the cup that held it and firm to the touch. She slid the lid across the top and flipped the cup expertly face down into the heating chamber. Then she removed the lid. Sand filled the chamber. Not one bit escaped. Already the heating chamber was too warm to touch. Frank knew his business. The tiny silicate grains would melt quickly. She would have to work quickly to catch the ball of melted sand just as the last stubborn grain became liquid. Too soon and unmelted grains could mar the clarity; too late and the glass could scorch.

She took a calming breath and began to hum. Her back twinged with unexpected tension. Well, it was her first making after the tainted mirror, after all. She hummed a calming note and relaxed, but that also cooled the chamber.

Frank looked up from the fire, a question on his face. Red coals reflecting off his spectacles gave him a demonic look. Of course he knew better than to ask aloud. Octavia shook her head and blew out a breath. The heating chamber returned to its former rosy hue and now her stomach clenched. She moderated her breathing and swallowed bile, her hands clenching against a wave of fear. The last time she sang the glass she fell into the molten ball, turning it monstrous. Now it seemed that all she could hear was the roaring of the monster as it rose, filling her vision.

The rogue mirror returned to reclaim her...

"Octavia! Octavia! Speak to me!" Frank shouted.

"Stop it." She pulled her arm free and struggled to sit up. "You're hurting me."

"You fainted. What happened?"

He pointed at the heating chamber. The pile of red sand was now a blackened muck, baked into the bottom of the heating chamber. Octavia flushed. She'd never messed up this badly, not even in her first days as an apprentice.

"I ... I don't know." She was too embarrassed to meet Frank's eye. "I began, then all I could think of ..."

"The *mortolo,*" Frank finished for her. He nodded grimly. "I thought so. I ... I could hear it in your voice. Maybe it's just too soon ..." He sat back on his haunches and polished his spectacles absentmindedly.

"Or perhaps I waited too long." Octavia cringed with shame. "The mirror is destroyed, we're all saved, there's nothing to fear. This is just business as usual. I should have started singing the glass again days ago to cure any nerves. I shouldn't be scared of a memory."

"Don't worry." Frank spoke in gentle tones. He put his spectacles back on. "We'll clean it up before anyone else sees it. I'd still rather do this than more laundry."

Queen Anula hissed. "So, it is as we thought ..."

"Might it not be merely an attack of nerves, Gracious Queen?" Clara asked.

"Singer Octavia is not of nervous disposition," Sandrigal pointed out. "Quite the opposite, in fact."

"Sandrigal, continue your observation. Keep me informed."

"It shall be as you command, Great Lady." The mirror's tones were as smooth and ingratiating as any courtier's. Clara bit back a smile as she followed her mistress out of the room. No one would could ever accuse the Queen's Scryer of lacking a personality.

Sandrigal's unblinking gaze focused on a patch of bright white cloud just passing his window. He had Queen Anula's consent; her command. He had no choice but to bring Octavia to Samoya. He could not do otherwise.

This was a most positive development.

Even so, the energetic connections would have to be perfect; Melampus' ceremony flawless. There were still a great many steps to take. Until he actually had the girl in his grasp he could not be certain of anything.

Patience.

Octavia's Journey   *by Lynette Hill*

Who's fault?

    Octavia writhed inwardly with shame. She did her best to appear calm while trying to explain to Grandfather what happened. A new brick chimney would have to be built under the heating chamber to replace the one she ruined.

    Master Verre sat behind the square desk in his office, the one peppered with animal heads and other strange designs. He hid his expression behind steepled fingers.

    "Octavia, do not blame yourself. This is my fault."

    "Grand ... Sir. How could this possibly be your fault? I'm the one who lost control."

    "Octavia, not everything is simply a matter of will. You have been through an extraordinary experience. Of course there will be consequences. None of us can pretend to be unaffected by what happened. The echoes of the *mortolo* still resound in the creation room. I should have foreseen this. I should have joined you in your first singing. Again I failed to protect you. I'm sorry."

    "Grandfather, it's not your fault. I lost control, that's all. I out sang the alarm cry during my test. I can deal with this. It may take some effort and focus ..."

    "Octavia, my dear, perhaps you should stop singing for a time while I consult the scholars of Tulum ..."

    "Grandfather, No! Just sitting around and thinking about my problems never helped me solve anything. I have to keep working with it until I find the solution."

    "Are you sure this is simply a matter of emotion?"

    "What else could it be?"

    Master Verre stood up. "Why don't you sing with me now? We'll use a portable brazier to make a flower."

    Octavia smiled. "That would be wonderful." She ignored her tightening stomach.

    Master Verre called Martin to assist as dragon and sent Laiertes to gather the necessary sand and coal.

    "Now, here is what we will do. Martin, you will observe as I create the *viridani* tones." The bald singer rubbed his freshly shaven head and nodded.

Master Verre paused a moment as if taking a breath, but Octavia knew he was actually waiting for Laiertes to leave. The red-headed apprentice seemed to know it too. He scurried out and shut the door carefully behind him.

"Now, Octavia, I will create the barrier tones. You will stand within them while making the flower."

Octavia kept her face impassive. Previously she had only read of the *viridani* technique. Named after Mother Piasa's murdered mate, it was used to create deep-throated booming sounds. The deep bass tones and their echoes off the sounding walls were meant to build a barrier of noise around a given area. Octavia wasn't sure she had the range to create the tones herself.

I'll find a way, she promised herself.

She would stand in the quiet space within the protective tones, in the eye of the storm as it were, and make her piece there. At least, that was the plan.

She exchanged nervous smiles with Martin as Grandfather began the tones. She couldn't call it singing.

It was hard to believe that such overwhelming noise could emanate from a human voice. The sound built up as a pressure in her ears. Just when the stress felt unbearable, it vanished.

She occupied a circle of absolute silence. Grandfather stood with his mouth open and moving. She saw his throat vibrate, but she heard nothing. Nothing, that is, unless she moved just a tiny bit right or left. There she encountered a pounding bass vibrato painful to the ears. Standing perfectly still in the center kept her in a place of complete silence. Grandfather nodded. *Time to begin.*

She poured the sand into the heating chamber over the coal bed and sang the melting tones. Taking pleasure in doing a simple thing well, she called the molten mixture out of the box and set it spinning in the air. She was safe inside Grandfather's protective tones.

Only she didn't feel safe. Terror caught in the back of her throat, skewing her voice. The ball of melted glass before her turned gray and expanded into the form of the all-devouring *mortolo*. It spun towards her, expanding as it moved. She was trapped by the wall of sound behind her, *there was no escape ...*

"Octavia, you will stop singing for the time being." Master Verre spoke in the most neutral tones. He refused to meet her eyes as he spoke. Octavia scarcely knew what to say. Grandfather and Martin saw nothing but the glass rise normally out of the melting box and her abrupt faint.
But how can I stop? How can I solve this ... whatever it is ... by doing nothing?
Told to rest, Octavia spent the rest of afternoon and evening pacing in her room, trying to find a solution.

The next day at supper Martin shocked them all by announcing his departure.
"I'm sorry ..." Martin's voice wavered as he stood up to speak. He passed one nervous hand over the stubble reclaiming his scalp and then hurried out of the kitchen.
Lanky Ted rushed out after him. Frank and Sylvia exchanged unhappy glances. The apprentices sat in an uncertain silence. On the whole, no one minded losing cranky Phyllis but Martin was well-liked.
That left Verre House with just four singers: Frank, Sylvia, Ted and Octavia. Halfnote glanced at Alma. The cook looked as disturbed as the rest of the staff. As was almost normal, now, Octavia and her grandparents were not at the table. Did Master Verre already know or would Alma have to tell him?

Unable to sing but determined to find a solution, Octavia stayed in her room. Resting, she told Sylvia to tell the others.
But how could she rest, while others sang? It drove her frantic that afternoon. The vibrations of *making* trembled through the stones of Verre House up to her room. Each pulse of song invoked the monster just as when she sang herself. She felt stalked, haunted, as at any moment she might turn and find the *mortolo* behind her. Just when it seemed unbearable, the song stopped. The overwhelming terror

vanished when the vibrations ended.

Relieved, she washed her face. At least she meant to. When she looked at the glass pitcher of water, the monster appeared. She stumbled backwards. Her eyes encountered her wash bowl. The monster appeared there as well. The *mortolo* vanished as soon as she looked away. The horror of the encounter vanished with it.

She sat on the edge of her bed, arms wrapped tightly around herself. She willed her thudding heart to slow. She did not look at her lamp because it was also glass. She tried the calming tones. Even these invoked the monster.

She heard Alma calling for supper. Supper would mean moving past the giant glass decoration in the stairwell and then eating from glass dishes using glass cutlery.

Sylvia tapped on her door a little later.

"Octavia, are you all right? Alma wants to know if she should send a tray up."

"Actually," Octavia said, "Could you ask Alma to come up, when she's free?"

"Oh. You want Alma to come up to your room? Are you sick? I can bring a tray. Do you want supper? Or at least some tea?"

Any food or tea would be served in glassware. *No!*

"Um, no thanks. If she could just come herself. I need to talk to her about something."

Below, in the apprentice room, Marissa, Annie and Alice huddled together on the twins' bed. They stared up at their creaking ceiling. Halfnote sat on the bed she shared with Marissa and started humming the calming tones.

"Shut up!" Marissa turned on her suddenly. "It's time somebody got upset about what's happening. Doesn't your grandfather care about the rest of us?"

"Marissa, calm yourself." Sylvia stood in the door. They all turned in surprise. The doe-eyed singer moved more quietly than anyone else Halfnote knew. "Master Verre is aware of the situation. There is no reason to believe anyone else is in danger."

No one said anything. Sylvia sat on the edge of Halfnote and Marissa's bed until everyone fell asleep. Or at least until the other girls fell asleep. Halfnote lay stiffly under her sheet, staring at the ceiling. It took forever for Octavia to stop pacing. And even longer for Sylvia to finally leave.

Of course Octavia will solve this.

The others were just being stupid. Halfnote knew her sister could do anything once she made her mind up. Octavia managed to complete her singer's test despite the interruption of the alarm tones, after all. No one had ever done that before. Of course Octavia would beat this. She could beat anything that got in her way.

Water reflects, but not the monster

Octavia shut her eyes and dashed water onto her face from the wooden bowl provided by ever resourceful Alma. An unshaded candle in a porcelain holder provided the only light in the room.

No. I will face my fears.

Octavia stared into the water bowl. Her reflection glared back with a steely gaze. She waited several moments, not daring to breath.

No monster appeared. Staring at the water she breathed in, then exhaled. No monster appeared.

Why not? My reflection is clear in the water.

She went and pulled the mirror out of her closet, face down. Took a breath and flipped it over. The *mortolo* roared out of the silvered face. She flung the looking glass back into the closet. The monster vanished. She held herself very tightly as her heart pounded out a desperate rhythm. She waited for her heartbeat to slow as she considered these events. The monster did not show itself in her reflection in the water. She peeked into the wooden wash bowl again just to make sure. No monster.

So, she could wash safely. That was something.

I may be mad but at least I can keep clean, she thought and allowed herself a wry smile.

Also, the monster vanished when she stopped looking into glass. That was something else to consider. The *mortolo* might frighten her, but it could not leave the glass.

At least, not yet?

Would she see the monster if she did not see her reflection?

She retrieved the mirror and pointed the silver surface away so that she could look at it from an angle. She made out the wall, her door still slightly open, a face peering through the gap. She dropped the mirror with a gasp.

"Halfnote!"

"Octavia? What are you doing?"

"Halfnote, you scared the life out of me."

"What are you doing?"

"What are *you* doing up here on the singers' floor? You know apprentices aren't allowed."

Halfnote rolled her eyes. "That's not what you said before."

"All right. But what do you want? I'm busy."

"We can hear you pacing. The girls are worried. Even Sylvia doesn't know what to tell them. But what are you doing? Why do you keep looking in the mirror and throwing it down?"

"I'm trying to understand what's happening. I see the *mortolo* in glass, but not in water. I want to know if I see the monster in glass only when I see my reflection or any time I look in glass."

"You said you didn't have a problem with your mirror."

"Yes," Octavia sighed. "I did say that. At first I just felt uneasy when I looked into the mirror or saw my own reflection. But it's gotten worse. Now I see the monster."

Octavia's Journey   *by Lynette Hill*

One last try

Despite Grandfather's command, Octavia felt she just had to try again. Her experiments with the mirror gave her a new idea. When she did not see her own reflection, she could endure looking at glass for a very brief time. What if she sang and visualized the piece without looking at it? She crept into the main creation room early in the morning, while everyone else was at breakfast.

Octavia stood in the center of the making platform and took in a deep breath. *Calm*, she told herself. *Calm and centered. Peace.* She searched for that point of balance within herself. She found it occupied by the memory of the whirling unformed mirror that had devoured her. It took all of her willpower to push that roaring memory away.

Begin again. Calm. Calm and centered. Peace. Stillness. Focus on the piece you intend to make. The piece you are making. She released the breath.

The form took shape in her mind's eye. Octavia intended nothing elaborate, just an ordinary daisy. She would spin out the petals and leaves. A simple piece. Any second year apprentice could make it. Even Robbie could, at least on a good day.

I am Octavia Breydon, a singer of Verre House. My ancestors learned to sing glass from the dragons.

Octavia slowly released her breath.

She looked at the cooling racks set against the white wall. They stood next to the worn black marble entry steps.

Halfnote hid under those steps to watch my test.

Octavia stood now in the exact same spot as for her test. She passed that challenge even as every piece of sung glass in Verre House cried out. No one, not even Grandfather, understood the meaning of the alarm. Too late they learned that the glasses warned of plague.

Although, Octavia realized, the glasses could also have been warning of the *Hygeia mortolo*. Here she stood, staring at the spot where she lost concentration to fall into the unformed healing mirror to create that monster. Her carefully cultivated sense of peace vanished. She sucked in her next breath too quickly. The pounding of her heart echoed in her ears.

I fell saving Grandfather. And survived. I am the only person ever to emerge alive from the clutches of the Hygeia mortolo. That thought made her dizzy.

I brought back the cure that saved all of Albermarle and Samoya and every country in-between from the worst plague ever known. Better. Her heartbeat slowed. She gently released the air from her lungs.

She thought of a pool of water, clear, still as a mirror. In her mind's eye, one small leaf dropped onto the surface of the water. Ripples radiated in every direction.

Legend said that the dragons used their fiery breath and magic to transform this room and others like it. They turned ordinary mountain caverns into the rounded shape perfect for glass singing. Some said the dragon Falafel, son of Piasa, formed these rooms out of love for the human Melinda. She was honored as the first glass singer. Nothing, not a monster, not even a *Hygeia paraphasis* turned *mortolo*, could destroy the magic of this place.

Of course I can do this. Mother says I was born singing. This is my inheritance. It is my destiny.

Robbie and Halfnote had kitchen duty again.

"You look upset," Robbie said as they scrubbed the breakfast dishes together.

Halfnote sighed. "I thought ... I thought things would be better now," she admitted. "I thought curing the plague would ... would solve everything really."

"Here, now, you two." Alma turned from her kneading to face them. Dough clung to the portly cook's fingers. "What sort of talk is this? If you remember, there was a time when we didn't know what to do about the plague. Everyone thought all hope was lost. But we found a cure, didn't we?"

"Octavia did," Halfnote whispered.

"You and Robbie thought you were lost forever in the tunnels with your father, but we found you, didn't we?"

"Yes ...."

"See," Alma returned to kneading, "Things happen and everyone gets scared because at first they don't know what to do, but then someone finds a solution."

"People still died in the plague," Halfnote objected.

"Bad things happen. But just because you can't think of a solution right now doesn't mean you won't figure it out in the future. There's always hope."

"Hope," Robbie repeated. He smiled.

"Hope." Halfnote sighed. She wanted to believe it.

Taking in a new breath, Octavia imagined the daisy alive in Alma's garden. It stood alone above green blades of grass in bright sunlight, its yellow center made brighter by its contrast to the white petals. Mentally she reached out, plucked the head from its stem and twirled it in her hands. She felt the tiny hairs on each petal with her fingers. The image was complete in her mind.

Octavia sang the making notes. She peeked through squinted eyes at the melted glass ball rolling in the air before her. It swirled into the form of a daisy. The molten flower took its shape. Each petal stood individuated; each dot of seed held its proper place in the center.

Perfect.

She closed her eyes quickly. Tension tightened her arms and shoulders. She allowed the reverberation of her tones to maintain her piece while she took breath. She began the completion tones.

"She's done it," Halfnote said. Robbie and Alma looked up at her. "Octavia." Halfnote waved a hand towards the making rooms. "Can't you feel the energy?" Cook Alma might not notice, but surely even Robbie could feel the vibrations. They tingled inside Halfnote's nose and ears.

"She's not done yet." Alma's eyebrows creased just a bit. "May the dragons guide her."

Halfnote and Robbie stared at Alma in surprise.

"You can feel what's happening?" Robbie asked. "But you're

not a singer."

Alma snorted. "How long have I lived in this house, child? Of course I feel the energies. How could I not?"

Smiling, Octavia belted out a triumphant b-flat, the first note of completion. Her perfectly formed flower exploded.

Molten glass flew in every direction. Octavia threw her arms up just in time to keep a scalding glob from hitting her face. She ran for the cooling bath and plunged her blistered arm into the water. The glass steamed, solidified and fell off. She kept her arm in the water until the stinging stopped, struggling to stop tears of pain and shame.

I don't understand. The last echoes of her triumph faded away. The notes mocked her with their perfection. Octavia listened intently but heard nothing amiss.

I did nothing wrong. Why is this happening? How do I correct a mistake if I don't know what it is?

Queen Anula blew out one impatient breath. Clara willed herself to invisibility.

"Foolish, foolish child," the Queen scolded the girl in the mirror. "Why do you torment yourself in this way? But how could you understand when your fool of a grandfather insists that you remain uninformed?"

She turned away from the looking glass. "It is a scandal of the worst kind, Sandrigal, that the glass singers of Albermarle should sink to this level of ignorance. I am ashamed of them."

"Indeed, my Queen," the living mirror agreed. "But Master Verre and most others of his rank believe ignorance will stop the creation of more *mortolo*."

"It only leaves them helpless when monsters do appear. But never mind. The girl is defenseless. I shall have her and she will do as I bid." Queen Anula's angry eyes focused suddenly on Clara. "No matter what that fool Fortis Verre thinks. I will have her!"

"Indeed yes, mistress," Clara murmured, curtsying. Anula snorted and left the room. Clara hurried after, one step behind.

Octavia's Journey *by Lynette Hill*

On the balcony

Octavia stood on the house's highest balcony. From here, as Halfnote often said, it felt as if you could see all the way to the port of Tulum and the ocean itself. Forest and farmland spread out beyond the giant lake that lay at the foot of the sheer cliff. It had been a day of uncertain weather; showers mingling with passing sunshine. Silver puddles glinted on the balcony's stone surface.

Oh to be a bird and just fly away.

After her last failure, Grandfather banned her even from entering a making room. He called a staff meeting and said that anyone caught helping her sing again would be instantly dismissed. Even if that person was Halfnote. Or Alma. Anyone.

She'd never seen Grandfather so grief-stricken.

How can I stop? If I stop before I find the solution, then I really am a failure. I don't know what else to do. I have no other skills. I am the greatest voice in three generations. What do I do, if not sing?

A stair creaked behind her. "Octavia?"

Octavia turned around. She'd expected Halfnote to come check on her but not ...

"Mother? When did you get back? I didn't think we'd see you again until next week."

"That was the plan, but we heard a most disturbing rumor in Haverley. Octavia, are you all right? What's happening?"

Octavia started to insist that all was well, then flung up her hands in an unusually helpless gesture.

"When I sing ... things go wrong. Things I don't know how to fix. I'm fine, I'm just frustrated. Yes, something's wrong, but I wish everyone would quit making such a fuss about it. I just need to work it out. Grandfather wants me to stop singing, but how can I? That's admitting defeat, isn't it? You might not understand..."

"Oh, I might more than you think..."

"Mother, don't patronize me. You made your choices. I need to make mine."

"Fair enough. But Halfnote tells me that you see the monster

Octavia's Journey   *by Lynette Hill*

now in every bit of glass you look at."

"Yes, that is part of the problem."

"*Part* of the problem? And when you hear others singing the glass, it makes you dizzy? Nauseous? When did you last eat?"

"I eat, Mother. I just come outside when they sing."

"You skipped breakfast and lunch," Halfnote said.

Honestly.

Octavia glared at her sister. Mother stepped between them.

"Octavia, if the *mortolo* still haunts you ..."

"Don't be ridiculous. The *mortolo* was destroyed."

"But it still haunts you."

"All right, so I see the monster. I know it's my imagination. I can't let fear beat me. Grandfather wants me to *stop singing...*"

"I see his point ..."

"No, Mother, no! I have to solve this. I have to. Who am I if I don't sing? What sort of life will I have if I spend it in fear of seeing a bit of glass?"

"Is it possible that you're simply trying too hard? Maybe you just need a rest."

"A rest? All I've done these last few days is rest."

"Have you? Just look at yourself in any mirror…"

Octavia flinched.

"I'm sorry," Mother said, her expression genuinely contrite. "I am sorry. I just meant that you look exhausted. Perhaps you can't solve the problem because you've simply been trying too hard. Take some time to step back and look at things from a different perspective. Why don't you join us on the river for a while?"

Halfnote smiled at this idea but Octavia didn't.

"I can't just leave. You know I've got to solve this."

"And if you can't?"

"Just because you quit singing doesn't mean I have to."

"Octavia, I didn't quit singing. I simply chose the life that is right for me. That is what you need to do."

"Then I should stay here."

"Haunted by a monster?"

"I'm working on it. At least I'm trying. Grandfather blocks me at every turn. How can I solve the problem if I don't face it?"

Halfnote started to speak, then shut her mouth. Octavia and Mama ... well, Octavia didn't understand why Mama chose to live on the river. It made perfect sense to Halfnote. Mama wanted to be with Papa and Papa wouldn't be happy here. No Khelani would live in a cold stone building when he could travel the river.

Sometimes Halfnote missed the river so much it hurt. She yearned for it the way she ached for her parents when they were away. But for Octavia, singing the glass was all that mattered. It was clear, as Mama often said, that Octavia had been born for Verre House. Octavia appreciated that Halfnote missed the river, but she never understood why Mama chose life on the Khelana over glass singing.

As for Halfnote, well, she did often want to return to her parents' raft. But she was also beginning to understand Octavia's obsession with glass singing. *If only there were a way to do both at the same time...*

Singing with Mama

Later, Halfnote found Mama standing on the podium in the main creation room. Mama wore a funny expression. Was she sad or happy? Halfnote couldn't quite tell. She looked a bit of both. Was she going to sing? There was sand in a barrow to the side but not in the making box. A coal bed had been laid in the brazier but no fire lit.

"Mama? Do you need any help?"

"No, thank you, Sweetie. I'm just remembering. I used to sing here too, you know."

"Do you miss it?"

"No, I don't."

"Really?"

"Really." There was no doubting that tone.

"Octavia does."

"Yes, she does." Mama gave her a speculative glance. "How

would you feel about it?"

Halfnote considered this. "Mama, can I tell you something?"

"Of course." Mama sat down on one of the steps leading to the podium and patted the space next to her. Halfnote happily plopped down beside her.

"Mama, when I was in the tunnels with Papa and Robbie; when the *mortolo* took Octavia, I saw it. I could see it. I saw the *mortolo* and Octavia inside of it. I saw their energy, streaming down through the tunnel past us."

Mama's eyes widened.

"What did you see? Can you describe it to me?"

Halfnote bit her lip and thought hard. "It was like ... the river, because it flowed down the tunnel, but not like the river because it wasn't water. The *mortolo* was gold, at first and then it turned red as it got hotter and hotter. And Octavia was like ... well ... like a cooler spot in the middle of the *mortolo*. She was just a blue blob. It didn't look like Octavia but somehow I knew that it was her."

"I think I understand. Octavia said she heard your voice while she was inside the monster. And Papa said you started singing in the tunnels. What happened?"

"I sang the counter clockwise swirl, Mama. I watched Octavia practice the swirl all those times for her test and because I know how the river flows, somehow I knew what to do. I used the swirl to keep Octavia away from the *mortolo* as it heated up. And I used the swirl to put cold from a pond between Octavia and the heat, so she didn't burn up with the mirror. Mama, are you all right?"

Mama's face went pale. "I didn't realize you were in such danger. Your father never mentioned this."

"I don't think he knew. He's not a glass singer. I know he didn't see anything. Papa didn't understand why I sang. He told me to stop but I didn't dare. I knew Octavia was in trouble."

"Does your grandfather know any of this?"

"We tried to tell him. But he was sick from the plague and so worried about Octavia; I don't know how well he *listened*. But Mama, what I mean is, before I didn't care about singing. I mean, I did it and I

Octavia's Journey   *by Lynette Hill*

was good at it and sometimes it was fun but ... but now I do care. When I sang the swirl, at first all I wanted to do was to save Octavia. But I sang and I put cold between Octavia and the *mortolo* and I felt ... I felt alive. I felt like I was touching life itself. Like, I don't know, like I could do anything."

And that part she hadn't told anyone. Not Papa or Octavia or Alma. Not even Robbie and he'd been there. For the first time she wondered what he had seen, there in the utter darkness.

"That is amazing," Mama said. "And truly, in spite of everything that's happened, you still want to continue at Verre House? Do you really want to be a glass singer?"

"Yes, Mama. Do you know, I don't think anyone's ever asked me that before."

"Yes." Mama's laugh was a short, sharp bark and not entirely pleasant. "I would be surprised if anyone had." They sat for a moment in companionable silence.

"Would you like to sing with me?" Mama asked.

"Oh, yes," Halfnote gasped in delighted surprise. "That would be wonderful. What shall we make? There's not much sand or coal. I'll go get some more."

"Oh, I think we can make do with what we have here. Let's make something small, a flower perhaps? A small rose?"

"A rose and a bee? Like in the story?"

"Oh, we are getting ambitious. Do we have enough sand?"

Preparations made, they stood and sang, Mama and Halfnote together. They spun out the rose between them. Their voices blended wonderfully. They sang, louder and louder, letting the room fill with the echoes of their echoes. When the melted ball of glass was ready, Mama winked at Halfnote.

Mama held the maintaining notes while Halfnote used the counter clockwise swirl to pinch off a tiny piece. Then they switched, so Halfnote sang the rose while Mama made the bee. They carefully brought the bits back together again, so that the bee kissed the rose, just like in the story. Halfnote found it hard not to giggle then.

The reunited piece dropped into the cooling bath with a

satisfying sizzle.

"Oh, well done!" Grandma stood in the door to the room, radiant with joy. Tears trickled down her cheeks.

"Grandma, why are you crying?"

"I'm just so very happy to see you singing with your mother. I never thought I should enjoy such a day."

"Oh, Mother." Mama sounded impatient. "You know I haven't stopped singing."

"Yes, my dear. But I have so longed to see you sing with your daughters. And so has your father."

"Hmmph. No doubt he would just criticize my technique again. Well, come on." Mama nudged Halfnote. "Let's see how our piece turned out."

It was beautiful, they agreed; a many-petaled rose on a small stem. The tiny bee perched on a leaf just below the blossom.

An argument overheard

That night after supper, Halfnote took a detour past the door to her grandparents' chambers. It wouldn't really delay her errand for long and she wanted to see Mama again. Obviously she couldn't help overhearing people when they raised their voices.

"Of course I don't blame her. But leave Verre House?" Something that sounded very old and incredibly frightening reverberated in Grandma's voice.

Halfnote thought she sounded like one of the queens Grandma so often played on stage. Grandma's voice held the power to keep a listener's attention in the same way that Grandpa's voice had the power to shape glass. Halfnote could not stop listening as her grandmother asked, "What did you have in mind?"

"Octavia could come with us," Mama said. "On the river."

"Fortis will not allow that." Danger echoed in Grandma's voice like thunder in a distant storm.

"It's not up to him."

"She is an apprentice of Verre House!"

"Octavia is my daughter, and, as you have apparently forgotten, a fully-fledged singer in her own right."

Halfnote shivered. She'd never heard Mama and Grandma argue before. Grandpa and Papa fought all the time, but not Mama and Grandma; Not with each other and almost never with anyone else.

"And what will she do on the river?" Grandma spoke so quietly that Halfnote strained to hear. The danger in her tones poised like a snake ready to strike.

"She will rest. And she can go to Tulum." Mama again tinged her voice with calming tones. "The best scholars and physicians are there. Father can hardly argue with that."

"There are faster modes of travel," Grandma pointed out, her voice dry. The danger had passed. Now Grandma sounded tired.

"Perhaps. But none more restful."

"Halfnote!" Alma called. "I need you."

Halfnote gave a guilty start and rushed as quietly as she could to the kitchen.

Did someone call me?

The other girls were already in their nightshirts. Marissa sat cross-legged on Annie and Alice's bed, deep in animated conversation with the twins. They all looked up with guilty expressions as Halfnote hurried in.

"It's just me," she said. No one responded.

The ceiling creaked. Octavia was pacing again.

Halfnote sighed and got ready for bed. None of the other girls spoke to her. She pulled the sheet over her head so she wouldn't have to deal with them. The house fell silent except for the floorboards squeaking above.

Sometime later Halfnote woke to the sound of whispering from the other bed. At least she didn't hear Octavia pacing.

"Do you really think Octavia's cursed?" Annie asked Alice and Marissa in soft but still clearly audible tones.

"She's not well, that is certain," Marissa muttered.

"I'm scared," Alice whimpered. "I want Peter to come back. I want to go home."

"So do I," Annie sighed.

Of course the twins missed their older brother. The pacing above began again. The girls on the other bed gasped. Halfnote flung back her sheet and sat up.

"Octavia's not cursed," she hissed. "She's just trying to work things out."

From her window Octavia could look past the branches of a widespread oak to see the clear sky. Eventually the full moon rose high enough to share its light with her. She thought of Mother Piasa facing impossible choices from her giant tree atop the mountain peak. From there the dragon mother must have had an amazing view of both moon and the southern plains. A lonely ache, different from her current woes, filled Octavia's heart.

She wrapped herself in a woolen shawl and hurried out of her room. It was late enough that most lights in the house had been extinguished. Indistinct voices emanated from the master's chambers. Even the kitchen stood dark. At least she didn't have to worry about confronting any monster-filled glass in the gloom.

Someone called her name from the master's chambers.

"What is it?"

No one answered. She paused to knock and heard her name called again from inside. The voice was muffled so she couldn't be sure who it was.

"Mother? Grandmother? Is that you?"

She followed the voice in, but still found no one.

Oh, honestly.

Movement caught the corner of her eye. She followed it around the corner into Grandmother's changing suite. Large mirrors covered all four walls. Grandmother used this chamber to try out the different costumes required for her theater roles. She often joked that she married a glass singer just so she could always have excellent mirrors. Something moved across the face of one silvered pane of glass.

"Grandmother?" Why wouldn't she answer? "Madame Verre, are you all right?"

Octavia realized that she was alone. No, actually, she wasn't. Mirrors surrounded her.

"No," she gasped. Why on earth had she come in *here?*

She turned to find the door, but couldn't. Everywhere she looked the swirling monster appeared. She turned frantically, again and again, but found only the monster.

Multiple reflections intensified its power. *Mortoli* closed in from all sides, ready to devour her. Octavia flung back her head and with the full power of her voice screamed the *Dragon's Cry.*

The mirrors shattered.

A stench like burnt hair filled the chamber. Clara blew out her breath to avoid taking it in. The chanting abruptly stopped. Two magi cried out in alarm.

"No!" Queen Anula shouted. "What happened? Why didn't it work? What's gone wrong?"

Melampus collapsed. His magi caught him, but their movements broke the circle. Every pore on Clara's body tingled as if lightning threatened. Then everything was ordinary again. They had failed.

"I'm sorry," Melampus gasped. "At the last moment, something interfered."

"What? What interfered?" the Queen demanded.

"I do not know." Melampus clung to his assistants for support, his face twisted in pain. "Octavia was with us. She was entranced. I could feel it. But then, something destroyed the spell."

"Again," the Queen ordered. "You must try again."

Melampus, terror in his eyes, shook his head.

"Alas, Oh Luminous One, the moon has moved out of alignment. The moment of power has passed. We cannot hope to succeed until the next full moon."

Queen Anula stood very still, fury in her eyes. Clara held her breath, fearing for the life of the chief magus.

"Then begin your preparations for the next full moon," Queen Anula commanded. "I will have her, whatever the cost. Whatever it takes, have it ready. Whatever blocked your way this time, determine how to overcome it. You *will* succeed when next we call Octavia, Melampus. Your life depends on it. The lives of all of your minions depend upon it."

Clara glanced at Sandrigal. The mirror hung serene on his wall. He reflected only the scene that lay before him: the ornate room misty with incense, the magus cowering in the arms of his robed assistants before the enraged Queen. Anula stood silhouetted against a sky rich with stars and now empty of the full moon. If the silver-faced scryer had an opinion, he did not share it.

And that, Clara realized later, was quite odd.

Octavia woke up the next day in her own room to the sharp scent of Alma's poultices. She felt the answering sting of treated cuts in her skin. It seemed that bandages covered nearly every inch of her body.

Grandmother, her hair an unkempt beehive, dozed in a chair next to the bed. She woke as Octavia struggled to sit up.

"How do you feel?" Grandmother put a cool hand on Octavia's forehead. "I don't think you have fever. Alma left you a cup of tea, but it must be tepid by now. Are you hungry? I can have a meal sent up."

"What time is it?"

Grandmother stretched and looked out the window.

"Just after mid-day, I think."

There was a light tap, then Mother walked in.

"Oh, wonderful. You're awake. How do you feel?"

"She's just woken up." Grandmother sounded cross.

"If it doesn't upset you too much," Mother said, "can you tell us what happened?"

Octavia touched that memory and flinched. "I was surrounded by the *mortolo*. Everywhere I looked. I couldn't escape. It was going to take me again; I was sure of it."

"We found you in my mirrored dressing closet," Grandmother said. "Why on earth did you go in there?"

"I thought I heard someone calling me."

"Who?" Mother and Grandmother asked together.

"I don't know." Octavia shook her head fretfully. "A familiar voice. I wasn't thinking about the mirrors. It felt like a dream. I don't understand. It was like walking into a trap. In every mirror the *mortolo* roared." She trembled just from thinking about it.

"Octavia." Mother's face paled. "Things are getting worse. For your own safety, you must leave this place."

"Not now, Melody," Grandmother snapped. "Let the poor child get some rest."

"My daughter is clearly in danger here." Octavia's jaw dropped in surprise at the steel tones in her mother's voice. "If you cannot keep her safe then I will."

"Safe on the river? As you kept Halfnote safe?"

"Please, Mother, Grandmother ..." Octavia looked from one fierce-looking woman to the other. This was almost as bad as being surrounded by the monster. "And people wonder where I got my temper," she said in a light voice, trying to ease the tension.

Mother and Grandmother locked eyes.

"Madame Verre, I would like to speak with my daughter privately now," Mother said.

Grandmother stood abruptly, her body stiff with disapproval. "I'll go tell Alma to send up some soup for Octavia. Would you like some, Madame Breydon?"

"Why, yes, I would." Mother calmly met her mother's angry gaze. "And tea as well."

Grandmother stalked out. Octavia waited until she could hear Grandmother's footsteps on the stairs before speaking.

"Mother, I don't think I've ever heard you and Grandmother fight like that before."

Mother gave her a guilty look. "Despite all of our differences, your grandparents and parents agree on one thing, Octavia. You,

Halfnote and Cadie are very precious to us all. We want desperately to keep you safe."

Melampus had failed. The sorcerer hadn't foreseen Octavia's instinctive response to the spell.

And neither did I, Sandrigal thought. And they had both underestimated the power of the singer's voice. They would have to take more care with their next attempt.

At least there would be a next attempt. Despite the cost, and the danger, Queen Anula was more determined than ever to bring the young singer to Samoya.

Patience.

He could still hope for success. And if the girl survived, she would be powerful beyond belief.

Halfnote and Annie sorted supplies in the top basement two days later when loud voices filtered down from the kitchen.

"That's Peter," Annie said. Grinning from ear to ear, she dropped her list and ran up the stairs.

Halfnote considered the number of things they had left to do and followed. In the kitchen they found the twins' older brother talking with Alice. The bearded young man had long, ropy muscles and a quick smile. Marissa considered that smile highly attractive, as Halfnote and everyone else in Verre House knew. Peter didn't smile now, though. Alma stood with her thick arms crossed. She looked deeply upset.

"Annie, there you are," Peter said. "Go pack your things. We're all going home as soon as you're ready. Pop doesn't want you to spend another night in this place."

The twins exchanged happy looks and ran upstairs.

"You're taking Annie and Alice out of Verre House?" Halfnote gasped, genuinely shocked.

Peter ducked his head. "When our parents heard about Octavia's troubles, they started to worry again. They're afraid the *mortolo* wasn't really destroyed."

"But what will the twins do?" Halfnote asked. "What about their apprenticeships?"

Peter brushed back his dark bangs. "I don't know."

That night, Mama asked Halfnote to join her for a private supper in the visitor's suite. Mama and Papa always stayed there when they were in Albemarle.

"Supper for just you and me?" Halfnote asked in delighted surprise. "No one else?"

"Just us." Mama smiled, but her eyes looked sad. "Papa and Mischa are down at the market, getting ready for our next trip. Alma is looking after Cadie."

Octavia, of course, remained in her own room, recovering.

Halfnote carefully took her seat at the table, doing her best to sit like an adult. She felt nervous. The table had been set just for two. Steaming serving dishes waited on a side cart. This was how Grandpa and Grandma dined, when they ate together in their own quarters.

At first they made small talk. Mama told a funny story about Cadie's attempts to catch a noisy frog. Finally, Halfnote put her fork down with her supper only half eaten.

"Aren't you hungry?" Mama asked.

"My stomach hurts." It seemed rude to be nervous when Mama was giving her a treat, but, well, she was.

"I don't understand. I thought things would be better now. We cured the plague. We destroyed the mirror and rescued Octavia. But it almost feels like things are worse now. How can that be?"

"Life's like that sometimes. It's like the river. You never know what you'll find around the next bend."

"But the river usually warns you. Ripples show you where the underwater logs are. The current picks up when the river bed narrows. Insects are a sign of standing water. Mama, is there something you want to tell me?"

Mama looked at her in amazement. Halfnote felt a little surprised herself.

"My, but you are growing up. I've missed so much. It seems like just yesterday you were the toddler chasing noisy frogs around the raft." Then Mama's expression turned sad.

"Halfnote, you know that we have a complicated family with a lot of different needs. It's hard to know what's right for everyone."

Halfnote nodded and held her breath.

"Octavia is going to spend some time with Papa and me on the river." Mama's voice turned gentle. "She needs help and maybe she can find it in Tulum. She needs to rest. And I think she needs to find a different view of what is important in life."

"But I have to stay here?"

"No, you don't *have* to stay if you don't want to. But I thought it best to ask first. What do you want to do?"

Halfnote blinked. She'd never really gotten to choose for herself before.

It was risky, Halfnote knew, to sneak up to her sister's room before everyone else went to bed. She didn't care. Octavia, still covered with bandages and smelling of medicine, welcomed her with a smile.

"Mama says you're going with them on the river."

"Yes," Octavia held up one bandaged hand. "It seems the wise thing to do at the moment."

"Some buildings on the riverbank will have glass windows," Halfnote said, her forehead furrowed in thought, "But at least you won't see the monster in the water."

"No. At least I hope not."

"How will you get to the lifts? Will you go tonight?"

"No, we'll leave early in the morning. Mother says we'll take the tunnels that Father knows. Apparently they lead all the way down to Lake Kerguelen, if you know which passages to take."

"Papa knows. But Octavia, Mama asked me if I wanted to come with you."

"I know. And you said no? Really? Are you sure?"

Halfnote nodded.

"But why? You love the river. You should go and I should stay here. This is all wrong."

Halfnote sighed. "What will people say about Verre House if we both leave? How will Grandpa feel?"

Octavia squirmed. "That's not your concern."

"Maybe, but I'm also worried about Robbie. He gets bullied a lot. He needs someone to show him how to be a glass singer. I've already taught him a lot when no one else would. Sometimes the others aren't very patient."

"I know you worry about Robbie, Halfnote, but he's still not your responsibility. It's good to care about other people, but you need to look after yourself too."

"I am. I want to learn more about glass singing."

Octavia looked at her younger sister in surprise.

"More than traveling on the river? More than spending time with Mama and Papa? And Cadie and Mischa?"

Now it was Halfnote's turn to squirm.

"I'll see them when they come back."

"You always miss them when they're gone."

"I know, but I'd miss Grandpa and Robbie and Alma if I go. Wherever I am, I'll be sad that someone's not there. And I really do want to learn more about glass singing."

"Why?"

"Why do you like singing so much?"

Octavia smiled wistfully. "I just do. Partly because it's what I'm good at and partly because I love the challenge. Learning a new technique is the best thing in the world. I love figuring out how to do it. I love making beautiful things; clever things. I look at a piece and I've made that. It's real and it's there and I can touch it. Over time I can see how I've improved in making things. Every new piece tells the story of what I learned and how I made it.

"And then I see what our great-great-grandparents made. I'm part of this great chain of beauty. It's fun to see if I can match them, or even beat them. Singing glass is all I've ever wanted to do. When I sing, I feel alive."

Halfnote nodded. "At first, I didn't feel like that. I knew you enjoyed it, but I just did what I was told. This house felt so cold when I first got here. Of course I knew how to sing. I learned from Mama and from you. But when I saw you inside the *mortolo*..."

"What did you see? I've always wondered. You were down in the tunnels with Father."

"I saw the energy with you inside it, just the way I see you now. The monster called to us the way it called to everyone. And I knew how to keep you safe. I knew because of all the times I watched you practice the counter clockwise swirl, and because I know the river currents. I did what I knew and it worked. I followed the flow and you were all right ... I felt ... wow."

"Wow, indeed."

The sisters smiled in unconscious reflection of each other. "I felt like I could do anything," Halfnote said. "Like I was magic. Like ... I don't know. But I'd like to feel that way again. I want to understand how that works."

Octavia's mouth quirked. "I'm jealous. What a journey you're about to take."

"I'm jealous too. I want to go on the river. But I don't know how to do both at the same time."

"Me either," Octavia said. "Imagine all of the stories we'll have to tell each other when I get back."

"Yes," Halfnote sighed. "Just imagine..."

Dragon tales

An eerie silence fell throughout Verre House after Octavia left. Master Verre retreated into his chambers and did not come out again. That afternoon, unusually, the apprentices found themselves with nothing to do. They knew that some new orders had come in, but no one assigned them any tasks.

Alma's kitchen chores were quickly dispensed with. No one dared to disturb Master or Madame Verre to ask what to do. There was even doubt about who between Sad-eyed Sylvia or Four-eyes Frank, as Dan dubbed them, was the senior singer left.

Octavia's Journey   *by Lynette Hill*

In ones and twos, the apprentices filtered out into the little wood behind the house. They climbed trees and threw sticks off the cliff and played tag. No one's heart was really in it. They ended up in a cluster under a great oak on the edge of the cliff overlooking Kerguelen Lake. The bare granite outcropping known as Piasa's Perch jutted out to one side. The astronomers' shelter atop the perch stood empty, of course, as it was still daylight.

At first Galliard, the oldest male apprentice, whistled a merry dance tune. No one felt like dancing, or even cheering up. He switched to a slower, ballad, then gave up whistling altogether. Hefty Marissa, the oldest apprentice overall, looked around at their little group.

"There's hardly anyone left. Do you think Master Verre will close the house? Where will we go if he does? I should take my singer's test in another year or two. I can't leave. My family can't afford to find me another position."

"Don't be silly," Halfnote said, more than a little frightened by the idea. Already she regretted her decision to stay behind. "No one's going to close Verre House. This is the place where glass singing began. Melinda, the very first glass singer, learned the first dragon songs from Piasa's son Falafel right here in this wood."

"Oh, please." Dan, second oldest boy apprentice and now third oldest overall, sneered.

"Stop it," Galliard told him. "I like the dragon stories. Go on, Halfnote, tell us. How did glass singing start?"

Marissa and the two youngest boys, red-headed Laiertes and little Robbie, chorused their agreement. Halfnote tried not to look too pleased. She loved telling the stories almost as much as she enjoyed hearing them.

"Well, all right. Once upon a time, the dragon mother Piasa and her sons Falafel and Capello lived right over there, on Piasa's Perch. Albermarle was still very small back then. A human girl named Melinda came to this grove to collect firewood. She was Kiera's niece."

"Wait," Laiertes said. "Who's Kiera?"

"Who's Kiera?" fat Marissa snorted. "Are you serious? She was the herbalist, the hunter. She was one of Father Bartholomew's original companions. She made the poultice that saved Piasa after the dragon mother was wounded by the poisoned spear. *Who* is Kiera? Really?"

"Hang on." Laiertes pointed at his brilliant red hair. "I'm from Canton, remember? I haven't heard all the dragon stories. That's why I'd like to hear this one."

Halfnote nodded. "Do you know how Albermarle began?" she asked Laiertes. "The story of 'The Great Friendship'? How the human Bartholomew met Piasa the dragon during a famine? They agreed to help each other and that's how the city came about."

"Sure," Laiertes said. "Everyone knows that one. But I've never heard how glass singing actually started."

Halfnote nodded. "So anyway, Melinda came here for firewood. Octavia says Melinda wasn't quite old enough to marry. Falafel was also still young, not yet full grown.

"As it happens, Melinda's home was one of those closest to Piasa's Point. The dragon sang to her sons at night. Melinda, living so near, heard Piasa's every song. They say the music invaded her dreams. She memorized the songs without even trying.

"Octavia says that Melinda was singing one of Piasa's lullabies when Falafel heard her. Melinda sang it to herself as she picked up wood. Falafel was entranced by the beauty of her voice. He crept up across the treetops and began to sing with her.

"Dragons love music. That's why dragons love gold. The dragons say it sings to them. They can hear its tones. Every metal, every substance has its melody. The dragons think gold's harmony is the most beautiful. That's why the metal workers have to stay down in Kerguelen village now. They make the metal scream, with all that melting and pounding. This upsets the dragons."

"But the dragons are gone," Dan pointed out.

"But they might come back."

"You don't really believe that, do you?"

"Why wouldn't I?" Dan's question didn't make any sense to her. He smirked as if he knew something she didn't, but instead of explaining he just shrugged.

"Oh go on," Marissa said. "Don't start that fight again. Tell the rest of the story."

"So, anyway, Falafel taught Melinda more dragon songs. He said that music is the language of dragons. Each chord is a word, or several, depending on pitch and tone and vibration. He taught her many chords and phrases.

"Melinda sang these songs to herself as she went about her daily chores. Funny things started happening. She would sing while she swept up river sand, for instance, and the dust pile would melt. Or the imported glass windows in the mayor's house would sing with her. There wasn't much glass in Albermarle back then, Octavia says. It was hard to make, easy to break and very expensive. The Khelani had not yet come up the river. There wasn't much trade with Tulum or the ocean kingdoms."

"No Khelani?" Galliard asked.

"No, we came later."

"From where?" Galliard hailed from Malmesbury but his mother was Khelani, Halfnote remembered. His townie father owned a large brewery there.

She shrugged. "Mama says we used to live in the chain of islands between Samoya and Tulum. Over time, trade brought us up the river. Anyway, Melinda told Falafel what happened when she sang. He thought it was funny. But his mother heard them. Piasa was furious that Falafel had shared dragon songs with a human. Imagine what it must have been like, to see a dragon mother angry with her son."

Everyone shivered at this, even cynical Dan.

"Even so, Falafel and Melinda continued their friendship and their singing lessons. Soon Melinda could sing the dragon language nearly as well as Falafel. As the years passed, Melinda became known as a great singer. People traveled for miles just to hear her. Tales of the strange things that happened when she sang spread. Melinda taught other villagers the dragon songs. She married and had children.

"But the dragons grew restless. There were no mates for the boys. Mother Piasa didn't like humans learning the dragon language. And three large dragons were too much for the growing number of humans to feed. People who moved to Albermarle from other places felt uncomfortable living so near to dragons."

Octavia's Journey   *by Lynette Hill*

"But the dragons lived here first," Laiertes said.

"I don't think it makes sense either, but Octavia says that at the end, some people were nervous about the dragons. I don't know why those people didn't go live in Kerguelen. Father Bartholomew had to post guards around Piasa's Perch to keep the peace."

"Wait," Dan objected. "That's ridiculous. What do you mean, 'too much for the humans to feed?' Why didn't the dragons hunt for themselves? They're dragons. They can do whatever they want."

"Don't you remember? That was part of the original bargain between Father Bartholomew and Mother Piasa. The humans agreed to provide food so the dragons wouldn't eat all the sheep in the southern plains. That's why the people of Kerguelen hated the dragons. The Kerguelens killed Viridian, Piasa's mate, because he kept attacking their flocks. The people of Albermarle kept large herds of sheep and cattle for the dragons so they wouldn't eat someone else's animals.

"That's one reason Father Bartholomew founded the city of Albermarle. But even a small dragon will eat a whole cow every day if it can. And the bigger the dragon, the bigger its appetite. Octavia said things became quite serious."

"So what happened?" red-headed Laiertes asked. "Why did the dragons leave?"

"Well, one day there was a great noise. Even the humans heard something. Some people said it sounded like a tone or a vibration. Some said it sounded more like a horn. Others said it was a voice, contralto, calling one note.

"The humans all disagreed on what they heard. Only Piasa knew what it meant. The dragons were summoned. People tried to ask who or where the summons came from, but the dragons wouldn't say. Maybe they didn't know.

"Mother Piasa called her sons to her. She announced that they had to leave, and at once. Father Bartholomew, who was quite elderly by then, made his last public appearance. Dressed in full ceremonial robes he called Melinda out of the crowd. She led the humans in singing the dragons' music back to Mother Piasa and her sons. The people sang the lullaby that so entranced them all.

"The citizens of Albermarle sang from the heart and everyone wept; even the dragons. Even Mother Piasa. Then the dragons flew off towards the northeast and were never seen again. Father Bartholomew died three days later.

"Some say Melinda flew off with Falafel, at least for a time. Others say he came back secretly to visit her. But where the dragons went and why, no human can say. If Melinda or Bartholomew knew they did not tell."

"But ... but ... what about glass singing?" Laiertes asked. "They learned the songs from the dragons, but how did people learn that singing would shape glass? Or that you had to heat the glass first? Or the sand, anyway? Or which chords would create a curve instead of a straight line? How to spread, how to twirl, all of it? Was it Melinda or someone else? Did the dragons tell her?"

"I don't know," Halfnote said. "Melinda is honored as the first glass singer so I always thought she was the one who figured it out."

"Maybe that's the story on the wall of the lowest basement," Dan said. For once he looked thoughtful instead of cynical.

"What?" The other apprentices stared at him.

"What are you talking about?" Galliard asked.

"Haven't you seen the figures in the lowest basement?" Dan asked. "I don't know why they're down there, but they are. Little glass dolls in a line on the wall; hasn't anybody seen them?"

"No," Galliard and Marissa said. Robbie glanced at Halfnote but she didn't know what Dan was talking about either.

"There's nothing on the basement walls," Laiertes sneered. "This is a joke, isn't it? We would have seen them. We've all been down there often enough."

"You're right," Marissa said. "Why decorate a basement?"

"It's not even the regular basements." Dan jumped up. "The very lowest one, beneath the regular storage. You know, under the room where they kept us during the plague. Surely I'm not the only one who knows about it. Come on, I'll show you."

Dan set off at a run. The others followed. They tore through the back door into the kitchen to find Madame Verre sitting at the table with

Sylvia, Frank and Alma. Alma was pouring out cups of tea.

"Oh, excuse me, Madame Verre." Dan skidded to a halt. The others couldn't help but bump into him and each other.

"Indeed," Madame Verre replied. "Of course I don't need to remind you that running in the house is forbidden. Where are you all going in such a hurry?"

An embarrassed silence followed.

"Um, well, that is …," Dan stuttered under Madame Verre's sharp gaze. Marissa elbowed Halfnote. She jumped and stepped forward, rubbing her side. Technically, as the eldest apprentice, fat Marissa should do the talking.

"Dan wants to show us something, Grandm …. I mean, Madame Verre. He thinks there are some glass dolls in the lower basements that tell the story of Melinda and Falafel. We haven't been given any work assignments," she added, just in case.

Madame Verre exchanged a look with Alma and then waved them on. "I'm glad to hear that you are putting your spare time to such good use." Her mouth crimped, as if she swallowed a smile. "Please be careful on the steps and take adequate light. Alma will call when she needs help with supper."

"Thank you, Madame," Halfnote said. The others chorused their thanks as well before clattering off. Halfnote glanced back at the foursome at the kitchen table. Frank looked unusually nervous, and frail Sylvia … well, she didn't look frail anymore.

Madame Verre and Alma smiled as the apprentices left. Sylvia did not smile. Neither did Frank. He took his spectacles off and polished them on his tunic.

Madame Verre's expression turned serious. "All right." She took a sip of tea. "What did you want to discuss?"

Frank blinked but Sylvia met Madame Verre's gaze calmly.

"Madame, I received a message yesterday. My auntie died in the plague. She was my last living relative. They burned her body with the other victims."

"Oh Sylvia, I am so very sorry."

"Thank you," Sylvia said in a nearly steady voice. "She was a happy woman. I miss her. But Verre House has been my home for so long now that I scarcely know the place where I was born. I ... I..." Sylvia took a breath.

"I began preparing for my junior master's test before the plague began. As I think you know, the date has been set; according to guild rules it cannot be changed for any reason. I don't want to leave Verre House until the appropriate time, when I am a full master. However, there is no one left to help me train so long as Master Verre remains indisposed. Frank's date hasn't been set, but he also needs to prepare for the test." Frank nodded and put his spectacles back on.

Madame Verre sighed. "Sylvia, Frank, Verre House needs you, now more than ever. However, if you choose to join Geoff and Lorraine or some other house, we can hardly blame you. We will write permissions for you to leave, as we did for the others."

"I don't like Geoffrey, Madame Verre. I never have. I love Lorraine like a sister but I never understood what she saw in him. I don't know why Master Verre trusted him. I don't want to join any enterprise that includes him. The flaws in his character always seemed clear enough to me."

Alma snorted.

"As bad as that? Sylvia, did something happen between the two of you?"

"Nothing ... improper. I wouldn't allow it. But that is the past. My concern is for the present ... and my future. Verre House has the best books, the best facilities, gifted apprentices who also need help. Teaching is as much a part of a master's preparation as practice."

"You wish to stay, then?"

"Yes, very much so,"

"And me," Frank said. "I don't care about Geoff one way or the other, but I'd rather train here. I don't want to start over somewhere else unless absolutely necessary."

"There's enough business, if we can meet the orders that come in," Sylvia said. "The astronomers and some jewelry makers still insist on using our glass. Frank and I will stay and do the work that comes in as long as we can adequately prepare for our tests.

"I would, with your permission, like to consult with other masters outside of this house. Geoffrey aside, I still want to work with Lorraine; at least talk to her. There are other glass masters in Albermarle; none of Master Verre's standing, but still quite skilled. If we could talk to them from time to time it would be helpful. I would like to consult with Mistress Franklyn, for instance, or Master Dylan. Of course we won't share house secrets."

"I know you won't," Madame Verre said, her voice rich with relief. "I am more grateful than you can know. This house needs you. Of course you deserve proper training. By all that's holy I promise, if Verre House cannot meet your needs we will make certain that you and the apprentices find good posts elsewhere."

The apprentice challenge

"But …" Frank said, and then looked at Sylvia.

"There is one other thing." Sylvia's dark eyes reflected true regret. "And I am so very sorry to say this." She looked at Alma. "It's about Robbie. He's a lovely boy, he really is. We understand why Verre House took him in after the floods, we really do."

"But," Madame Verre cut in, "He's not really glass singer material, is he?"

"No." Frank looked relieved. "He doesn't know how to find a pitch, he can't stay on key and he has no sense of rhythm."

"These things can be taught. He has improved, in his time here. And I must say that I've never known Master Verre to be wrong about an apprentice."

"Yes, perhaps," Sylvia said, "with time and patience Robbie might improve a little more. In normal times, I would be willing to work with him. But not now, not with everything else that's going on. We can't afford to take the time to correct his mistakes. The wasted materials, the time spent cleaning up instead of singing … it all adds up.

It delays everyone else."

"He's an excellent dragon," Alma said. "He can build a fire and maintain a steady heat better than any other apprentice. Better even than you, Frank."

"No one makes a career as a dragon alone," Sylvia said. "And I am so sorry to say this, Alma. We aren't asking Madame Verre to send him away. Just, could you keep him in the kitchen? Train him up as a cook? He definitely has talent in that area. I mean, does he have to be a glass singer? If it's the wrong place for him, better to accept that now while he's a boy. There's no shame in being a cook. Dragons know we'd all be lost without you, Alma."

"I'm glad to hear it. For a moment there I thought you were trying to replace me. Of course I'll take Robbie on. That boy has more potential than any of you realize. I'll stake my life on it."

When the apprentices reached the second basement, Dan led everyone over to the darkest corner behind the stairs. Galliard whistled in surprise, then helped him roll a heavy barrel out of the corner. Marissa retrieved a bundle of candles. She lit each one before handing them out. Even Halfnote was surprised to see the half-sized door hidden by the barrel. The apprentices ducked through it to find narrow stairs leading further down.

The damp rock wall reminded Halfnote of the tunnels under Verre House, only this wall was cleaner. The air here was stale, but at least it didn't smell like a sewer.

"Who would bring anything here?" Laiertes asked. "I'd hate to have to carry anything on these stairs."

"The dumbwaiter comes down here." Halfnote pointed to a slot in the far wall.

"We don't all fit in the lift," fat Marissa muttered.

At the bottom of the stairs the apprentices found a large area that looked more like a cavern than a room. The walls and floor remained more or less in their natural state. They spread out, holding up their candles for maximum light as they explored.

"Oh, I don't like this," Laiertes gasped. His candle shook and hot wax dripped onto his hand. He dropped his light and of course it went out. "Oh no. It's too dark."

"It's all right," Robbie said. He found the dropped candle, lit it and handed it back to Laiertes. The red-haired boy stood rooted to the floor, his hands shaking. Robbie sang the calming tones until Laiertes stopped trembling.

"Thanks," Laiertes managed. He scrambled back up the stairs and out of the basement.

"Here they are," Dan called, "See, like I told you."

The other apprentices clustered around to look at the line of little glass dolls. It began in one corner close to the floor. Galliard squatted down for a closer look at the pieces, and gave an appreciative whistle. The first few dolls, images of Falafel and Melinda, stood clean and clear. A line of small squares, each bearing the incised image of a person or symbol, came after the figurines. The squares followed a line around the room, slowly rising until they reached the stairs. There the line vanished. The symbols told the tale of Albermarle's founding. "But why put these here?" Galliard asked. "They didn't even finish smoothing the floor. Why add decorations no one will ever see?"

"But that's not the beginning," Robbie said, holding his candle high. "Look at these tiles here, near the lowest step. Look at the tones etched into them. It's just the basic scales, from middle C."

Whether it was the lingering effects of the calming tones or because they were all relaxed from playing, Halfnote could never say afterwards. But in a supremely rare moment of self-confidence, Robbie sang out the scales as written on the tiles. His voice, a boy's high tenor, resonated flawlessly off the walls.

"Wow, Robbie," Marissa said. "That's really pretty. I wish you could sing like that all of the time."

Halfnote couldn't see Robbie's expression in the dim light, but his head ducked down.

The tiles surprised them all by trembling. A small cloud of dust glowed white in the light of their candles. Then, as one, eight tiles flipped over to reveal a new line of glass figurines. Beside the figures a new line of tiles continued along the wall near the floor. Each depicted a different individual. The apprentices gasped in delight and crowded together for a closer look.

"That's not right." Dan sounded more bewildered than sullen. "These don't show Melinda and Falafel."

"No, they aren't," Galliard said. The older apprentice held his candle up for better light. "This one shows Mother Piasa's mate Viridian. Isn't that right, Halfnote? He was an enormous green dragon with a pair of giant horns just like this tile shows, wasn't he?"

"Yes. That's how the stories describe him, anyway."

"This one shows his death. He was killed by an iron arrow shot by the people of Kerguelen after he ate all their sheep and scorched their pastures. This tile shows Mother Piasa resting in her oak by the Perch. Why the stories insist Mother Piasa nested in a tree and not underground like any normal dragon is beyond me."

"It's a story, Galliard," Marissa said. "It's not meant to be taken too seriously."

Galliard winked at her and continued down the line of tiles. "These show Father Bartholomew and his companions setting out from their village. Father Bartholomew and Mother Piasa haven't met yet at this point. This is the very beginning. See, this tile shows a field of wilted barley. I think this symbol is meant to show how cold it was, even in the summer that year. This one shows starving villagers."

"But, wait." Dan frowned. He held up his candle and ran his hand across the rock wall. "It's changed. Where are the dolls of Melinda and Falafel?"

"Look," Marissa said. "The dolls that were here first have flipped back to show their tiles. Maybe they come and go."

"They turned over when Robbie sang," Halfnote said. "Maybe you have to sing other tones to turn the others."

"Whoever made these figurines knew what they were doing," Galliard said. "Look, it shows the basic scale from middle C. These show the beginning of the story and the beginning scale all at the same time." Galliard sang the scale. The tiles didn't move. He frowned.

They were still trying to figure it out when Sylvia made her way down to the basement.

Octavia's Journey   *by Lynette Hill*

"Wow." Sylvia's dark eyes expanded in surprise. "This looks like the apprentice challenge. I thought that was just a story."

"What's that?" Dan demanded. "Why put it here?"

"Well, if I understand it correctly, this is just the start. They say the challenge was built into the walls when Verre House was constructed. These dolls should run throughout this whole building, all the way up to the attic."

"Well, I've never seen them before," Marissa declared. "I've helped clean this house from top to bottom for the last five years and I've never seen anything like these tiles or dolls. I never even knew this sub-basement existed."

"What's it for?" Galliard asked.

"The challenge is meant to be a training aid," Sylvia said. "At least, that's what Lorraine told me. It's supposed to teach all the skills necessary to become a glass singer. Supposedly, if you succeed in turning over the entire set of figurines, all of the dolls will reveal themselves and then they sing for you."

"Singing dolls?" Dan asked in a skeptical voice. "Do you mean they whistle?"

"Hmm, that does make more sense, especially down here," Sylvia said. "But the story says they actually sing all of the songs that Melinda learned from Falafel from first to last in order. Whoever completes the challenge will receive a great gift and Verre House will stand renewed."

"How is that even possible?" Dan asked.

Sylvia shook her head. "I confess I don't know. The first singers, they knew their business. So much has been forgotten ... But look. Someone's started it. Well, you'll just have to finish it now, so we can all understand how it works. Who did it?"

Everyone turned to look at Robbie.

"Great," Dan groaned. "Now we'll never find out."

"Stop it," Halfnote snapped. "Robbie sang the scales well enough to start the challenge. You all saw him."

"Sure, the *basic* scales," Dan grumbled. "*Anyone* can do that. What about the rest of the tiles? Well, go on, genius; show us how well you can do the rest of them."

"There's no need to be mean, Dan," Sylvia said. "It's not Robbie's fault ..."

"Go on, Robbie," Halfnote urged. "Show them. Look at the tiles. It's the next scale. It starts with the middle C-sharp, a quarter step up from middle C. You can do it."

Robbie stared at her, his eyes wide with panic.

"Yes, you can. Look, the first note is the fire starter note. You use it every day to light the oven. Here, listen to me."

She sang the notes. The tiles didn't move. She glared at Robbie. He shook his head.

"Halfnote," Sylvia said, her eyes sad, "leave him alone."

But she kept singing. Echoes of her voice filled the chamber. Galliard started singing. Marissa joined in. Finally, Robbie sang very quietly. The tiles still didn't move. Everyone but Halfnote stopped.

"Halfnote." Sylvia's voice was gentle. "I think he has to do it by himself. Your tones are getting in the way."

She stopped. She crossed her arms and glared meaningfully at Robbie. He swallowed. The echoes of her tones died off. He took a breath and sang the scale. He made it a quick, rising trill that began with middle C-sharp and bounced seven more notes up the register. The next eight tiles trembled, then flipped one by one.

"Wow. I didn't think he could do it," Marissa said.

Halfnote stamped her foot. "He can do all sorts of things, if people would stop making fun of him."

"All right, everybody," Sylvia said. "This is really interesting but we have work to do. Robbie, Alma needs you in the kitchen. Everyone else will come with me to the main creation room. We need to talk about our tasks for tomorrow."

Madame Verre stayed at the kitchen table after Frank and Sylvia excused themselves. Alma boiled another kettle of water and refreshed the tea pot.

"Well, that's a relief," Madame Verre said after Alma sat back down. "I thought we were about to lose Frank and Sylvia. I don't know what we would have done. Have you heard from Ted?"

"No, but a friend saw him at the lifts yesterday."

"At the lifts? What, working as a porter?"

Alma nodded.

"That's dreadful. He can do better than that. Ted's a talented singer. It's bad enough that he left without saying good-bye. Why didn't he join Lorraine and Geoff?"

"Maybe he doesn't like Geoff either."

"Franklyn sent word that her studio could use an experienced hand. We should tell Ted that he has our permission to seek a new glass singing post. In his right mind, Fortis would die of embarrassment at the idea of a Verre House singer working as a porter. Right now I doubt that he would even care. All he does is sit in his chair in the dark, brooding. Why I insisted on marrying that stubborn old goat all those years ago I can't remember."

"I believe you said that he made you laugh."

"Mmm. Youth. Alma, Fortis would never allow the thing I'm going to do next, so don't tell him. I'm an actress, not a glass singer. I'll deal with this the way a theater handles a haunted stage. This house needs a cleansing and the sooner the better."

"Perhaps tonight, even," Alma said with a smile.

"Yes. I've already asked around. I think we can get a good crowd in after the last shows. Theater people are always up for a good party after a performance."

"I can put on a nice spread, but we need more wine."

"Send Galliard and Dan. They'll have to hurry before the market closes. Dragons know we've wasted enough of this day. Next time you have a chance, talk to Ted. Invite him for supper. Make sure he knows we're still his friends. Whatever he thinks, we do still feel an obligation. Tell him he's welcome back any time."

Steps sounded on the stairs from the basement as the apprentices and Sylvia trouped back up. Everyone but Robbie headed off towards the creation rooms.

"Excuse me, M...madame. I'm to h...help Alma."

Octavia's Journey   *by Lynette Hill*

A cleansing

Halfnote stared at the ceiling. It did not creak. Marissa snored in the other bed. Halfnote didn't mind sleeping alone on this warm night, but she wondered how it would feel in the dead of winter.

Why did I choose to stay?

Octavia had only been gone a day and already Halfnote ached at her absence.

If I was on the river, I wouldn't learn more about singing the glass. I wouldn't have learned about the apprentice challenge. And honestly, what would Robbie do without her? *He never stands up for himself. And Grandpa ...* she really didn't know what to think or do about Grandpa.

She hadn't quite fallen asleep when the noise began wafting up the staircase. She heard the front door open and close and open again; then laughter and the sound of many people talking. She didn't recognize any of the voices.

"Do you hear that?" Marissa sat up and rubbed her eyes. "What's going on?"

"I don't know."

As they peeked out of their doorway, Sylvia came down the steps, still wearing her work dress.

"What is it? What's happening?" the singer asked.

Drumming started up from what could only be one of the creation rooms. A pair of flutists began a wild duet. They danced through the gaily dressed crowd, still playing. Everyone gathered wore a mask or face paint. Halfnote didn't recognize anyone.

"I think they're actors," Sylvia said. "What are they doing here? It's a party, but why didn't anyone tell us?"

Marissa and Halfnote followed the singer down. Across the way the boys and Frank were coming down as well. They looked equally bemused. A line of masked dancers snaked out of the crowd, drawing in new members as they turned and twisted. Some played tambourines or wore bells on their wrists and ankles.

"Join us," the laughing leaders called and everyone did. Dancers zig-zagged through the reception hall before drawing the whole crowd into the main creation room. Drummers and other musicians lined the walls. Around the making platform tables struggled to hold an amazing amount of food and drink.

"It's like Octavia's celebration," Robbie murmured.

Except with more dancing, Halfnote thought. And she didn't seem to know any of the guests. She and Robbie clung to each other in the middle of the increasingly manic dancers until a fortuitous turn of the line brought them to Alma. She also wore a mask and a great red cloak but there was no mistaking the portly cook's large frame. She pulled them away from the other dancers and gave them each a sweetbread. The line of dancers was generally breaking up anyway. They clumped into small laughing groups of people that helped themselves to food and drink. The guests all seemed to know each other. The musicians continued to drum and play, each new song more frantic than the last. The noise grew louder as voices and music reverberated off the walls.

Alma put her arms around them. "Something's about to happen. But don't be afraid. We're all safe."

The door to the creation room slammed open. All music and talking stopped. A horrible looking horned and hairy creature stood in the doorway, pounding its chest. It leaned out and roared around at the crowd. Followed by a pair of horned and equally hairy minions, the creature leaped into the room. All three ran around howling and growling at everyone. People screamed and pretended to be afraid. The creature, actually a man dressed in a costume made of smelly wolf skins, leered at Alma and her charges.

He sniffed around them like an aggressive dog and then ran off to frighten others. After the creature and its companions made a full circuit, they jumped up onto the making platform and began helping themselves to the food. They smashed it into their mouths and smeared it all over their hairy bodies.

"Now that's just disgusting," Marissa said. She'd joined them unnoticed. In fact, all of the apprentices now huddled around Alma. A nearby drum began a soft but insistent beat. Other drums joined it.

Octavia's Journey   *by Lynette Hill*

Members of the crowd began to shake their bells at the creatures. They roared and raged as if pained by the drumming and jingling. The crowd began to call out and bang their cutlery against their plates. Someone threw a raw egg at the chief beast and it splattered against the back of his head. The air filled with food and shouting as the party-goers turned against the make-believe beasts. At first the creatures roared and threw food back, but the partyers banded together and soon prevailed. Drumming and jeering, they drove the howling trio of monsters from the room.

    The door slammed shut and everyone cheered. Musicians began a lively tune and everyone danced. Fresh supplies of wine and food passed from hand to hand.

    "All right, you lot," Alma herded the apprentices to the door. "Back to bed."

    As they left, members of the crowd shook the apprentices' hands or patted their heads and shoulders.

    "Blessings," they called. "All good to you and yours." The apprentices passed Frank and Sylvia, who didn't appear to see them. The singers laughed and carried on an animated conversation with a group of masked guests. The apprentices left the room to a chorus of good wishes. Out in the corridor they found bits of food ground into the floor and smeared across the walls. The trail led out the main doorway, which still stood open to the night air.

    "Oh, I'm not looking forward to cleaning this up tomorrow," Laiertes said.

    "Don't worry about it," Alma said. "Straight off to bed, all of you. We'll deal with everything in the morning."

    Halfnote thought she was too excited to rest but in fact she fell asleep even before Marissa began snoring. The somber chanting that rose up later from the main creation room invaded her dreams as the buzzing of bees. In her night vision she chased one truly annoying bee through all the rooms of Verre House from the lowest basement to the highest attic. Then, in the way of dreams, she found herself in Octavia's room, staring at the mirror that used to hang over the wash basin. The furious buzzing came from the mirror. She drew cautiously closer and peered into it. Something with large eyes stared back.

"Wake up." Marissa shook her. "It's late. Alma is calling everyone to breakfast."

They found Grandma sitting at the head of the table in Grandpa's usual seat.

"Today is a new day," she announced. "Today we put the plague and all that came after behind us. We miss those who are gone, but we who are still here must stand together. We have orders to meet, we have skills, we have all necessary resources. We remain, in Verre House, in a most fortunate position. The honor of this house is at stake. In everything we do we must maintain the standards of the house that gave birth to glass singing.

"Now, attend to Sylvia. She has your assignments."

To everyone's surprise, these did not include cleaning up. They found the creation room and all of its surrounding corridors freshly scrubbed and scented. They all looked so spic and span that for a moment Halfnote wondered if the party had been a dream.

A spy reports

Clara knew the importance of the message before the clerk finished decoding. The king's scribes didn't realize their efforts revealed yet another code. She snatched the parchment up as soon as the secretary finished. She rushed immediately to the Queen's quarters, not caring what gossip her haste might spawn. She paused outside the door just long enough to calm her breath before entering.

"My Queen. Your man in Albermarle reports."

"At last. Read it."

"To your most Immanent Radiance ..."

"Yes, yes, what is the message?"

"The events you hoped for have come to pass. Singer Octavia left Verre House in the company of her parents on the morning of the day that I write. Even now she travels south on the Khelana River, ever

closer to Samoya. ...

"At last," Queen Anula laughed gleefully. "As Melampus foresaw. She comes to us. Already she is on her way. I shall have her. See, she is drawn. She cannot help herself. Melampus' spell was more successful than we realized. I knew such power could not be thwarted. Come, Clara, there is much to do."

"Great Lady, there is a little more to the letter."

"Well, quickly woman, read on."

"Brightest Star, there is a persistent rumor that the House of Verre is in disarray, cursed by the monstrous mirror after all.

"They say that the mortolo *revenged itself by taking Singer Octavia's talent in payment for the plague's cure. Grand Master Fortis Verre is said to have shut himself up in his chambers, distraught. Several of the senior staff quit or have been dismissed. Verre House, once acclaimed for its role in stopping the plague is now shunned as cursed. Some say that the Singer Octavia is mad, haunted by visions of the* mortolo. *Some even say that the demon mirror possesses her.*

"Our spies follow Singer Octavia and observe, awaiting your further instructions. Others continue to watch Verre House.

"I remain your most humble servant..."

"Excellent. They have done well."

"Yes, Illumined One. Is there a reply?"

"In a moment. Sandrigal!"

"Yes, Oh Beautiful Queen?" the mirror responded.

"What of this rumor, that Octavia's talent was taken by the *mortolo*? Is it true? Is she possessed? Is she mad?"

"It is as you observed for yourself, Illustrious One. All of Octavia's efforts to sing the glass have gone wrong since she returned from the tainted mirror. This is the cause of the rumors. She is no doubt quite frustrated, but she is not crazy."

"Excellent. Clara, here is my reply..."

Octavia's Journey   *by Lynette Hill*

Kitchen boy

No one made any formal announcement about Robbie's new role in the kitchen. Several days passed before most of the other apprentices realized he didn't work with glass anymore. The rest of the staff stayed busy making wine bottles, jewelry settings and new telescope lenses. Halfnote tried to find time to talk to Robbie but she kept getting called away by Frank and Sylvia.

No one said anything about it, but they all enjoyed not having to do kitchen chores anymore. Dan protested when Sylvia told him to wash up after breakfast one morning.

"What? Why me? That's the kitchen boy's job."

"What do you mean, 'kitchen boy?'" Galliard asked. "Do you mean Robbie?"

"Alma and Robbie left early for the market," Sylvia said. "You certainly eat your share of their cooking. Like it or not, the dishes still need to be washed. Bring a load of coal to the smaller making room after you finish here."

"See you later, kitchen boy," Galliard called cheerfully as the other apprentices left. Dan stomped out the back door with a bucket to get more water.

Halfnote sighed. She missed working in the kitchen. Well, she missed spending time with Alma and Robbie anyway. She also felt a twinge of jealousy at the thought of Robbie enjoying the sights and sounds of the market without her. And to think she could have spent this fine day on the river with the rest of her family. What had she been thinking when she chose to stay here?

Octavia's Journey   *by Lynette Hill*

On the river

    Octavia knew from the moment she boarded her parents' raft that joining them was a terrible mistake. She stood to one side holding Cadie while Mother, Father and cousin Mischa lashed down their cargo and prepared to leave. Even her cousin, orphaned by the great floods of two years ago, now appeared as comfortable on her parents' raft as if he'd been born on it.

    And I am as out of place as a fish trying to live on land. Oh why did I agree to this?

    She barely knew where to sit or stand. Her parents, Mischa and even Cadie moved about the raft with the ease of long practice. She felt always in the way. The bobbing of the craft even in quiet waters kept her always off-balance. The constant breeze teased at her hair and clothing as if it deliberately mocked her. She had no idea what was expected. Actually, *nothing* seemed to be expected of her. She hated feeling so helpless. *Useless.* Is this what she could expect from the rest of her life?

    "Just rest," Mother said. "Be still and enjoy the view." Octavia gritted her teeth against the calming tones.

    I am not a child.

    Mother and Father might remove the glass from their raft, but they couldn't take it all out of the world. As Halfnote predicted, that first day they passed building after building displaying giant glass windows. Octavia sat in the shelter staring at the water.

    So much for avoiding my problem.

    Eventually they moved into less settled areas. Octavia's breath and heartbeat settled. A mirror on a passing raft caught her eye long enough to fling a monster at her. A moment's horror and then it was gone. Octavia lay on her back and stared at the sky. It was late in the day now; the sun moving toward the western horizon.

    How can I live like this?

    Would she live in seclusion for the rest of her life, made hermit by this horrible curse? Would she be that crazy woman in a cave?

After that first horrible day things did improve. Leaving behind Lake Kerguelen with its over-populated shores, they traveled now through farmland and forest. The hamlets they passed were too small and poor for glass windows. Other craft were fewer and further between. She began to learn the trick of it, looking away at the first flash of light that indicated danger. On the third day, her trouble became not avoiding glass but simple boredom.

"Mother, I have never been so idle. How can you do this?"

Mother smiled. "It is a different rhythm. See how you feel about things in a week."

I'll be dead of ennui in a week.

Octavia tried to shove that thought aside as unhelpful.

Think of sitting and watching as a new technique. That idea didn't help much. *No technique lasts all day.*

Even the process for creating a healing mirror was meant to be completed within an hour, before voices became strained. But some complex pieces did take several days, her more sensible side noted. Some objects would be worked, put aside to harden and then worked again. Some of these pieces took several weeks, depending on the number of layers.

This meandering southern half of the river would, eventually, take them all the way to great seaport of Tulum. Father said that the current at this point ran so slowly that almost anyone could walk faster than the river. It generally took a horse and rider about a month to travel from Kerguelen to Tulum. The same journey would take them around three months on the raft.

Octavia watched her mother through lidded eyes.

I have never understood how Mother could choose the river. Just because she likes living on it doesn't mean that I will. Just because Father is Khelani...

"Mother, she asked, "don't you miss Verre House?"

Mother smiled, though her eyes looked sad. "No sweetheart. I miss you and Halfnote, and my parents but ... no. Not at all. For me, Verre House was a prison."

Octavia barely knew what to make of that. *A prison?*

Octavia's Journey   *by Lynette Hill*

"You don't miss singing the glass?"

"I still sing."

"You do? I thought ..."

"I still sing, sweetheart. I don't make a business of it, but I enjoy the art. Of course I do. I make needed things, gifts ... cutting blades, bowls, trinkets. We often decorate the raft with chimes and sun catchers. Just not on this trip." Mother grimaced as if regretting her words.

No, not this trip.

Flat fields of wheat and barley stretched out as far as she could see on the eastern bank. Tall trees graced the much hillier western bank. They'd caught the weather perfectly. Here in late summer strong sunlight still warmed the days.

I should enjoy this. The scenery is beautiful.

Later, Octavia paced restlessly up and down one edge of the raft. She could resolve nothing floating down the Khelana at a snail's pace. She was trapped on a square of wood with nothing to do but think.

Oh why did I agree to do this?

Her rippling reflection, unhappy but unmarred by the monster, stared back at her from the surface of the river. *I am safe here. Safe from solving my problem, anyway ...*

She offered to help pole the raft, just to burn off some nervous energy. Father's eyebrows rose, but Mother caught his eye and gave a small nod.

"It's shallow enough here," he agreed. "Have you watched how we do it? Look out for obstacles and keep an easy rhythm."

He demonstrated by pushing the pole down until his hands neared the top. Then he pulled it out and spun it around to quickly grab the other end. Mucky water flowed over his hands and arms. He stabbed the water again, letting the pole pull away a little with the current. When the pole struck bottom he shoved down with all his might. His biceps bulged as he pushed.

"Sure you want to do this?"

"Oh go on," Mischa called from his post at the tiller. Cadie sat with him, 'helping.' "Let her do something useful. There's no room for passengers on this raft."

Father grinned. Octavia turned her back on Mischa. She felt restless and irritable, but that was hardly Father's fault. Or Mischa's. She took the pole and slid it into the water. It hit something solid sooner than she expected. The impact stung her hands. She only just managed to hold on. She pushed with all of her strength and the pole slipped. Apparently she pushed on a rock. It rolled and drew the pole unexpectedly away from the raft. Unbalanced, Octavia fell into the river with a mighty splash.

She kicked to the surface, happy to discover that she still knew how to swim. Father jumped in after her.

"Are you all right?" He treaded water beside her.

"Of course I am."

Octavia swam to the raft where Mother helped her climb on. She ignored Mischa as he howled with laughter. Father disappeared beneath the surface for a moment. He swam back and flung the pole onto the raft before hoisting himself on board.

"Next time, try to hang onto the pole."

Having begun of course she had to continue. By sundown, when Father insisted on taking over again, she felt as if she had spent more of the afternoon in the river than out of it. The pole kept sticking in mud or sliding off rocks. She didn't see obstacles like submerged trees or boulders in time to avoid them.

"But how can you see them? They're under water."

Father pointed at a smoother part of the river. "See those little ripples just over there?"

"No. I just see sunlight."

"The ripples in the water affect the reflecting light. Look how the sunbeams sparkle there. When you see the light just above the surface move like that you'll know there are ripples there. The ripples tell you that there's something under the water. When you can see the ripples, then you can start poling again. For now, just sit on the prow and watch. Look for the little ripples."

"That was Halfnote's job." Octavia wasn't sure whether to feel insulted or amused. "She loved this, sitting on the front and watching." Then she sighed. "Halfnote should be here, not me."

Octavia's Journey   *by Lynette Hill*

"Yes, Halfnote should be here." Father jabbed his pole into the water with much more force than necessary. "You should both be here, so we could be a proper family all together again."

"So why didn't you bring her?"

"Your mother insisted that we give her a choice. Having given her that choice, your mother says that we must of course abide by it." Father continued with such energy that Mischa, who poled the other side, called out in protest.

"Come back to the tiller," Mother told Mischa. "Paul wants to push the raft by himself for now. I need to start supper in any case."

"Father..."

He paused and gave Octavia a wan smile.

"In the very first weeks of our marriage, your mother and I made an agreement. She has to listen to me on the river and I have to listen to her in town. Of course, when we made our pact, I didn't realize how much time we would spend in Verre House. Or that I would leave my children there."

He started poling with renewed vigor.

"Father," Octavia said, "I'm really happy there. It's the right place for me."

"So everyone tells me. And Halfnote?"

"She did choose to stay. We talked about it. She wants to learn more about glass singing."

"I know," Father sighed.

"We'll be back there soon."

"It's three months to Tulum by raft. We won't return to Albermarle until next spring at the earliest, if we go all the way there and back again."

Oh...

Octavia's Journey   *by Lynette Hill*

A busy night

Halfnote woke with a strong need to pee. As she tiptoed back to bed Sylvia slipped past the door. Where was the singer going at this hour? Sylvia paused at the foot of the stairs to look around. Halfnote froze. The singer crossed the hall and vanished into the darkness.

Just as Halfnote started to move again, someone else appeared out of the shadows. Robbie headed for the kitchen. Now where was *he* going? Surely he got all of the snacks he wanted during the day. That was one of the perks of working in the kitchen, after all.

Halfnote followed. To her surprise, Robbie turned away from the kitchen and took the steps to the storage basements. He didn't even take a candle. Halfnote kept one hand on the wall for balance as she followed. She was half way down when a light flared below.

Halfnote made it to the bottom step before it vanished. Fortunately, the candles were still stored on the shelf by the door along with spare steel and flint. She found one and lit it by feel.

"Robbie," She called softly. What could he be up to? She continued down the stairs to the second basement. Robbie was nowhere to be seen. A noise led her to the little door that Dan had showed them. It stood open. A faint glimmer of flame reflected off the moist steps. Shaky tones reverberated up those same steps. Robbie's voice squeaked and cracked. Was he trying the apprentice challenge after all?

She found Robbie squatted next to the line of figurines, trying to decide what to do next. The scales on the first wall simply ran up the notes from lowest to highest. The notes on the next wall displayed several variations of the calming song. Again, easy enough, even for him. The little dolls on the first wall showed Mother Piasa and her mate Viridian. They flew up to Piasa's Perch, made their nest and laid their three eggs. The last figurine showed Viridian stuck through by an arrow and falling into a barley field. The next wall showed Father Bartholomew and his companions setting out from their village.

After that came the meeting of Father Bartholomew and Mother Piasa. The combination of characters also indicated a step up in the difficulty of the notes.

Halfnote held up her candle to look. "Wow. You've already finished two walls."

"They were easy." Robbie shrugged. "The real challenge begins here. It combines notes and asks you to hold for different intervals."

"You can do it."

"My voice wobbles. I'm not always sure of the key."

"Don't worry. I'll help you."

Are you Khelani?

Octavia sat on the prow of the raft contemplating the current. As the days passed, she deciphered the messages in the river. She was beginning to understand the meaning of sunlight sparking just above the water, or a point of stillness in a turbulent flow.

A nearby splash caught her attention. Another Khelani raft, flying the flag of a rival clan, headed upriver against the current. It passed so near that she could simply step across if she wanted. The passengers, apparently a family including two teen-age girls, whistled and called cheerful insults. Mischa stopped poling long enough to pound his bare chest. He laughed and yelled back. A mirrored sun catcher flashed bits of monster and Octavia looked quickly down, her pleasure in the moment destroyed.

A head suddenly popped up out of the water.

"Hi," a smiling boy said. He held on to the raft with one hand and wiped water from his eyes with the other.

"Hello." Octavia shakily returned his smile and willed her heart to slow down.

"Are you Khelani?" the boy asked.

A shout from the other raft caught his attention. The boy let go and swam off. Octavia watched as he pulled himself onto his own craft in one smooth motion. He waved to her as their rafts passed out of sight from each other.

Octavia ran a hand across her hair, still tightly bound in glass singer braids. Most Khelani women wore their uncut hair in a soft bun or ponytail. Mother created her own adaptation of the Khelani hairstyle by weaving colored beads and bits of shell into a bun. Octavia considered what tangles the ever-changeable river breezes might create in her fine locks and decided to keep the braids.

Am I Khelani?

She certainly didn't enjoy river life in the way that the rest of her family did.

I know who I am. I am Octavia Breydon, a singer of Verre House. My ancestors learned to sing from dragons. I am the only person to ever return alive from a mortolo. *I healed thousands with the knowledge I brought back.*

These thoughts did not cheer her as they usually did.

If I never sing the glass again, who am I? What will I do?

Octavia blinked and looked around. At some point the movement of the raft and the warmth of the afternoon had lulled her to sleep. The raft now bobbed by the riverbank, docked among many others. It looked as if they stopped among a whole village made up of Khelani rafts. Smoke and cooking smells filled the air. Cheerful voices chattered and called in every direction.

"Where are we?"

How long had she slept? Sunlight filtered low through the trees. Clearly it was late in the afternoon.

"Tondo," Mischa said.

"What's Tondo?"

"It's a meeting point. Nobody wants to take the rough water that's coming up in the dark, so everyone camps here overnight. Your mother said not to wake you. She thinks you need to get more rest. Your parents have gone to talk with the clan elders. Tomorrow we'll be back on the river. Tonight we celebrate."

"What are we celebrating?"

"Meeting up, what else?"

Octavia clung to Mischa's arm for balance as they stepped from raft to raft on their way to shore. Apparently the path was predetermined.

Octavia couldn't tell how everyone else knew where it was but all who headed to shore or came back again followed the same route. No one seemed to mind the parade of people using their rafts as a walkway. Families carried on cooking and washing as if this were the most normal thing in the world.

Octavia smiled at the number of girls who called greetings to Mischa. Like most of the Khelani males here he was shirtless and barefoot, wearing only knee-length breeches. Her cousin, Octavia realized, was quite good-looking. Just a year younger than herself, Mischa already stood a head taller. He was nearly as tall as Father. The bicep she clung to for balance was tight with the long muscles built by hours of poling, swimming and handling cargo. His black hair, newly washed, hung straight and glossy to his shoulders. His bright eyes only made him that much more attractive.

Few people looked past him to Octavia, although she did get one or two curious glances. One motherly looking woman leaned over to her another and asked rather loudly, "Who's that townie girl with Melody's boy?" Octavia flushed and looked away. She made unexpected eye contact with a gray-headed man just as she and Mischa stepped onto shore. The man gave her a friendly nod.

"Well, Mischa," he said, "who's your pretty friend?"

"Uncle Tal!" Mischa's ever-present grin widened. "Don't you recognize her? This is my cousin Octavia."

"Octavia? Paul and Melody's Octavia?" Uncle Tal's expression changed from cheerful curiosity to awestruck amazement. "Dearest Octavia." He took her hand in both of his. "Welcome. We are all so very grateful to you."

"Who is it?" A woman carrying a load of wet clothing paused to ask Uncle Tal. "What's her name?"

"It's Octavia." Uncle Tal pulled her over to the washer woman. "Paul and Melody's Octavia. You know, she fell into the mirror and brought back the cure to the plague."

The woman gasped and the crowd milling about them all gasped with her. "Oh," the woman said. "Oh, Octavia."

Octavia gave her a polite but nervous smile. The woman

Octavia's Journey   *by Lynette Hill*

dropped her bundle of newly cleaned clothes onto the mud of the riverbank as she reached out to touch Octavia. Startled, Octavia pulled back. The woman's hands flew to her own face, then to her belly and then back to Octavia's arm.

"Octavia. You saved us. You saved my children. Thank you. May Hamsa ever bless you."

"Um." Octavia looked at Mischa for help. He looked equally astonished and uncertain. Others hurried over, some herding children.

"This is my Alan," a bearded man said. He held up a boy about two or three years old. "He was on death's door when word of the cure came. In three days' time he was playing again as if he'd never been sick. Thank you."

"Th ... that's wonderful."

"All thanks to your bravery." Uncle Tal patted her shoulder. Others crowded up as well, touching her and calling thanks.

"My whole family," the woman with the dropped washing bundle said. "My husband and five children; my sisters and their families. And me. You saved us all. May Hamsa bless you and all your descendants forever."

"It wasn't just me," Octavia said. "My sister Halfnote saved me from the mirror. Without her I would never have been able to bring the cure back."

"But you entered the mirror to save your grandfather," Uncle Tal said. "What courage that took!"

"That was an accident. It shouldn't have happened."

"And when you returned with the cure," the laundress added as if she hadn't heard, "you shared it. You didn't keep it to yourself the way a greedy townie would. You told everyone." The gathering crowd called their agreement.

"Well of course I shared it." Octavia flushed. Did anyone seriously think she might have done anything else?

"Here." Another middle-aged woman pushed forward three children of various ages. "Look here. These are my brood. Hania and Zoe and Jane. They're alive because of you. Thank you. Surely Hamsa must bless you."

"I'm so glad they're all right." Octavia stepped back to avoid the crush of the crowd but found the river blocked her escape. "Uncle Tal, it's lovely to see everyone, but we're supposed to meet my parents for supper. They'll wonder where we are."

"Of course, of course," Uncle Tal said. "I'm very happy to show you the way."

Taking Octavia's arm, he easily found a path through the massed onlookers. As they moved past people reached out to touch Octavia. The chant of her name and calls of "thank you" and "you saved us" filled the air. Octavia found herself nodding and smiling to what seemed like hundreds of people. Mischa, holding tight to her other arm, looked as daunted as she felt. It took an eternity to move the few feet from the riverbank to her parents' fire.

Octavia flung herself into her father's protective embrace. "I don't know what to do," she murmured against his solid chest. She didn't want to upset people, but what could she say? It had all been an accident. She wasn't a hero. And she couldn't help anymore anyway.

"It's all right," he told her. "These are our friends."

Uncle Tal appeared to be taking charge of things.

"Everyone," he announced, "this calls for an extra special celebration. Where are the musicians? Where are your tastiest dishes? Tonight let us dance and sing to show our appreciation for Octavia's bravery and sacrifice."

Everyone cheered and suddenly the mass of people staring at Octavia dispersed in all directions. As late afternoon faded into evening, she greeted people, tasted special dishes and applauded an amazing variety of dancers, jugglers and singers. A line of people, most known to her parents by name, came by to shake hands and thank Octavia. Many were relatives that she'd never met.

"It's like your singer's party." Mischa spoke through a mouth full of nutty pastries brought by a well-wisher. Octavia cringed at the reference. This felt nothing at all like the gathering that celebrated her promotion from apprentice to singer. There she knew she deserved the accolades from people she knew well. Here she felt like a fraud.

Mischa looked confused when she tried to explain.

Octavia's Journey   *by Lynette Hill*

"But you did bring the cure back. Even if you did fall into the mirror by accident and even if Halfnote did help you get back out. You did find the cure and you did share it with everyone. You didn't keep it to yourself or try to sell it. Of course they're grateful. Of course you deserve this."

"But of course we told everyone," Octavia said. The thought of doing anything else, the idea that she might hold the dying to ransom, as it were, appalled her.

Eventually the evening's festivities came to an end. The cascade of well-wishers trickled away. The bonfires at each end of the clearing burned down to glowing red embers. The tempo of music changed from rowdy to wistful. People straggled off in all directions. At the last a muscular older man wearing formal Khelani breeches and embroidered shirt sang a blessing on the evening. Octavia found herself caught up in his wonderful baritone. For once she could appreciate a bit of music for its own sake, without thinking about how to use it to make something.

It appeared that they intended to spend the night where they sat. On one side, Father spoke quietly to an elderly man she had not met. Mischa, sprawled on his back on her other side, snored softly. Octavia settled against Father's shoulder and closed her eyes. Father put his arm around her. Octavia sighed. Her eyes fluttered shut and she slid easily away into a deep sleep.

Why Robbie persists

Halfnote sighed and kicked off the sheet. Fat Marissa snored away in the other bed, as annoying as any buzzing bee. None of Halfnote's usual tricks for falling asleep were working. Clouds covered the sky so she couldn't count the stars. Unable to lie still any longer, she slipped out of bed and down to the basements.

Robbie barely acknowledged her. He squatted beside the wall, staring at it. Halfnote followed his eyes to the next line of tiles. They showed Nimos holding two large money bags as he rode astride Mother

Piasa. Traditionally, the image of Nimos indicated a minor key. And complexity, as the merchant's son was a controversial character in the story of Albermarle.

"Robbie," Halfnote said again. He just nodded.

"Can I help?" She didn't know what else to say.

Robbie shook his head. "I need to work this out for myself."

Fair enough, Halfnote thought, but she doubted that he could handle the tones required by this next line of scales alone. "It's a minor key," she said.

"I know," Robbie snapped.

Halfnote blinked, surprised and a little hurt by his tone. She was just trying to help. "You just need to ..."

"Halfnote ..." Robbie sighed and shut his mouth.

"Are you all right?" She'd never seen him so irritable.

"Y...yes. I just ..."

"It's hard, isn't it? I didn't know it would get so hard. Look at this one ..."

"Halfnote. Stop it. I have to figure it out for myself. It doesn't count if you do it for me."

She rolled her eyes. Why was he being so difficult? Of course he needed her help.

"Why are you still doing this, anyway?" she felt more than a little irritated herself. "I thought ... I thought you were happy in the kitchen. Do you really want to be a glass singer after all?"

Robbie sat still for quite a long moment.

"I like cooking," he said. "I like being with Alma. When I came here no one asked me if I wanted to sing the glass. They just assumed that I would. My Ma was a cook too, you know. My Da, he hunted. Ma cooked the meat he brought home. She sold meals to people on the river."

"Were they Gorani?"

He shrugged. "I think Da might have been. He didn't look Gorani. He was short and dark like me, but he had their ways. He had the Gorani accent. Ma, I think she might have been a townie, but I don't know which town. Our house was wooden, not stone like most Gorani houses. It stood on stilts out over the river. People could come right up to Ma's window in their rafts or boats to buy a meal. The Khelani were some of our best customers."

"Do you miss your parents?"

"Sometimes," Robbie admitted. "Sometimes I barely remember them. I wish I knew more about them. I mean, was Da really Gorani? I don't know. If Ma did come from a town, well, which one? How did they end up in our house on the river? I don't think I ever met their parents or any other kin. Even if I do have any living relatives I don't know them. I wouldn't recognize them if they came to Verre House looking for me. You have all of Clan Breydon. You know your mother's ancestors back to Father Bartholomew's time. You know who you are and where you come from. I'm just me."

Halfnote barely knew what to say. Shy, hesitant Robbie never spoke at length, never spoke without stuttering, and almost never mentioned his parents. The boy speaking to her now seemed a completely different person.

"After the floods Papa told all of Clan Breydon to look out for your family," Halfnote said. "Mama says the waters were so strong that they changed the Khelana's course. Nothing looks the way it did before. No one's sure where your house was. They're only certain that it's not there anymore. But they did look."

Robbie sighed. "I know. I'm grateful to be in Verre House. I'm grateful your family took me in. I ... I wanted to sing for them. I wanted to sing well for Master Verre, to thank him for giving me a place. It's hard, not doing well. It's frightening. I feel like I'm letting Master Verre down when I sing badly. For a long time I was afraid he would send me away if I couldn't sing."

"Of course Grandpa won't send you away. And you *can* sing. I've heard you hit every note perfectly. You just need confidence. Tell Grandma you don't want to be in the kitchen anymore."

"I am happy in the kitchen. I like being with Alma. Sometimes when I think of my mother, I see Alma's face instead."

Halfnote frowned. "Now you really don't make sense. If you're happy in the kitchen, why try the challenge? Why bother? No one cares if you don't sing."

Octavia's Journey　　　　　　　　　　　　　　　　*by Lynette Hill*

Robbie fell silent again. Halfnote watched as the flickering light of their candles fell across the glass figurines. One figure would stand out for a moment, then fall into shadow. What would happen if you put the candle inside the glass dolls, she wondered. What kind of patterns would the colors make on the white walls? Would you see an image of the figure or just random colors?

Robbie sighed. "I want to thank Master Verre for taking me in. I want him to know that I am grateful and worthy of his charity. And I want Dan to stop calling me 'kitchen boy' just because he thinks I can't sing the glass. Halfnote," he looked at her directly for the first time. "Go back to bed. You can't help me anymore. I have to do this by myself."

She made it all the way to the top of the basement stairs before bursting into tears.

"Halfnote." It took her a few minutes to compose herself enough to see who spoke.

"Come and have some tea, dear," Alma said. The portly cook sat at the kitchen table with a steaming kettle, two cups and a plate of cookies. "What's the trouble?"

"Robbie doesn't want me to help him anymore. He told me to go away. I could be on the river now, with Octavia and Papa and Mama. I stayed to help Robbie and Grandpa and they don't care. Robbie doesn't even want me around and Grandpa's too sad about Octavia to notice."

"Ay, that's hard, that is," Alma said. "And I don't think we can change any of those things right now. Sometimes people have to work things out for themselves. The best thing we can do is get out of the way and let them get on with it. I'm fairly certain they'll come back to us when they're ready. Waiting is hard, though. What can we do to help Halfnote feel better in the meantime?"

After Halfnote left, Robbie yet again considered the line of glass dolls set into the wall. He ran his finger over the figure of Father Bartholomew. By tradition, Father Bartholomew was described as a most handsome man, with "hair black as midnight; eyes blue as the midday sky." Robbie's Da had dark brown eyes and hair and a way of simply vanishing into the forest shadows. According to the legend, Father Bartholomew had been a man who enjoyed much singing and camaraderie. Da had been a man of silence. He spoke rarely, even to his own wife and son.

But now and again Da would take Robbie by the hand and lead him somewhere. "Rabbit run." Da would point at a nearly invisible line in the undergrowth. Or "muskrat," for a footprint in the mud nearby. Or, taking a few hairs caught in brambles, Da would hold them to Robbie's nose so he could catch the musky scent. "Lady fox, ready to make babies." Robbie would sniff and nod. They walked in silence through the marsh that lay between forest and river; Robbie careful to step only where Da pointed.

Robbie pictured the ramshackle wooden house where his life began. It stood on stilts out over the edge of a muddy bend. Before coming to Albermarle he'd lived his entire life in that house. He'd not left it once, not until the floods carried him away.

From a wide balcony next to her kitchen, Ma traded sweet breads and smoked meats for iron nails, flour, spices and occasional coins. Most of her customers were Gorani miners and Khelani traders. Robbie spent his days in the kitchen helping Ma, or outdoors weeding their large garden. In the mornings he chased the goats around, to catch them for milking; in the afternoons he chased them again, to keep them from eating Ma's vegetables. On other days he sat in the wide front glassless window, watching for customers while Ma kneaded and baked. When a Khelani raft or Gorani boat darted across the river toward their house, he rang a large copper bell to call her.

Robbie's small, slight father did not look like a traditional Gorani. He looked almost nothing like Father Bartholomew and not at all like the musclebound mountaineers who steered their skin-clad boats past the house with a few casual flicks of a wooden oar. Even so, Da had the Gorani manner.

After Father Bartholomew found the way past the impossible cliff, many Gorani descended into the rich lowlands and intermingled with the people of the plains. Many still made their living from the fruits of tree and mountain. Some worked as miners, or, by extension became metal workers. Others became builders, skilled in the use of stone and lumber. A few brewed the thick ales and ciders popular among Gorani and townspeople. Some intermarried with the Khelani and took up trading. Those who stayed in the mountains maintained their traditional ways, hunting and herding, prospecting and mining.

As a daughter of the Khelani, Halfnote could count as near family any member of Clan Breydon and as distant relation any member of a dozen or more other allied clans. Regardless of whether any actual blood tie existed, in times of trouble she could confidently invoke the bond of kinship with thousands of people up and down the river and so get help. So could any other Khelani. And as a daughter of the House of Verre, Halfnote could, at need, seek aid from any glass house between Albermarle and Tulum.

It wasn't just Halfnote who was rich in relations. Red-headed Laiertes came from a sprawling family who farmed the far-off hills of Canton. Marissa could count on seeing at least some of her twelve siblings on visitors' days whether she wanted to or not. The twins had been pulled out of Verre House by a family deeply concerned for their well-being. Robbie had no such wealth of kin. No cousins or grandparents, even. His parents must have had parents, of course, but he didn't know who they were … or where. Even Sylvia, so recently bereft of family, knew her home village.

The flood wiped Robbie's past clean away. That giant wave had appeared out of the darkness without warning. It washed him out of his warm wooden home into this cold house of stone and glass. It was highly unlikely that his parents still lived. Of course, his own survival seemed an equally impossible miracle, yet here he was.

He remembered very little of the flood itself; only its ending. A small hand grasped his own and pulled him out of the water. Fresh air burned in his lungs as he took his first breath. Then he wiped his eyes clear to see Halfnote standing by the water.

"Are you a water spirit?" he asked. He didn't remember her answer, only the way she looked at him with bright, amazing eyes.

If not to Verre House, where might he have gone, after the floods? Could he have found shelter among the Khelani? Certainly the river traders who visited his parents' house cheerfully called his mother "sister" in the same way that they greeted each other. They freely gave friendly kisses and gossip. They often offered advantageous trades of goods and tips on what might make a better profit next time. Ma often tucked extra buns and sweetmeats into the baskets of Khelani welcoming a new child or facing illness.

And it was the Khelani who, unasked, drew their knives and rushed to help Ma when thieves tried to take advantage of Da's absence. Robbie shivered. He didn't like to think about that day.

After the flood he just followed Halfnote. Master Verre accepted his presence as if it had been pre-arranged. Naturally no one questioned Master Verre. So here he was, still following Halfnote.

Did he have a direction of his own? He'd been so close to drowning when she pulled him back to life it seemed impossible to do anything else. At first he thought she must be a sprite. Ma always left little offerings to the sprites of water and forest as she went about her day. The first warm roll from baking, a ball of new cooked rice, a splash of wine just after uncorking the bottle; all of these went into a dish on the altar she kept in one corner of the living room. Here she prayed daily, for safety, for health, for enough of everything to get through to the next day. It had not been enough, Robbie thought, to save her.

"It saved you."

Startled, Robbie looked around. The basement was empty except for him, and yet not. For a moment it seemed as if his mother's spirit stood before him, hands on her hips in the way that she had when he misbehaved.

"The spirits saved you and brought you to a rich man's house. That's good enough for me. What are you doing down here? You're not feeling sorry for yourself, now, are you?"

"I miss you." Robbie found himself weeping.

If he had survived the flood without meeting Halfnote, he might still have met the men who took them to the nearby village. If Halfnote had not been there, he would not have come to Verre House. Even so, he might still have found a place among the river traders, perhaps even with someone who remembered his parents. He might have found a place where no one cared if he could sing or not.

"Doesn't matter," his mother's shade told him. "You're here now, boyo, and glad I am of it. What might have been is washed away and all we have left is what is."

What is. "I am Robert Dinaldo, an apprentice of Verre House," he said aloud. The ethereal image of his mother disappeared as he spoke. The sound of his words vanished with her. His tones carried little weight in this stone place. The otherwise skittish glass figurines held their places. Still, Robbie thought, something shifted. Movement occurred, even if he couldn't say where.

Deep in the Forest

She resisted the shaking, not wanting to leave her dream.
"Octavia, I'm sorry, but you have to wake up."
It was Mother. Octavia reluctantly opened her eyes. Only embers remained of the great bonfires. In the dim light she could just make out the huddled bodies of many sleeping people. A baby fussed somewhere. Mischa still snored on his back. Even the rowdier singing back in the trees had died out. What could she possibly want?
"What's wrong?"
"Nothing, but I need you to come with me."
Still half asleep, Octavia followed Mother down a path leading away from the main clearing. Dotted throughout the trees, small campfires illumined their way. After a few minutes they left the last fire behind. Mother traveled on without hesitation while Octavia stumbled to keep up. Soon Octavia followed Mother on sound alone. She was about to call out for help when a small light appeared just ahead. Mother exchanged words with someone. Another smaller light bounced towards Octavia. She realized Mother was trying to hand her a beeswax candle.
"This place is sacred," Mother whispered. "Do not speak except to answer a question."
They stepped into a circular clearing. Around the edge of the

Octavia's Journey   *by Lynette Hill*

open space Octavia saw little points of light. These were candles held by Khelani women. Most of the women looked middle-aged or older. Mother guided Octavia into the center of the circle. There sat a gray-haired woman hunched over with age. Two younger women stood behind her, one to each side. Mother took Octavia's candle and pushed her toward the ancient woman.

"My daughter Octavia, Mother Lara," Mother said.

The ancient woman took hold of her hands and stared into Octavia's face. Octavia looked from the old woman to her mother, uncertain what to do.

"Welcome, Octavia of Clan Breydon, daughter of Paul and Melody," Mother Lara said in a voice husky with age. "Your people are happy to see you. We are so grateful for your gift of healing. We offer a gift in return, in the hope that it will ease some of your burden."

Octavia started to speak, but Mother caught her eye and shook her head. A strange sort of humming sprang up. Mother Lara smiled and stared deeply into Octavia's eyes. The women's voices sounded more like wind in the trees, or the water of a far off stream.

The crone held up a small mirror. It was a plain silver oval with no edging. Octavia flinched, but Mother Lara forced her to look into it. No monster met Octavia's gaze. Instead, she saw Uncle Tal's face.

"Thank you," he said. "Thank you for saving us." His image transformed into the woman who dropped her clean laundry onto the mud. "You saved us. Me and my whole family. May Hamsa bless you." She was replaced by the old woman in Physician Cornelius' office. Another person followed and another, all expressing gratitude.

Octavia's internal chaos woke up and howled in pain. The monster rose up from within her. Pulsing golden strands of energy sprang up with the humming. The bright strings dazzled her eyes. As the *mortolo* emanated out towards the women it met the energetic strands. These lines wove into a net which wrapped around the creature. It roared and fought, but could not escape.

Octavia turned in alarm. Mother gestured for her to hold still. The net shrank, pulling the monster with it. The web of energy tightened around Octavia but did not hurt her. She held up her arms and watched the strands as they crisscrossed her skin. The lines vanished into her body. When the last bit disappeared she stood in darkness. She blinked but could not clear her dazzled eyes.

"Octavia."

She started awake and found herself back in the main clearing, between Father and cousin Mischa. Mother and Cadie slept next to Father. Only ash remained of the great bonfires. A bright ray of sunlight cut through the leafy canopy to hit her right between the eyes. She appeared to be the first awake. So who called to her?

Hanging beneath her dragon's head pendant, she found a river pearl, whitish, bumpy and roughly moon-shaped. Whenever she touched it or looked at it she again heard the many voices expressing their thanks. Why a pearl, she wondered, and not the little silver mirror? Even so, she was grateful for the reminder. Whatever her current situation, at least she *had* helped people.

Bottling

If there was a more boring job than making jars and bottles, Halfnote couldn't think of it. Melt, spin, hollow, drop in the cooling bath, repeat. Wine bottles, beer bottles, jam bottles, bottles for medicines. The work seemed endless.

"How many more do we have to do?" Galliard sounded about as listless as Halfnote felt.

"It's that time of year," Sylvia said, which really didn't answer the question. "Harvest will be on us before you know it. Then everyone will be desperate to make preserves, bottle new wine and so on in time for the mid-winter's celebrations. We have to meet these orders to prove Verre House is a trustworthy supplier."

"But why do we have to make the bottles one at a time?" Halfnote asked. They were spread out in the main creation room. Frank and Dan maintained the fires of four small braziers while Halfnote, Marissa, Sylvia and Laiertes sang the bottles into shape. Galliard quickly netted the finished products and placed the bottles on the cooling racks. Working in tandem they completed a new bottle every few seconds.

Dan snorted. "Do you know a better way?"

"Yes, like this." Impatience and pride fueled Halfnote's voice as she spun her new ball of melted sand. Trilling the counter clockwise swirl she divided her globe into three smaller orbs precisely equal in size. A trio of new bottles dropped into the cooling bath with one satisfying sizzle.

Everyone stared. Sylvia came to herself first and snatched the net out of Galliard's hands. She retrieved all three bottles and examined each one closely before putting them on the racks.

Halfnote held her breath, barely able to keep her sense of excitement in check.

"Too thin." Sylvia tapped one with her fingernail. "The sides are too thin." Halfnote's heart sank. "We'll need to use a larger ball of glass to make multiple bottles. Halfnote, that's amazing."

Sylvia grinned at her. Halfnote's heart climbed back into its proper place.

"Where did you learn ... oh, what a ridiculous question; from Octavia, of course. But can you teach everyone else how you do it?"

Halfnote matched Sylvia's grin. "You just have to think about how water flows. Have you spent any time on the river?"

"Don't be stupid," Dan snapped. "We're not Khelani." Galliard smacked him on the back of the head. "Ow! What was that for?"

"Some of us are," Galliard said. "My mother, for instance."

"Enough," Sylvia commanded. "Halfnote and I will sing while everyone else watches. Once you feel you understand the technique, raise a hand and we'll see if you can join in."

"But that's a master song," Dan complained.

"Stop whining, Dan," Marissa hissed. "If Halfnote can sing it then so can we."

"Sure you can," Halfnote said. "It's not hard. I don't know why someone didn't think of this before."

Dan rolled his eyes.

"Because masters don't usually make bottles," Sylvia said. "And you simplified the swirl tones in a way I would never have considered. Now come on everyone. Lunch is in an hour."

If ...

Octavia and her family left Tondo as soon as they woke up. Others cast off as well, though many remained. The rapids, frightening to Octavia, posed little challenge to the raft's crew. Soon they floated serenely on down the river again, at peace with all the world.

Octavia took her place on the prow of the raft. She ate one of the hazelnut pastries presented to her the night before. It tasted wonderfully of cinnamon and honey. She ate another and stretched out in the sunshine. This late in the season every warm day was a blessing. The weather would turn colder soon. She watched the currents and replayed the previous night's events in her mind.

Had it all been a dream? Her hand found her dragon's head pendant. Beneath it still hung the gift of the Khelani mothers: the moon-shaped river pearl. "Thank you," the voices breathed again in her head. "You saved us."

Mother sat down beside her.

"How are you feeling?"

"Last night, was that real?" Octavia asked.

"Yes, indeed."

"What did you see?"

"Probably not the same thing that you did. I saw the wise women singing. I saw you start to glow, and then a dark cloud surrounded you. It vanished and you glowed a little while longer. And then everything was normal again. What did you see?"

"Mother, if it's true ... the monster is inside me."

"Yes."

"And now it's bound inside me."

"Yes."

Octavia's Journey   *by Lynette Hill*

"So why didn't we just let it go?"

"Hmm, yes, well, you saw what happened the last time the *mortolo* got loose."

"You agreed to this? You knew what was going to happen and you told Mother Lara that it was all right? Without asking me?"

"I didn't know exactly what would happen, no. But I did ask Mother Lara for her help. You are now safe from the *mortolo*. As safe as you can be, anyway. We did not bind it to you. You already held it. We could not take it out of you. We cannot free it. Instead, we caged the monster so it cannot harm you or anyone else."

"But now what? Do I spend the rest of my life with this creature inside me? Can I now return to normal? Can I sing the glass again?"

"Mother Lara assured me that all will come to pass as it is meant to in the normal order of things."

"By all the dragons, Mother, what does that mean?"

"I'm afraid it means we will both have to remain patient for a little while longer."

"What do you mean 'we'? I'm the one carrying the monster."

"And I have to watch you carry it. I have to sit helplessly by watching you suffer. I have no cure for this, no herb. If only we had a healing mirror to consult."

"That's how I felt when you had the plague."

The pain of those memories burned afresh. At least they did find a cure for the plague. If she had to choose between her song and her mother's life... Octavia stared into the river, seeking her own reflection. It did not show the monster. She put her hand to the pearl and heard the voices again: "Thank you. You saved us."

"Mother, even if I never sing again, I will always be glad we cured the plague."

At least, she wanted to be glad of that.

But what do I do now? If I cannot sing, who am I?

She spent the rest of the day on the prow, staring at the river. It widened and deepened. Traffic increased. In this heavily populated area, she encountered glass fairly often. Each time a window appeared, however, the rough river pearl glowed and filled her eyes and ears with the thanks of the people she saved.

Cadie snuggled up against her and napped there for most of the afternoon. As the afternoon passed she heard Mischa whistling cheerfully behind her.

Things could be worse. Now I have some defense against the monster. And, dragons be thanked, I am not an orphan.

Father and Mother poled through a turbulent patch. Mischa turned the tiller according to the directions they called out. After an hour or so the trio switched places.

Halfnote always talked about how much she loved sitting at the front of the raft, watching the river. This was how her younger sister learned about the flow of currents. It was from doing this that she knew how to save Octavia from the tainted mirror.

And ultimately, that is what saved the lives of all those people at Tondo. Halfnote saved them.

Well, it had been a joint effort. If she hadn't fallen into the mirror, if Halfnote hadn't known how to call her back, if the others hadn't been able to destroy the mirror, if, if, if …

So many choices led to that moment. If Samoya's Intan hadn't come to Albermarle, would the plague have reached the city anyway?

If they had made the mirror when the Samoyans first asked, how many more lives would have been saved?

If the city council had not banned the making …

If Grandfather's cousin hadn't died all those years ago while attempting to make another healing mirror …

If Geoffrey hadn't taken the Samoyans' bribes and given them to Father to purchase supplies despite the quarantine …

If Father had gotten Halfnote and Robbie to safety …

What if, before the plague, someone asked me to give up my talent in exchange for saving thousands of lives? What if Mother Piasa in all her glory returned to ask me for this sacrifice? I would have agreed, wouldn't I? I couldn't let all those people die.

Fine. Let's say I gave up my talent to save everyone, including Grandfather, Mother and Grandmother. I traded my talent in exchange for their lives.

Octavia's Journey   *by Lynette Hill*

Octavia tried to consider this an acceptable bargain. She tried not to think, *'why did it have to be my glass singing talent?'*

Acceptable or not, it's done.

Grandfather might bow or shake hands to signify an agreement. Khelani traders made a great show of slapping their hands together before shaking hands. They created a very public display so that everyone around knew that a deal had been sealed. Bile rose in her throat, but she forced it down again.

She remembered the awful washer woman who couldn't stop touching her at Tondo; the shy, confused children pushed forward by their grateful parents.

I saved Mother. I saved Grandfather and Grandmother. I saved Galliard, Laiertes, Melissa and the twins. I saved all those people in Tondo. I saved thousands of people I will never even meet in places I will never visit.

Fine. Great. She couldn't be unhappy about that.

But what do I do? If I am no longer a singer, who am I?

She leaned over to peer into the river.

"I'll tell you who I am," she told her reflection. Cadie woke up and watched her with a frown. "I am Octavia Breydon. My ancestors learned to sing the songs of dragons. I outlasted the alarm tones to pass my singer's test. I am the only person ever to return alive from the belly of a *mortolo*. And I am the person who will find the solution to this new puzzle. I *will* create a new life and make something of it."

And thanks to the wise women of my father's clan, I have a new tool to help me do that.

"Tavi." Cadie held out her arms, wanting to be held.

As the skies remained clear and the temperature warm Father allowed the raft to continue on after dark. He and Mischa took turns keeping watch overnight but nothing disturbed their lazy progress.

Octavia woke to see a light shining further down the river. At first she thought it might be the moon, just rising into view. But the waxing moon glowed high overhead. The light reflecting off the river came from an oil lamp at the front of a raft moving towards them. Her eyes focused on the glass container. *Oh.* She took in a breath as the swirling gray clouds of the monster coalesced on the face of the glass. Her heart pounded furiously.

Between her and the lantern covering, another pinpoint of light appeared. It began to spread. Octavia squinted her eyes against the glow. As she watched, this illumination widened into a silver oval. Instead of the monster's storm clouds, she now saw Uncle Tal mouthing the words 'thank you.' As before, he faded away and face after face appeared, all expressing their gratitude.

She began humming the calming tones and felt the monster respond. It arose in her mind a whirlwind of anguish, bound in the golden net. In her imagination she gave it eyes. Using every bit of self-control that remained to her, she stared back into those eyes; those coal black, furious eyes. She held that stare for one heartbeat, two, three. She took a breath. The monster expanded. Every cell of her body cried out in despair. Another heartbeat, beat, beat. Breathe. The monster grew.

I cannot bear this.

How big could the monster grow? Curiosity gave her strength. She watched now as if from a distance.

Will it outgrow me? Will it devour the raft and all I love?

Three heart beats, breathe. *I should stop this.*

The monster pulsed to the rhythm of her own heart. And again. Breathe. A slash appeared under its eyes. A mouth. A mouth that twisted into the most horrible grimace. Breathe. The monster did not grow further, only steadied in form. It remained a roaring horror. It was alive and it stared back at her. Breathe. Three more heart beats. Breathe.

It seemed that she observed all of this from afar: the monster and the girl, watching each other. Terror. Hunger. Rage. Breathe. Terror. Hunger. Rage. Breathe. Between them, shimmered face after face mouthing "thank you."

I am not destroyed.

A loud wailing cut through the air. *Cadie!* Octavia started awake. The monster vanished. Octavia found herself still on the raft, her back against one of the shelter's poles.

It will rain soon...

Mother grabbed her hands. "Are you all right?"

Octavia smiled at her. "Yes I am. I am not destroyed. It was a fair exchange, Mother. My song for your lives. You were right to bring me on the river. The world is a much wider place than ever I knew. I don't know what I'll do next, but I will find something to do … next."

A visit from the guard sergeant

Madame Verre stepped into the kitchen. "Alma?"

She found the portly cook offering tea and a plate of cookies to Sgt. Chevalier. The muscular city guard jumped to his feet as Madame Verre entered the room.

"Oh, hello, Sergeant. Is everything all right?"

"Yes Madame, I was just … ah … checking in."

"I'm sorry I didn't call you, Madame," Alma said. "The sergeant just came by to make sure that all is well in Verre House. Isn't that right, Chevalier?"

"Yes, Madame." The red flush on his cheeks faded. "My patrols report no disturbances in this area this past week. There have been no more lines at your gate or sight-seers trying to climb the walls. I wanted to make sure we hadn't missed anything."

"We are most grateful to you for the city guard's vigilance, Sergeant," Madame Verre murmured. "I do agree that things appear to have settled down."

"Yes. We'll continue the extra patrols for another week or so. Thank you for your time, Madame. Unfortunately, duty calls." The sergeant whipped his cap back on, bowed to them both and hurried toward the front door.

"Alma, see Sgt. Chevalier out why don't you? Come find me in the office suite when you have a moment."

Madame Verre smiled at Alma when she returned.
"Chevalier? Really?"

Alma dimpled. "He is a most honorable man. And quite conscientious in his duty."

"So you have no personal interest? I mean, he is such a fine looking man. He's got that strong jaw and those interesting hands. Those could turn a weaker woman's heart. How many characters have I played whose love stories began with less?"

"And what if he has caught my eye? What if I do have a 'personal' interest?"

"It's about time. You've been alone for far too long."

"I am hardly alone, here in Verre House."

"Mmm. At any rate, please be sure to tell the sergeant that he is always welcome. And if he or anyone else should ask, please tell them that we do not interfere in the personal lives of Verre House staff. So long as they conduct themselves honorably and honestly, of course."

"I shall endeavor to do so, Madame."

"You might let Sylvia and Frank know that too. They seem worried that I'll catch them out and disapprove. I think they make a lovely couple. We can't afford to send them away in any case." Madame Verre's expression changed. "You aren't thinking of leaving us, are you? I don't know what I'd do without you, Alma."

"Of course not, Madame. I've lived here in Verre House longer than … well longer than anyone but Master Verre. And I could not leave while he is so … unwell. I have taken what steps I can to help him. The plant grows." Alma nodded towards the seedling in the glass cloche in the window. The Lady Sigil had not blossomed, yet, but its leaves brushed the top of the cloche. It would need a larger container soon.

"It looks healthy, but is it enough?"

"Growth takes time. The blossoms arrive when they will. Master Verre has been hurt a second time close by the old wound. That sort of damage is difficult to overcome. I cannot make up his mind for him. Still, I think we are making progress."

"I hope you're right. I haven't seen it."

Octavia's Journey   *by Lynette Hill*

New Friends

Galliard and Laiertes caught up with Halfnote as she left the kitchen after lunch.

"Come on," Galliard said. "We're all meant to spend the afternoon in reading lessons."

"But Master Hardy was here yesterday."

Now that she was free of kitchen work and filling bottle orders had become more manageable, Halfnote spent two afternoons a week in lessons with the other apprentices. Master Hardy of the scribe's guild came twice weekly to drill them in letters and languages.

"Did he give you an assignment to copy out before his next class?" red-headed Laiertes asked.

"Yes." Halfnote wrinkled her nose. "In Tiniquan. From 'The History of Ost Oropa and Its Surrounding Seas.'"

"I thought you liked history." Galliard winked at Laiertes.

"I like stories. Not lists of rulers and royal houses and who conquered who."

"You mean 'who conquered whom.'"

Halfnote rolled her eyes. Laiertes led the way to a smaller office next to the master's chambers. Textbooks filled the shelves that lined the walls. A giant south-facing window let in ample sunlight for reading.

"Do you know your letters for reading and writing in Albi?" Galliard asked.

"Of course I do." What a question. *Of course I do.*

"Excellent." The older apprentice slapped a large, square-shaped book in front of her. He flipped it open to an apparently random page. "Read that paragraph."

Halfnote stumbled through a sentence. As she began the second Galliard snatched the book away.

"Excellent." He plopped another book in front of her. "How's your Tiniquan?"

"Not as good," Halfnote admitted. She managed to decipher the sentences as requested. "Are you really meant to teach us?"

"Yes, he really is," Laiertes laughed. "He's the tutor when

Master Hardy isn't here."

"And why not?" Galliard demanded in an unflappably cheerful tone. "I, as a privileged citizen of Malmesbury, was tutored from a young age in Albi, Tiniquan and both styles of Cromarty by my father's mother, the chief scribe of Bou Arta. Every day I thank all the dragons that Master Verre heard me singing at the spring planting festival and offered me an apprenticeship here. Otherwise I might have spent my entire life stuck behind a desk, with hands permanently stained by ink."

"All right." Frank appeared in the door. "It's just you three this afternoon. You're here until supper. Make it count. I don't want to hear a sound out of this room until we're done singing."

"As you can see we've already begun." Galliard indicated the book in front of Halfnote.

The moment Frank shut the door, Laiertes picked up a small glass ball from the windowsill and stuck it in his pocket. Galliard felt up the window edge and undid the clasp so it swung open.

"What are you doing?" Halfnote glanced guiltily at the door but it remained closed.

"Tutoring you and Laiertes in Tiniquan. Laiertes has already learned quite a bit, so you'll have to catch up. For the rest of the afternoon, speak only in Tiniquan."

"But ..."

Galliard cheerfully put a finger to his lips and clambered out the window after Laiertes. He beckoned to Halfnote. Hesitating only a moment, she followed. In less than a minute they climbed a tree, crossed the wall and dropped down into the street outside.

The next two hours flew by as they strolled through the woodcarvers' district, Galliard whistling a cheerful tune. Laiertes and Galliard would point and name something. Halfnote struggled to remember the words. Her head began to ache with the strain, but as the afternoon passed she managed a few sentences.

After a while Galliard pulled out a purse of purple velvet and bought them all sweets from a street vendor.

"Where did you get money?" Halfnote gasped in Albi.

"My father sends me an allowance," Galliard replied in the same language.

Halfnote's eyebrows rose. This was a new concept. The only way she knew to get money was by selling something.

"How would you ask that in Tiniquan?" Galliard asked.

"I don't know." Halfnote rubbed her aching head. "How does walking around talking teach me to read?"

"You know your alphabet. Once you know the words, you'll recognize them when you see them on the page."

"Besides," Laiertes added, "do you really want to spend a sunny afternoon like this inside reading?"

Well, actually, Halfnote had to admit, no she didn't.

"But it is time to go back." Laiertes held up the now opaque ball. "Our two hours are nearly up."

They made it back to the study room with no time to spare. Frank opened the door just as Galliard closed the window.

"I bet you three are ready for a break," Frank said. His eyes narrowed when he looked at Halfnote. He didn't say anything but appeared to be trying not to laugh. As they left the room Laiertes whispered, "Quick, comb your hair. There are leaves in it."

Ella, the new maid, had the unfortunate habit of chattering when nervous. Upon hearing that Intan Negarawan had accepted his great-grandmother's invitation, she carried on non-stop.

"Is it true, what they say?" she whispered to Queen's Companion Clara. "Did Queen Anula really try to murder the Intan? More than once? Why would he agree to meet with her if that's true? Why would she want to kill her great-grandson?"

Clara eyed the girl. She had only joined the Queen's service a few days ago. "Excessive speech will not endear you to our mistress," the Queen's Companion warned.

Ella managed to stay silent for a whole minute.

"They say the conference room is always locked, except when the Intan and the Queen meet there. Is it true? And only Chancellor Razak has a key? They say the Intan's men bring all the furniture with them, and take it away again after ..."

"Yes, well, look on the bright side," Clara attempted a light tone. "That means less work for us." In fact, King Negarawan's precautions were far more extensive than Ella suggested; far more thorough than any single individual was meant to know. But anything spoken of in the palace of Samoya was known to the Queen's Scryer and so, of course, by the Queen. And Clara.

"But why does the Queen want to kill the Intan?" the apparently clueless chambermaid bubbled on. "And why does the King allow them to meet, if it's so dangerous?"

Clara considered the pretty young servant once again. Ella seemed bright, intelligent, cheerful.

"Of course King Negarawan prefers a resilient and resourceful heir. It is the King's belief that the Intan will grow stronger by facing his most dangerous enemy. When the Intan encounters lesser foes they will seem less daunting and so easier to defeat."

"Queen Anula is the Intan's most dangerous enemy?" The chambermaid looked as if she didn't quite believe her ears. "But why would she kill her own great-grandson?"

Sandrigal cleared his throat.

"Enough," Clara hissed. "The Intan comes."

Ella looked around, bewildered.

"How can you know that? Have you the sight?"

"Go to your duties, child."

Despite the heat of the day, the Intan arrived in full leather armor under a closely woven and hooded cloak. His thick gloves reached all the way back to his elbows. Strong glass spectacles protected his eyes.

Every detail of the meeting followed strict rules also set down by the King. To the right of the Intan stood his chief councilor, Razak, and Razak's secretary. The secretary, a pale, nervous man, diligently took down every word and gesture of the meeting. Mirroring the scribe in position and action, the Queen's female clerk captured it all as well. To the left of the Intan stood his latest bodyguard, a scarred giant of a man said to be able to kill just by breathing on his intended victim.

Mirroring him stood Clara. Queen Anula explained this as a gesture of light mockery. "He believes you are no match for his brawn.

We both know that he is no match for your intellect and beauty."

Clara considered her opposite with a practiced eye. He was too proud of his strength. He looked only for foes as obvious as himself. Better to face this great lug than the Intan's half-brother and *mahout*, Maru. Now *he* was a worthy adversary.

At the king's command, the rest of the room stood empty. All other courtiers and companions waited in the stairwell outside. Again by the King's order, closest to the door waited the best squad of the Intan's bodyguards. They were meant to rush in and retrieve the Intan at the first sound of danger.

To match them, Queen Anula set one chambermaid. The Queen's maid had orders to knock and enter at her call, in case anyone should require a cup of tea.

"My dearest Laki," Queen Anula declared as the Intan entered. "Do take a seat before your bodyguard decapitates me for smiling too broadly in your direction."

"Ona, it's good to see you again."

"As always, it's been too long," Queen Anula pretended to sulk. "But at least this time you have good reason. Tell me about your visit to Albermarle."

The Intan had grown in the months since his last visit, Clara noted. He was taller, more muscular and more certain of himself. Even in the presence of his great-grandmother.

"I found both the weather and the people there cold," the Intan said in his usual grating tenor. "They do not respect the glory and authority of Samoya. The art was as unusual as you mentioned, but hardly worth the trip."

"Really? Nothing caught your eye? Not even that young glass singer who brought back the cure to the plague? I hear that she is actually quite attractive."

The Intan gave a nervous laugh. Perhaps he hadn't matured that much after all. "Ona, you know that my first three wives are already chosen. How often have you scolded me for wanting a pretty bride over one who enhances the power of our house?"

"My goodness, how mature you're becoming. Accepting your

responsibilities at last. It does my old heart good to hear this."

The Intan regarded his great-grandmother warily. Councilor Razak cleared his throat.

"I fear our time together has come to an end," the Intan announced, jumping to his feet. "Father requires my presence at the reception for the new ambassador from Wy-an. Is there anything else you require, Ona, before I go?"

"No, my dear. I wanted only to look upon you again and congratulate you on your successful mission."

To Clara's surprise, Queen Anula sounded genuinely sad.

The Intan's eyes darted around. Clearly he believed he'd missed something. When no threats materialized, he all but jogged out, his guards close behind. Chancellor Razak and a squad of mercenaries waited in apparent courtesy as Queen Anula made a great fuss of needing Clara's help to rise and slowly leave.

As they exited the meeting chamber the rest of the Queen's household gathered around their mistress. Clara took Ella's arm and pushed her towards Chancellor Razak.

"I regret to inform you, Chancellor, that this girl is unsuitable for the Queen's service."

If the chancellor was disappointed by the loss of his latest spy his expression didn't show it. Clara knew the girl would most likely be executed for her failure.

Sorry Ella.

At least Ella's family would be compensated for her loss. They would survive.

"Your family remains safely hidden in Malmesbury," Sandrigal reassured Clara later. "The hunters have all but given up the chase."

Mischa and Father poled, whistling and chatting to pass the time. Mischa suddenly whooped and shouted at a raft. The individuals aboard, too far away for Octavia to make out, responded with calls and whistles. Mischa turned to Mother.

"Aunty Melody, it's Tamisin!"

Mother smiled. "All right. If Octavia will replace me on the tiller, you can go."

"Sure," Octavia said, curious. Before she could ask 'who is Tamisin' Mischa had stowed his pole on the floor of the raft and jumped backwards into the river.

"Where's he going?"

"A girl," Mother sighed, picking up Mischa's pole.

Father laughed. "That's how it is with the young." He glanced from Mother to Octavia and suddenly looked embarrassed. "With the young Khelani, anyway," he amended. "What's for lunch?"

Octavia rolled her eyes. "It's all right, Father. You don't have to blush on my account. You should see what goes on at Verre House once the lights are out."

"Really?" Mother arched an eyebrow the way Grandmother always did in a theatrical moment. She winked at Father. He grinned.

"I mean, well, not me ..." Octavia spluttered.

For some unexplained reason, Mother and Father found this incredibly funny. They kept smiling at each other and giggling at odd moments until well past supper.

Honestly.

Time to create the next piece?

Madame Verre sat at her dressing table, brushing out her thick, lustrous hair. She watched her husband's mirrored image. He sat in a high-backed chair set at an angle to look out the window at the back garden. Though the room still held the heat of the day he pulled a shawl around his shoulders as if ill.

"Alma spoke to Ted again. He still works at the lifts."

Master Verre did not respond. His wife continued brushing.

"She gave him your message. Ted is adamant he doesn't want to return, or take a post with another glass house. He says he just wants to be left alone. Alma told him we've written his parents."

Still watching the back garden, Master Verre nodded.

"Fortis, you have a message from the astronomers."

Master Verre still said nothing.

"Rafique asks that you meet him at the look-out on Piasa's Perch this evening well before moonrise. He says it is important and pertains to the matter at hand. Fortis! Are you listening?"

"Yes, yes. Can't you go? I have a headache."

"I am not Fortis Verre."

"What could be that important?"

"He said 'the matter at hand.' I would assume he means Octavia's plight."

"I doubt it."

"Fortis, Rafique is your oldest friend. The astronomers have been our strongest allies from before the plague. At times they have been our only allies on the council. We can hardly afford to offend them. If Rafique says the matter is important, it must be."

"All right, I'll go."

"Thank you. I think I feel a bit of a tickle in my throat. Perhaps I should let my understudy take the stage tonight. Dragons' know she's ready. She'll be great in her time."

Master Verre just stared out the window. Madame Verre gave a vexed hiss. "Fortis, do you fear death?"

"I welcome it."

"Fool. How dare you squander such a gift?"

"What gift?"

"Octavia saved your life three times over."

"It should have been me. The mirror should have taken me. There, I've said it. Are you happy now?"

"I hardly think so. If *you* had fallen into the mirror, we would all have died of plague. Octavia had the nerve and the will to fight her way free and so bring us the cure. You didn't have the strength. And," she added before he could respond, "that is most certainly *not* your fault. There is no way you can blame yourself for the plague. That guilt lies with the Samoyans, if anyone."

"Of course I'm grateful to her," Master Verre growled. "But I don't deserve to live. Octavia's plight is my fault. This is where my pride has brought us. I'm the fool, but Octavia pays the price."

"Fortis." Madame Verre put down her brush and turned to glare at her husband. "Octavia still lives and so do you. Pig-headed idiot. Your pride nearly cost us Melody. Will you drive Octavia away as well? What if there is no cure for her?"

"Don't say that."

"She's not dead, Fortis. She is not ill. Neither are you."

"She cannot sing."

"Is that all you care about? What if she never sings again? She still lives. She is still our granddaughter."

Master Verre's face turned a deep shade of red. Abruptly he stood up, dropped the shawl and stalked out of the room.

Halfnote was drawing water from the well when she heard the back gate open. She looked up just in time to see Grandpa, wrapped in a hooded cloak, leave. The gate clattered shut. Had Grandpa even seen her? Where was he going? It was too late for market; too early for the theater or for a normal social call.

She didn't have time to find out. They needed more water for the cooling baths in both creation rooms. At the moment the city's physicians were ordering all of their glass from Verre House. Frank thought it was because the healers felt guilty about running away from the plague. Sylvia believed they hoped any remaining resonance from the healing mirror would make the new pieces more effective. Whatever the reason, Verre House had more complex orders to fill than usual and fewer to staff to do it.

Halfnote picked up her buckets with a sigh. She could have gone back to the river. Neither Grandpa nor Robbie cared that she stayed. She hadn't spoken to either in days. It didn't do, Mama always said, to let old hurts get in the way of new enjoyments, but still ... she missed them.

"Halfnote, what took you so long?" Dan demanded when she reached the second making room with her last bucket. "You kept the whole team waiting. You weren't flirting with that stupid kitchen boy again, were you?"

Master Verre did not see Halfnote as he left. He did not bother to take a light, despite the growing darkness. His feet knew this path nearly as well as he knew the way from his chambers to the kitchen. The night sky promised to stay clear. A bit of blue still stained the west when he reached the astronomers' lookout. From here they had a clear view of the heavens in almost every direction. As evening fell, lighted homes created their own constellations out across the southern plains.

"Fortis!" Chief astronomer Rafique greeted Master Verre with a relieved smile. "How happy I am to see you. I feared you might still be too ill to visit. Please, take a seat. Will you have tea or a mulled wine? Something to take the chill off?" The astronomer gestured to an apprentice. The girl hurried to produce the offered beverages.

Master Verre accepted the mulled wine, allowing the heat of the glass to warm his hands.

"You said it was important."

"Even so, old friend, you are not yourself these days. The recent troubles have taken their toll. It is said that you have not left Verre House since ... well, since Octavia left with her parents."

Master Verre's eyes narrowed. "What of it? Surely I have as much right to privacy as the next man. Is every moment of our lives subject to idle gossip?"

"Of course it is." Master Rafique clapped Master Verre on the shoulder with a hearty laugh. "After you saved us all from the plague? Your every move is watched and debated. The people of Albermarle believe you glass singers hold our lives in your hands. They may even be right. I have something special to show you. Joan?"

"Yes, Master Rafique. All is arranged as you asked."

"Excellent. Thank you, Joan. Now, Fortis, I believe you know your constellations well enough to find Lyra, just there. She is just rising above the trees."

"I know where to look thanks to you, you mean." He forced himself to smile.

The chief astronomer led Master Verre over to a large telescope, one of several set atop the giant rock. The glass master dutifully bent down to look through the eyepiece. He found the constellation easily enough, gasped and took a second look.

"Is that really a new star? How is this possible?"

"No, not new. It is actually quite old." Master Rafique bounced on his toes, beaming with delight. "The ancients would say that Lyra has opened her eye. She sees. She has turned her head, perhaps, to look directly upon us. This only happens once every thousand years, according to the written records."

"Why has this happened?"

"Who can say? It is part of the universal pattern. We know the stars move. We strive to determine the meaning of their movements. It is not just that Lyra's eye has opened, but the location of the opening and the movements that will follow. Its opening has always been a sign of hope to those who sing with dragons. The star is ascendant and will continue rising for some time. Verre House could not receive a more optimistic omen."

"This is a good sign for Verre House?"

"Yes. Surely you know enough to understand that for yourself. This is a most excellent portent for the guild of glass singers in general, and for Verre House in particular. Interesting, that it appears just now, don't you think?"

Master Verre still smiled when he left the lookout an hour later. Of course he knew it was irrational to seek signs in the stars. He appreciated the scholarship and passion of his friend Rafique but ... Master Verre never quite trusted the so-called omens said to be found in nature. Why should the powers of the universe concern themselves with one man or even one family? Why would they care enough to write him personal notes in the stars?

And yet ... why should an ancient but hidden star reveal itself in the constellation Lyra at just this moment? Rafique said the eye would shine for another century, if it followed old patterns.

Master Verre turned away from the path that led home. Instead he made his way to the cobblestone road into town. He pulled the hood of his cloak up around his face to avoid being recognized. He let his

Octavia's Journey   *by Lynette Hill*

feet choose their own path as his thoughts meandered.

Octavia still suffered. And that was his fault. If he'd been stronger, if he'd agreed to make the healing mirror sooner, when they all had greater strength ...

None of it mattered now. The past is the past, as Rafique said. The patterns continue. The stars still move. A new chapter is being written even as we stand and watch. The question is no longer about what you did then; the question is what will you do now? That piece is finished. What new piece will you make?

Master Verre found himself outside the entrance to the great lifts. Ted still worked here as a porter. Despite Alma's best efforts to bring the young man back to Verre House, Ted preferred hard labor to singing the glass.

Octavia was not the only singer troubled by the *mortolo*. Ted's was another career cut short by exposure to the tainted mirror. Not a soaring talent, perhaps, but competent. A nice baritone. And working as a glass singer certainly would profit him more than the manual labor of a lift porter.

I have been remiss. Too self-indulgent in my sorrow.

Great oil lanterns kept the entrance brightly lit even at this time of night. Several generations of Verre House singers created most of the glasswork on display here, Master Verre realized with pride. Could Rafique be right? Lyra's eye had opened to look upon Verre House; surely this could only bode good for glass singers.

The past is past. Time to create the next piece.

A helpful porter, bulging with the muscles developed by a long career on the lifts, escorted him to the masters' cramped, paper-filled office. The porter naturally carried the scent of a man who did hard physical labor. His smell was nothing, however, compared to the aroma that wafted out of the masters' office. How many generations of sweating workers had filled that space?

The deputy master, a veritable giant half a head taller than the porter and nearly twice as wide, introduced himself as Karl. He hurried to clear a seat in the cluttered chamber for his guest. Even sitting, Master Verre looked up to speak to the deputy lifts master. Karl

Octavia's Journey   *by Lynette Hill*

insisted on serving tea and cookies. The lifts master carefully poured steaming liquid into clear glass cups smaller than his own hands. The ginger fragrance did help to make the room's enveloping aroma more tolerable. It took some time to get through all of the polite amenities before Karl would discuss business.

"I am 'onoured by your visit. 'ow may I be of service?" Karl finally asked. Master Verre smiled and put down his cup.

"A young man, one of my singers, has come to work for you while he deals with a personal issue."

"'e's not stolen somethin', 'as 'e?"

"No, no, as I said, a personal matter. He's a good man. A hard and honest worker. I have a message for him."

"Ah. A girl, is it? We get a lot of them. What's 'is name?"

"Unfortunately, it's nothing so simple." Master Verre forced a laugh. "He is Ted Voclain. As I said, a good man, an honest worker. Is he here today? Can I speak to him? Of course I'll pay for the time he is away from his duties."

"Oi, course you can talk to him. No payment required. I'll call Oskar, the porter master. 'e'll know Ted."

"We should speak in private. I don't wish to call unnecessary attention to his situation."

"A course." Karl hurried to his door and shouted out, "Oi, Oskar, get in 'ere. Master Verre needs a word!"

The glass master gratefully followed Oskar, a balding man somewhat shorter but just as wide as Karl, out of the fragrant office. They found Ted bent nearly double under a wooden trunk. Master Verre tipped another porter to take the trunk on to its destination.

Ted looked down at his feet. "I'm sorry I didn't come speak to you, Master Verre. They said you were sick."

"Don't give it another thought. I was unwell. I am recovering. Let us step outside a moment so that we can talk privately. I've cleared it with the lift master."

They found a quiet spot next to a balustrade on the cliff edge. A breeze came up from the south. Moths whirled around an oil lamp. Tall, wiry Ted looked thinner and more muscular than Master Verre remembered. A half-healed bruise shadowed one eye. He did not, Master Verre noted, wear his dragon's head pendant.

"Ted, as a singer of course you are free to leave Verre House. I'm sure Lorraine would be happy to take you in as she has the others. But I am concerned about your well-being. The *Hygeia mortolo* shadows others who met it. I am haunted by it. Does it distress you?"

Ted looked away, then took a breath to calm himself.

"I glimpsed the monster," Ted managed to say, though Master Verre strained to hear his words. "I saw Octavia fall into it. I should have caught her, pulled her back. But I was afraid. I stayed behind my shield. Now I'm afraid I'll see the monster again if I sing. I still have my talent and Octavia does not. If only I had caught her. I do not deserve my place in Verre House. I cannot bear to sing the glass any longer. I simply cannot bear it."

"I understand," Master Verre said. "No one will force you to try. But I do feel some responsibility for your plight. We can certainly find you a better position than this. You have a fine voice. Madame Verre has friends in the musicians' guild. She could get you an audition. Or, if you do not care to sing at all, perhaps we can speak to the Scribes' Guild. If I remember correctly, you write with a fine hand and have a good command of languages."

Ted looked away, a muscle in his cheek twitching.

"You don't have to decide now." Master Verre textured his voice with calming notes. "If you prefer a different opportunity, I will help you in any way that I can. Where do you sleep? We still have the things which you left."

"I share a room with other porters." Ted took a breath. "And I thank you for your concern, Master Verre. You are very kind. I … I'll think about it."

Master Verre gave a reassuring smile, though inwardly he felt unhappy. Ted clearly suffered. "Visit Verre House any time. Everyone misses you and worries about you. At least give Alma the chance to feed you again."

Ted smiled. "I do miss Alma's cooking. I'll think on what you've said, Master Verre, and come by in a while."

"Excellent. Everyone will be happy to see you."

The fragrant deputy lift master waited for Master Verre.

"Ever'thing all right?"

"Yes, yes. As well as can be, anyway." Master Verre handed Karl a purse, forcing it into his hand when the well-muscled giant tried to wave it away.

"Look after Ted for me. Keep the bullies off of him. He faces some difficult choices. I would not see him harmed."

"We don't allow bullying," the deputy master said, pretending to be affronted. "But I'll keep an eye on 'im. You 'ave my word."

Alma was so surprised to see Master Verre when he walked into her kitchen that she gave out a small shriek and dropped her tray of fresh-baked rolls.

"I do beg your pardon, Alma. I'm just back from a long walk and would love a bit of tea in my chambers." His eyes twinkled almost mischievously, Alma thought, as he helped her retrieve her baking. Her heart skipped a beat. Was this truly the hopeful sign that it appeared?

She sent Robbie in with a heavy tray that included cheese, cold meat and bread.

"It seems I've seen a lot of you lately, Robert," Master Verre said as the boy filled his cup. "How goes your singing? What projects have you been given?"

"S...sir, I only work in the k...kitchen now."

"What? What do you mean? You are an apprentice glass singer. Who put you in the kitchen? Did you ask to go there?"

Master Verre stormed into the main creation room. Robbie, running after him, called out a desperate warning.

"S..sir! W..wait! They're still s..singing!"

The glass master, his face red with fury, flung the door open the instant the vibrations finished. Frank and Sylvia stared back at him, their faces white with shock.

"What is it, sir?" Frank asked.

"You had no right to decide this without me. You cannot take

Robert's apprenticeship away without my written permission."

"We didn't send him away..." Sylvia began.

"I am still the master of Verre House. I decide who sings here and who does not."

"Oh really? I didn't know you still cared what happens in this house, *Master* Verre," Sylvia snapped back with sudden fire. Her face reddened nearly to the same shade as the glass master's. "Those who sit idly by have no right to judge those who carry the burden in their place. Octavia's loss was great, yes, but do the rest of us have to lose our careers as well? Grieve as you will, but life goes on. This house would have closed if Frank and I hadn't stepped in. We can't do everything. Coddling Robbie was that step too far. Your own wife gave up the role of a lifetime to look after your interests."

Drawn by the noise, Halfnote and every other person in the house clustered around the door. They all stared in astonishment as normally soft-spoken Sylvia matched Master Verre bellow for bellow.

"Sylvia." Madame Verre's tones all but drew blood. "You do not speak for me. I choose my roles, not you or anyone else. Even Fortis does not choose for me."

The Verres shared a look indecipherable to the rest. Master Verre turned to Frank. "And you, Frank? Do you agree with Sylvia?"

Frank looked around in every direction, as if desperate for an exit. Then he took a breath and stepped up beside the other singer. They joined hands. Ever after Alma would say that this was the true moment of their marriage.

"Yes I do, Master Verre," Frank said in a shaky voice. "I'm sorry," he added with a nod to Robbie, "but I do."

Master Verre's expression softened. He crossed his arms and regarded his clustered staff. Guilt replaced anger in his eyes.

"As you say, Sylvia, life goes on," he said. "One person's loss should not destroy another's chance. I want Robert to continue training as a glass singer ... should he choose to do so."

All eyes turned to Robbie. He flushed a bright red and stared down at his feet. Halfnote reached out to take his hand but he refused to notice this.

"Sir, no, it's not fair. Not to him or anyone else," Sylvia said. "He makes a fair cook but he's hopeless at singing. I won't have him."

Alma put an arm around Robbie's trembling shoulders.

"Just in case it needs to be said, I stand with this boy whatever anyone chooses. If you send him away, you send me with him."

"What do you say, Robert? Do you wish to continue singing the glass or are you happy in the kitchen?" Master Verre asked.

Robbie swallowed hard. "I l.like c...cooking, M..."

"Who would want him anyway?" Dan howled with laughter. "Listen to the idiot. He can hardly talk, much less sing. The kitchen's the only place for a dummy like him."

A cold and angry light dawned in Robbie's eyes. He raised his head and glared directly at Dan as he spoke.

"But I w...*want* to s...sing for you, Master Verre."

"Well said, Robbie." Alma silenced Dan's mocking laughter with an angry glance.

"Excellent." Master Verre smiled. "Robert will rejoin your crews, Sylvia, while I tutor him."

"No," Sylvia said. "Absolutely not. I will not have him. He'll have to finish the apprentice challenge before I take him back."

"The challenge?" Master Verre blinked. "That's just a story."

"No it isn't, Grandpa," Halfnote jumped in eagerly. "We found where it begins in the basement. Robbie's already started it."

"You mean I found it," Dan snarled. "I found it. I showed it to all the rest of you. It's supposed to be *my* challenge. It just needs to be reset so that a proper singer can use it."

"I'll take Robbie back when he completes the apprentice challenge," Sylvia repeated.

"If the stories are true, there are several levels to the challenge. It's meant to take a singer from raw apprentice all the way up to full master and beyond," Master Verre said.

"Then he'll return when I say he's ready."

"That's hardly fair, Sylvia," Alma said. "You're already dead set against him."

"Indeed," Master Verre murmured. "I prefer an impartial judge.

Master Gibb and Madame Donatello will oversee your junior master test. I'll ask them to hear Robbie on the same day. They are fair-minded. If they are satisfied; if he demonstrates the skills and knowledge they normally expect of an apprentice of his age and experience, then he will rejoin our crews. Agreed?"

Sylvia took a breath. She looked at Robbie. He still glared defiantly at Dan.

"Fine," she said. "But someone else will have to train him. I'll not give him one more second of my time until he proves he's worth it. Master Verre, I'm sorry to lose my temper but you ask too much. I cannot lead the work crews, train the regular apprentices, prepare for my own junior master test and take on a special case like Robbie. It's too much."

"Of course I will tutor him," Master Verre said, "but no one sings the glass alone."

"He'll have to," Sylvia said. "I won't take him back until I know I can trust him."

Master Verre reddened. "I am still the master of this house."

"And I have my career to consider," Sylvia snapped. "My test date is set. You know better than anyone that it cannot be changed. Since it was determined we have endured plague and all that came after. These next few days are my last chance to prepare. Robbie is just that step too far. I will not add him to my burden."

"Fortis," Madame Verre touched his shoulder. "We are of course very grateful to Sylvia and Frank for the way they have taken things in hand. Verre House couldn't have gotten through our recent difficulties without them."

Another look passed between husband and wife.

"Very well, Sylvia." Master Verre relented, though clearly unhappy. "But if Masters Gibb and Donatello consider his singing to be acceptable ..."

"I'll welcome him back with open arms," Sylvia said.

"We'll hold you to that," Alma said.

"Good luck, Robbie," Frank said. Robbie had the strangest expression on his face, Halfnote thought. As if half of him was determined to succeed -- and the rest of him just wanted to disappear through the floor.

Oleny

They docked that day at a little market town called Oleny. Mother and Father left Cady on the raft with Octavia and Mischa. Mischa spent most of the warm, muggy afternoon tickling Cady and making faces at her. The little girl giggled happily until collapsing into a nap. As Cady slept, little bubbles blew up and popped on one side of her mouth. Mischa lay on his back, whistling tunelessly.

Glass glittered everywhere: in windows, as sun catchers on rafts and boats, even floating in the river as discarded bottles. Mother and Father considered bypassing the town despite their business there, but Octavia insisted they dock. She needed the experience of confronting her nemesis. She would have to return to some town sometime. Everywhere she looked, she saw glass. And every time she saw glass, the pearl warmed against her neck and the voices of gratitude blocked the monster from view.

Even so, the process took its toll. After half an hour or so, Octavia turned her back on the town and its windows. She sat, as usual, against a shelter post, watching the river and looking away from the passing boats. At some point, she would have to consider a new occupation. Nothing within sight appealed to her.

"So how did your visit go with Tamisin?" she asked.

Mischa grinned. "I enjoyed it."

"Will you see her again?"

"Oh yes, Hamsa and the Khelana willing, our paths will cross again. They always do. Perhaps even tomorrow."

They lapsed into another comfortable silence.

"Octavia," Mischa said after a while, "Tell me a story."

"What? A story? What kind of story?"

"Oh, I don't know. One of your dragon stories. Like your

mother tells. Halfnote says that you're an expert on dragon stories. Were there any dragons around here?"

Octavia thought a moment. How far down the river had they drifted from Piasa's Perch? Surely they were well past the field where Viridian fell, even past the market town where Bartholomew and his companions bought the first grain and sheep to save dragon and human from famine.

"I don't know of any." Octavia sifted through her memories. "Dragons living in this area, I mean. But Piasa and Viridian came to Albermarle from somewhere. They fled something. That much is clear. I always thought they came from the south."

"Why did they settle in Albermarle? I mean, there's so much more food here."

"Well, originally, there was plenty of food in the mountains as well and fewer people. The dragons wanted their privacy. The escarpment kept them safe from the people of the south. The people of the north, the Gorani, they lived in the mountains and farmed the little valley meadows. In good times, in normal times, they had no reason to go near Piasa's Point. The drought and cold that brought Piasa and Bartholomew together was highly unusual. All the stories agree on that. They say there was still frost in the fields on Midsummer's Day."

"What caused it?"

Octavia shrugged. "What causes any weather? You might as well ask where the Khelana River comes from. Why does all this water choose to flow here?"

"The old people say it comes from the ice dragon of the north. He's so cold he breathes water instead of fire."

"Don't the Khelani say the river is a dragon, their dragon?"

Mischa shrugged, then frowned. "Some say that. But Octavia, why do you say 'the Khelani' like some ridiculous townie? You are Khelani, through your father. We are your people. The Khelana River is also your dragon."

Octavia flushed. "Of course you're right. Mother and Halfnote would certainly say so. I just feel so disconnected. It's been so long since I've ridden the river. I have no balance. The way I lost my calm point in singing, I've also lost my balance here. I don't feel at home anywhere at the moment." She sighed. "I envy you, Mischa, your sense of place. You're so at peace. How do you manage that, after ... everything? How can you still be so happy?"

Mischa cocked his head at her. "What do you mean?"

"That is," Octavia already regretted her question, "you lost everything in the floods; your whole family. And here you are today and every day, laughing and talking. Even chasing a girl. You seem so happy. How can you be?"

Mischa looked away. He sat as still and quiet as Octavia had ever seen. He went so long without speaking that she began to fear she'd irreparably offended him.

"I'm sorry. I am sorry. I shouldn't have asked that."

Mischa shook his head and looked back at her, tears streaming down his cheeks. He shook his head and wiped his eyes, clearly struggling to speak.

"When the floods hit, when ... after ... the thing I could still hold on to, my shelter in that storm was the knowledge that I am Mischa of Clan Breydon. The clan sustains me. They care for me. Your parents, Aunty Lilly, Uncle Tal, everyone. They held me up when I couldn't hold myself up. When I was able to look outside of the overwhelming flood of grief, I still had my place in the world. Maybe it would help you feel better, if you knew that ... if you could remember what it means to be Khelani.

"Do you remember, at your celebration," Mischa said in a husky voice, "I asked if it bothered you that I live with your parents while you live in Verre House?"

Octavia nodded.

"I couldn't imagine living in that cold, horrible place."

"Cold and horrible? Verre House?"

"Why would you want to live there when you could spend your life on the river? Your mother always said it was your destiny. You were born singing." He shrugged an apology as she winced. "Sorry. I just meant, this," he spread his hands to indicate the breadth of the river, "this is my destiny. For better or worse, I am Khelani.

"I live when so many died. My survival," Mischa shrugged again, "was pure chance. When I watch the river, I see a pattern in the current and I have a part in it. In Tulum, among the waters of the sea, still there is a pattern and I have my place in it. In the forest, among the trees, the wind blows and I see patterns in how the leaves flutter. I may not understand the purpose of it all but there is a pattern and I have my place in it."

"That's what Halfnote says," Octavia said. "She sees how the currents flow. She understands the currents that occur in glass making because she understands the river."

Mischa nodded. "The only place I do not see a pattern is in town. There I see only chaos. In town I see angry, unhappy people bumping each into each other without meaning or purpose."

"In town, you see no pattern or purpose? Not in craft or ... or the bringing together of resources? Commerce is a balancing act, after all. Places with too much of something trade it for things they don't have enough of."

"Maybe I don't see patterns in any town because I have no real place there. I don't belong there."

"You have your purpose," Octavia said, jealous. "You know your place in the world, Mischa. Me, my purpose was snatched away. I must find a new one. I just don't know how or where."

"Perhaps the river will bring you to it," Mischa said.

"Perhaps. That's what Mother seems to think."

He nodded, watching her with dark, expressive eyes.

"Octavia, have you ever been to the rapids of Lochsa?"

"Perhaps," she said. The name sounded familiar. "Before I went to Verre House, but that was a very long time ago. We'll reach them tomorrow, won't we?"

"Perhaps the next day or the day after, Hamsa willing. They are the worst rapids on the Khelana River. Perhaps they are even the worst rapids in the whole world. Have you heard the joke about them?"

"Um, no, I don't think I have."

Mischa grinned mischievously.

"How do you get past the rapids of Lochsa?"

"I don't know, Mischa. How do you get past them?"

"Any way you can." He broke into hearty laughter. "Any way you can."

The Queen prepares her trap

Queen Anula, her eyes glued to the scene provided by her ornate scrying mirror, blew out one impatient breath. Clara pressed her back flat against the wall, willing herself to invisibility.

"So, they approach Lochsa. These rapids have a great whirlpool, do they not?" The Queen turned away from the looking glass and snapped her fingers.

"Where are my maps and reports? Where are my experts? Who knows that area? I must have a full description of this part of the Khelana River. She will come to me," The Queen's angry eyes focused suddenly on Clara. "She is very nearly in my hand. I have but to close my fingers. I will have her!"

"Indeed yes, mistress," Clara murmured.

The Queen strode out of the room, shouting for Melampus. Clara followed a cautious step behind.

Melampus's chief assistant tapped a long, spindly finger on a map spread across a large rosewood table. "Here is Oleny. Here, Vara Nasim. And here, the Lochsa Rapids. And yes, my Queen, your recollections are correct. The rapids do include a powerful whirlpool.

"As you noted, the combination of the energies of the full moon and the power of those swirling waters in concert with our magical command should be impossible for any power to overcome. If we could bring her to overlook the whirlpool at just the right moment, I do not believe the girl could resist."

He spread his long fingers across the points on the map, calculating distances. "The waters of the Khelana flow quite swiftly just prior to the rapids. Even so, under normal circumstances, I do not believe their raft could reach Lochsa in time for our needs."

"Must it?"

The skinny monk stood twice as tall as his mistress. The point atop his hooded robe only made him seem that much taller. Even so, he appeared a shrunken man in the presence of Queen Anula. Her determination filled the room. It pressed almost physically against every other person there.

"Given previous events, my Queen ..." he swallowed. "Yes."

"Then make it happen. Speed their craft. Create a new current in the river, if need be."

"It will take great power..." he murmured, momentarily lost in new calculations. Queen Anula snorted. The monk paled. He bowed so low that the tip of his hood brushed the table edge. "It shall be as you command, Oh Gracious Lady."

The Queen tutted as she left. Clara just managed to keep up.

Private tutoring

Master Verre surprised everyone by joining them for lunch and ate a full bowl of stew, Halfnote observed with approval. He cheerfully enquired into everyone's projects. At the end of the meal, he called Robbie back.

"If you will meet me in my study after cleaning up, please."

When Robbie arrived he found Dan loitering just outside the study. Dan rushed him, hitting Robbie hard with his shoulder. They both fell to the floor.

"Why don't you look where you're going, kitchen boy?"

The office door opened. They both jumped to their feet.

"Ah, Robert, just in time," Master Verre said. "And Dan. Did you want to join us?"

Dan recoiled as if bitten. "I'm not a stupid kitchen boy. I don't need *special help*."

"As you will," Master Verre replied in a mild voice. "Aren't you meant to be working with Frank this afternoon?"

Dan dashed off.

The lesson, it turned out, consisted of breathing exercises.

"Now then, I understand that you told Halfnote not to help you anymore," Master Verre noted.

"I h...have to d..do it myself, s..sir, or it doesn't c.count."

"I do admire your sense of independence, Robbie, but we all need help sometimes. Duets and choral singing are the larger part of the glass singers' art. Now, the first technique is something that you can do while going about your other chores. This is a four-part exercise which will help you maintain a calm demeanor. Practice it as often as you think of it, and particularly just before you begin any singing."

Dan stormed into the making room, his face a thundercloud. Frank took one look and told him to replace Laiertes as dragon. Dan set the charcoal bed of the temporary brazier afire with one strike of flint and steel. The flames billowed up. Dan jumped back just in time to avoid setting himself on fire. Frank snatched up a damping lid and quickly slid it into place over the minor conflagration.

"Right." The singer paused to wipe his spectacles. "A few rounds of calming tones first, I think. Dan, a dragon needs passion, yes, but control as well. Channel that temper."

Dan muttered something inaudible, but the calming tones mellowed his expression and eased everyone else's concerns. The making began.

Robbie now found he often had an audience when he worked on the challenge. He tried to send the others away, but they refused.

"No one sings alone," Galliard pointed out. "You need to get used to being observed. Certainly the judges will watch you."

Dan made a point of monitoring Robbie's progress as well. At first he tried to interfere, making mocking noises as Robbie struggled to find his pitch.

"Oh no you don't," hefty Marissa snapped. "Robbie gets a fair chance." In a move so fast that it startled everyone, she twisted the bully's arm behind his back and marched him out of the basement. Somehow Galliard's whistle both mocked Dan and applauded Marissa all at the same time.

"I can't believe you did that," Galliard told Marissa with a laugh when she returned.

"Oh please." Marissa sat back down as if nothing had happened. "I have six older brothers and three younger ones. And they would have put up a fight. Dan's nothing but hot air."

"But why are you still working on the challenge?" Halfnote asked Robbie. "You're going to be tested by Master Gibb and Madame Donatello. Grandpa said so."

Robbie shrugged. "It helps me. It's a good teaching device."

Frank and Sylvia did not join his audience. In fact, Sylvia actively avoided Robbie. One evening, however, Robbie found Frank squatting just outside the door to the lower basement. Frank banged his head on the low ceiling hard enough to send his spectacles flying. Robbie retrieved them while Frank ruefully rubbed his head.

"You dropped something else." Robbie pointed at an item in the corner that glinted in the light of their candles.

"Actually, I didn't drop it," Frank said. His cheeks reddened as he picked up the glass pitch pipe, made in the shape of a curvy letter F. He blew into it to produce several notes.

"I made this pipe for my singer's test." He grinned. "Octavia isn't the only singer who wanted to impress the judges.

"As I'm sure you know, most people who apprentice in Verre House already have perfect pitch. I'm one of the few who had to learn how to find and hold a note after I arrived. Maybe you can learn from my experience.

"Here's what you do..."

Dan stood in the shadows at the top of the stairs and scowled. Why did everyone want to help that idiot kitchen boy? So he'd had a difficult life. So what? Didn't everyone?

Why don't they feel sorry for me? I've had it hard too.

The apprentice challenge had been his. He'd found it. Yeah, the stupid kitchen boy found the right notes first, but that was just an accident. Dan wasn't going to let anyone steal his chance.

I'll show them.

He just needed a good hammer.

Hope

Late the next night Octavia sat again against a shelter support. She watched the interplay of moon and clouds. Mischa lay nearby, asleep on his side. Mother, Father and Cadie slept together in a little huddle under the shelter.

Octavia considered the dark waters of the flowing river. Warm night air pressed uncomfortably against her skin. A lantern flared.

As before, she hummed the calming tunes. The monster awoke and opened its eyes. It stared at her through the golden net created by the mothers of Tondo. Octavia held its gaze and counted her breaths.

Terror, Hunger, Rage, breathe. The pattern remained the same. Again the monster grew until it appeared that it would surely break free of the net. Just when it seemed too much, the monster stopped growing. It held its gray, nauseating, tumultuous shape and glared back at her with coal black eyes.

Terror, hunger, rage, breathe. Terror, hunger, rage breathe. This was easily the most painful thing she'd ever done. The black eyes sharpened their focus. Would the creature speak?

It appeared that she had gained control. She struggled to maintain her breathing. Now what should she do with the beast?

What if the monster breaks free? What then?

The monster expanded as she panicked, straining against the net. The calming notes did her no good at all. The heating notes also had little effect. She tried the swirling notes, faster and faster, but the chaotic twirling of the monster did not change. Octavia began the counter clockwise swirl.

The *mortolo* opened its mouth in a soundless howl. It shrank a little. Octavia continued the notes for the counter clockwise swirl and the creature continued to shrink. *Of course.* That made a kind of sense. Everything was reversed with the monster as if it were a reflection in a mirror. She continued to shrink the beast until it vanished from sight. Was it gone altogether? She tried the calming notes. The chaotic entity appeared, a little smaller than before. Its tumultuous nature had not changed, but the control she now felt diminished her own terror.

Progress. This was definitely progress. She shrank the *mortolo* again, imagined a thick iron trunk lined inside with mirrors and dropped the monster into it. She slammed the trunk shut and locked it with an imaginary key.

She opened her eyes. Her heart pounded. She felt incredibly energized and exhausted all at the same time. *I'm on the right path. But this is so dangerous. If I get it wrong* ... She shuddered to think where that could take her. A *mortolo's* appetite was insatiable. And if the net did fail .... *So much for acceptance*, she thought with a wry smile. She'd found an even more painful emotion: the one called 'hope.'

"Well done, Robbie," Galliard cheered that night as another row of tiles flipped. "You sang that line perfectly just from reading the notes. The judges won't understand why anyone ever had a problem with your singing."

The next day Robbie almost dropped a dish in surprise when Frank asked him to join the afternoon work session.

"It's just more wine bottles," Frank said, "but the repetition will do you good."

Halfnote didn't think she was the only person who realized that Sylvia was out of the house that afternoon on a personal errand and not expected back until late.

The Liar's Revenge

The next morning they docked at Vara Nasim, one of the largest cities between Albermarle and Tulum. Water craft of all description crowded the docks. Octavia heard at least three different bands playing loud dance music, apparently indifferent to the overall discord they created.

"Oh dear, I had forgotten about the festival," Mother said. "It's the Liar's Revenge."

"The what?" Octavia asked.

"It's a story-telling festival. It's put on by the local guilds for actors and story-tellers and the like. Basically it's an excuse to throw a party while the weather is still reasonable. It's very popular."

"You two should attend," Father said. To Octavia's great surprise he handed her a fat purse that rang with the particular melodies of gold, silver and copper coins. "Your mother and I have business to take care of, but that shouldn't stop you and Mischa from enjoying the festival. Don't worry, we'll take Cadie with us. Everyone's been far too serious on this trip. Go have some fun."

"Just watch for pickpockets," Mother added as Octavia tucked the purse away. "They'll be out in force on a day like this. And you, Mischa, put on shoes and a shirt. This is Vara Nasim, after all."

Mischa made a face but quickly pulled on ankle-length trousers, soft leather boots and a newish blue tunic decorated with silver embroidered flowers. After a bit of rummaging, Mother found a green town dress and held it up to Octavia.

"Do you like this one? The color certainly suits you. It should fit, with a few quick stitches. I bought it from a dressmaker here a few months ago, so you'll be right in style."

"It's lovely, Mother," Octavia said, delighted. "I don't think I've worn anything like it before. But is it long enough?"

"It'll take just a moment to let the hem out and stitch it up."

"Octavia," Mother murmured more quietly when the others were distracted, "will you be all right in town?"

Octavia fingered her pearl. "Yes, Mother. Don't worry."

Octavia's Journey   *by Lynette Hill*

"I'm your mother. I'm required to worry."

Octavia laughed. "It's really all right, Mother. I've been practicing with glass on the river. The pearl protects me. I'll be fine."

You look nice," Octavia told Mischa as they left the raft.

"And you." Mischa grinned and offered her his arm.

The streets were full of people from everywhere. The fragrance of cooking meat, exotic spices and flowers filled the air. One smell Octavia couldn't identify kept catching in the back of her throat.

Drummers and jugglers and all sorts of other entertainment showed out in every direction. Octavia barely knew where to look first. A parade of giant puppets and their brightly dressed handlers wound its way through the crowd. Tiny acrobats dressed as mice – were they children? Dwarves? Some of both? – flipped and did cartwheels at the feet of the giants to give the impression of small creatures scurrying away from the puppets' great feet. Enthusiastic bands positioned here and there created a cacophony of dance music.

"Keep hold of my arm," Mischa shouted into Octavia's ear as they pushed their way through the crowd. She nodded and took a firmer grip to show that she'd heard. A puppet king's enormous hand swooped down. The crowd around them ducked and shrieked in appreciation. Up close Octavia could see the blue silk fabric of the king's sleeve fluttering in the breeze. The painted papier-mache hand was attached to slender wooden sticks by stout red stitches of cotton thread. The giant fingers, each one wiggling independently, brushed gently across her head.

"Ooooh. Lucky you," the woman next to her laughed.

"What?"

"That's good luck, that is," the woman slapped Octavia on the shoulder. "A pat from the king. Means you're coming into money."

Octavia smiled and nodded back. The enormous king and its entourage of tumblers moved away from them, followed by the shrieks of the crowd. She'd never heard an accent like the woman's, or seen that type of dress. Halfnote would know, she thought, where the woman came from and what that style of dress meant. Eyelets dotted the orange and yellow fabric.

Around the waist the woman wore a black leather belt decorated

Octavia's Journey   *by Lynette Hill*

with little mirrors. The round bits of glass reflected the bright sunlight. All around the belt, the mirrors flashed as the woman twirled. Round and round and round. Swirling light all around. Swirling monsters roared out at her. They came and went too quickly for the pearl to react.

    Octavia swayed dizzily. The roaring whirl of the *mortolo* filled her vision. She tore her eyes away from the woman's belt and came face to face with another enormous puppet, the figure of a young maiden. Tiny mirrors, meant to represent diamonds, covered her tunic. Orange silk billowed in the wind, blocking out all other sights. Each little mirror peered towards her like a small, hungry eye.

    "Octavia!" Mischa shouted. "Octavia!"

    She stumbled backwards, shoved this way and that by the crowd. A group of boys chasing after the puppets pushed between Mischa and Octavia. They also blocked her view of the tunic. Octavia came to herself with a start, but it was too late. She couldn't see Mischa or even the woman with the mirrored belt. All around her strangers danced and laughed and called out to the puppets and each other. Octavia whirled in panic, shouting Mischa's name. She looked for an edge to the street, a kiosk, anything that might make an island to protect her from the crowd's surging current.

    Pushed and shoved from one place to the next, she stumbled. Octavia willed herself to stay upright for fear of being trampled. She called for Mischa but her words vanished into the overwhelming noise of the crowd. The wall of a building loomed suddenly to one side and she pushed toward it. Her heel hit something hard and she careened backwards. She fell against somebody, probably more than one somebody. Something hard and sharp hit her in the back.

    Tangled up with someone else, Octavia found it impossible to stop falling. Her hand hit something rough but solid. She'd found the wall. She managed to get her back against it and blindly apologized to whomever she was stepping on before her feet found the ground.

    She pressed against the brick wall for support. She closed her eyes to block out the tumult of the crowd and her own rising sense of disappointment. The protection provided by the mothers of Tondo didn't solve everything.

Octavia's Journey   *by Lynette Hill*

"Are you all right, dearie?"

Octavia opened her eyes to find an old woman looking at her with genuine concern.

"Festival too much for you, dear? It has that effect on some people; all that noise and nonsense."

"I guess. I'm all right now, though. Thank you for asking."

The crowd hurried off in pursuit of the parade. As the street cleared the store front on the other side came into Octavia's view. A giant picture window filled her vision. She stared at it. The window was glass. Of course it was. She could see her reflection in it. She could see the reflection of the old woman and the building behind them. So why didn't she see the monster? What sort of glass was this? Was it glass?

"Octavia!" Mischa ran up. "Thank Hamsa. I thought I'd lost you. Are you all right?"

"Yes, yes. I just got caught up in the crowd. Thank the dragons that you found me." Octavia turned to speak the older woman but she was already trundling off down the road with her bags of shopping. Octavia turned back to Mischa.

"Mischa, do you see the window across the street?"

"Sure ... um, Octavia, are you sure you're all right?"

"Yes. I'm fine. It's the first piece of glass I've seen that doesn't show me the monster. Why not? I was overwhelmed by the little mirrors on the puppet. Why doesn't this giant window bother me?"

"Um, maybe because it wasn't sung?"

"What? What do you mean, not sung? It's glass." Octavia hurried across the street to get a closer look. It was, she had to admit, an incredibly shoddy piece. Why on earth would the guild allow work of such terrible quality? The pane of glass was thicker at the bottom than the top, with visible flaws dotted all around. She tapped it with a fingernail, then placed her hand flat against the pane. Definitely glass. Definitely incredibly poor quality glass.

"Octavia," Mischa grabbed her arm. "You're starting to scare me. Why don't we leave the window alone?"

"All right." Octavia let Mischa lead her away. "What do you mean, not sung?"

"Well, it's blown glass isn't it? Not everyone can afford sung glass. What would you charge to create a window like that?"

"My window would be clear and unmarred. Mine wouldn't break. That piece looks so fragile I don't doubt it would shatter if you threw a rock at it. What fool put such a shoddy piece by the roadway? One stone kicked up by any horse's hoof will destroy it."

Mischa shrugged. Octavia realized that her cousin was not alone. A slender girl in Khelani dress stood behind him, smiling shyly.

"Hello," Octavia said. She gave Mischa a questioning glance. To her great surprise the ever-confident Mischa actually blushed.

"Um, Octavia, this is Tamisin. She's ... ah ... a friend. From Clan Loire. And Tamisin, this is Octavia. My cousin from Albermarle, the glass singer."

"Oh, you're the one who cured the plague," Tamisin gasped. "Thank you. We are all so grateful. You saved us. Most of our clan was already sick when word of the cure came. We can never thank you enough. If there's anything I can ever do ..."

Octavia did her best to keep smiling despite the clench in her gut. "It's fine, really. It wasn't just me. My sister Halfnote, the rest of the house staff all helped make it happen. Finding the cure really was a joint effort. But there is something you can do for me," she added.

"Yes, of course, what is it?"

"Please, treat me like a normal person. I am, you know."

Tamisin broke into a beautiful smile, a near match to Mischa's ever-present grin. *No wonder he finds her so attractive.*

"Yes of course."

After that the trio got along very well indeed. They spent the rest of the morning wandering from entertainment to entertainment, taking in story-tellers and circus acts. There was even a display of exotic animals which included a trio of elephants. The elephants, at the direction of their handlers, danced in a circle, then showed off their great strength by pulling flat carts filled with giant logs.

"Did you meet Maru?" Octavia asked Mischa.

"Who's that?"

"When the Samoyans came to Verre House, they brought an

elephant. Maru was its handler. The elephant was amazing."

Mischa laughed. "How did they get it up the lifts?"

Octavia grinned. "Everyone asks that. 'Very carefully,' that's what Maru said."

Tamisin didn't look amused. "People say it was the Samoyans that brought the plague up the Khelana."

"I don't know if they did or not," Octavia said. "Everyone in their party seemed healthy when they arrived. The prince was desperate to find a cure. His people were dying. What else could he do?"

Tamisin still frowned. Mischa pointed to the acrobats in clown paint who pretended to use the elephants' trunks as jump ropes. Soon they were all laughing again.

As the day progressed it became very clear that Mischa and Tamisin were besotted with each other. Octavia felt more and more like a third wheel. Mischa and Tamisin giggled together constantly and snuck kisses when they thought Octavia wasn't looking.

Throughout town they found many more examples of 'blown' glass in windows and doors. Sung glass appeared mainly as small decorative pieces such as lamps, mirrors, wind-catchers and the like. Octavia was appalled by the poor quality of 'blown' glass but grateful that she didn't have to see the monster in every direction. In hindsight, coming into town might not have been the wisest move. And yet, she was coping. And discovering blown glass was definitely worthwhile. Why hadn't Grandfather or Mother ever mentioned it? Or Halfnote?

Early in the afternoon they bought honey-coated hazelnuts and sat on a bench next to a stream in a small park. Octavia found the somewhat quieter surroundings a relief. Looking around to avoid watching Mischa and Tamisin as they kept sneaking kisses, Octavia saw tall spires peeking over the trees that lined the park. Of course, Vara Nasim's university. The school was known, among other things, for the quality of its library.

"Mischa, do you mind if we split up? Mischa!"

"Erm, yes, what do you need?" He came up for air after another kiss. Tamisin giggled.

"That's Vara Nasim University over there, isn't it? I'd like to go visit their library."

Tamisin wrinkled her nose. "Why do you want to go there?"

"I'd like to see what books they have on, well you know, I'd like to look at their books. Listen, we'll meet up at that restaurant down by the docks, the one with the big elephant's head on its sign. You remember that one, don't you?"

"Um, your mother might not like it ..."

"Honestly, how much trouble can I get into in a library? I know the way to the docks from here. You two clearly want to be alone."

"Oh let her go, Mischa." Tamisin squeezed his arm. "We can meet at the pub later. I know where it is. You can't miss that sign."

Hammered

"Do you need anything from the market, Alma?" Dan asked.

"No, dear, but thanks for asking. We went this morning." Alma blinked and turned around for a second look at the boy. Yes, it really was Dan asking the question. "Is there something you need?"

"No, I just wanted to help out," Dan said. He dashed out of the kitchen, nearly knocking over Halfnote and Laiertes as he left.

"What's he up to," Laiertes asked. "Dan never just wants to help anyone but himself."

"Oh, now, let's not be so hasty," the cook said. "Perhaps he's learned a thing or two in his time here. Don't you two have lessons this afternoon?"

Halfnote smiled. 'Lessons' were quickly becoming one of her favorite parts of the week. They found Galliard whistling a complicated piece that Halfnote didn't recognize as he waited for them in the study room. He already had their books out.

They were just about to leave when Sylvia poked her head in. "Is Dan here?"

"No," Galliard said. "Why?"

"When did you last see him? He's meant to be singing with me in the main creation room this afternoon."

"Just after lunch in the kitchen," Halfnote said. Laiertes nodded agreement. "He asked Alma if she needed anything from the market."

"Dan did?" Sylvia looked as surprised as everyone else. "That's odd. Well, he'll be in trouble when he does turn up. Come on, Galliard, you'll have to take his place. Laiertes and Halfnote will just have to get on without you."

Neither of the younger apprentices wanted to go into town without Galliard so they settled down to an afternoon of reading. Time passed very slowly indeed.

Laiertes straightened up. "Did you hear something?"

"Like what?" Halfnote stretched, happy to take a break.

"I don't know exactly," Laiertes frowned. "A bit like someone yelling, and then a heavy thump. Or maybe two thumps."

Halfnote listened carefully, and then shook her head.

"Someone's still singing, but I don't hear anything else. Still, it is late. Look how long the shadows are getting outside. Why hasn't anyone called us?"

"Let's go see." Laiertes shut his book. "Maybe they forgot."

While that seemed highly unlikely, Halfnote put her book back on the shelf and hurried out the door with Laiertes. Robbie all but knocked them over as he dashed up the hall from the kitchen area.

"Quick," he gasped. "Where's Master Verre? Dan's hurt."

"We heard a noise in the lower basement," Alma explained later to the assembled staff. "We went down the stairs and found Dan on the floor, unconscious. I sent Robbie for help. It looks as if the hammer bounced off the wall and back into Dan's face."

Alerted by Robbie's shouts, Master Verre and Frank had rushed down into the lowest basement. Frank carried the still unconscious Dan up to bed in the visitor's chambers while Master Verre sent Laiertes running for Physician Cornelius. Once they were certain that the boy would recover, they left him in the care of the physician and Madame Verre. Everyone else followed Master Verre back down into the basement. Even Alma, who normally looked after the household's ill and injured, chose to go back into the lowest basement. There, in the flickering light of their wax candles and oil lamps, everyone saw the result of Dan's actions.

"Why was Dan banging on the wall?" Laiertes whispered.

"Not the wall," Alma said. She glanced at Robbie. He stood pale with shock. "Or, not just the wall. Dan destroyed one of the tiles and the doll underneath it. He broke the last figurine on this level of the apprentice challenge."

The other apprentices huddled together on the last steps of the lowest basement in the same place where they usually sat to watch Robbie sing. Now they were a shocked audience to Dan's deliberate destruction. Robbie stood next to Halfnote, still mute.

Sylvia knelt down by the shattered fragments of the tile and picked up the remains of the figurine. The glass doll had broken into three large pieces. Galliard whistled at the sight.

Frank used a small mirrored lamp to peer into the gap left behind by the destruction.

"This is amazing," he said. "There's a whole network of small tubes in the walls. I thought this was all solid stone. Someone bored a small channel through solid rock to install the figurines and the tubes that connect them. What craftsmanship. The tiles are perfectly inset over the tubes to blend in with the natural rock."

Sylvia sobbed. Frank turned and put an arm around her.

"This is my fault," Sylvia wept. "I'm so sorry Robbie. You've been doing so well. I really did want you to complete this level."

Robbie still said nothing, but Laiertes frowned in confusion.

"I don't understand. Why is *Sylvia* so upset? She didn't break the doll. Dan did it."

"Well, she feels guilty, doesn't she?" Marissa hissed a little too loudly into his ear. "She sent Robbie to the kitchen, and she's always felt pretty guilty about doing that."

She has? Halfnote wasn't sure she agreed with this statement. Sylvia never looked guilty to her.

"Then Robbie started the challenge. And then everyone started helping Robbie and his singing got a lot better," Marissa continued.

"She felt like maybe she could have done more for him. But she has to pass her junior master test to continue in her career, so she can take of herself. Her last relative died in the plague. She doesn't show it, but I think she's really sad about that. Sylvia feels alone, now, and scared."

Now all of the apprentices stared at Marissa. She gave up trying to whisper. Even Robbie was listening.

"But Robbie's alone in the world too. So she feels terrible about being mean to him. But she didn't feel like she could back down from what she said to Master Verre. And she could see that Dan was getting really jealous. She knew he was bullying Robbie but she didn't know what to do about it. And now Dan's broken the challenge and Robbie can't complete it. Sylvia feels terrible."

"And you know all of this how?" Galliard demanded. "Do you read minds, too?"

"Are you kidding? I have twelve brothers and sisters. If that doesn't teach you something about human nature nothing will."

"So what happens now?" Laiertes asked.

Galliard shrugged. "The agreement was that Robbie prove to the judges that he can sing as well as expected of an apprentice of his own age. He just has to sing about as well as you do, Laiertes.

"He has to find his pitch and stay on key and hold the note without wavering for 30 seconds and show proper breathing technique. He'll have to demonstrate that he can lift and spin a liquid ball of glass. His dragon skills aren't in question. Everyone knows he's amazing with fire. He just has to sing in tune.

"Robbie never had to finish the challenge to regain his place, so this ... this is senseless. What was Dan thinking, Marissa, since you understand people so well?"

Marissa shrugged. "How would I know? Dan's an idiot."

"I'll fix this," Sylvia declared. Her voice resonated off the wall. "I swear I'll fix this. I'll make a new doll to replace the broke one. I'll repair the challenge. The new figurine will be my test piece."

"I'll help you," Frank said.

Sylvia buried her face in his shoulder.

"Come on everyone." Marissa stood up. "Let's go upstairs."

"What will happen to Dan?" Laiertes asked.

"Master Verre fired Geoffrey for taking bribes," Galliard said. "I don't think he'll have any trouble sending Dan home for breaking a precious Verre House artifact."

Halfnote waited for Robbie as the rest left. He hadn't spoken in so long that Halfnote began to worry that he might not speak again.

"You only have to sing about as well as Laiertes," she repeated Galliard's words. "And you already do. Just remember to breathe the way Grandpa showed you, so you can stay calm. You still have a few days to practice, you know."

At the Library

Octavia worried that the university or its library might close on a festival day, but luck was with her. A passing scholar directed her to the main door. The library filled the main part of two towers. Octavia kept her eyes averted from the windows (made of proper sung glass, she was both relieved and distressed to see) as she hurried up to the entrance. Inside, Octavia took in the sweet scent of parchment and ink and smiled. A wide desk blocked her way into the library proper.

"May I help you?" The clerk behind the desk wore silver and gray robes. They matched almost exactly the color of his elegantly trimmed hair and beard.

"Yes. I wondered if you had any works on glass singing."

"Of course. What college are you with?"

"Oh, um, I'm not with any college."

"Oh dear." Light from a nearby lamp reflected off the man's well-oiled beard. Octavia focused on his face, to avoid looking at the glass. "Only scholars and teachers affiliated with the university may use these facilities. Next, please."

He looked past her to the person next in line.

"But ..." Octavia wanted to protest.

"And you are?" The man peered down the short haired woman

in worn blue student robes who stood behind Octavia. The young woman, surely not much older than Octavia herself, leaned heavily on a crutch with a padded hand grip and elbow rest. She wore large spectacles with thick black wooden frames and even thicker lenses. The blown glass lenses looked of such poor quality that Octavia's hands positively itched to replace them. Any third year apprentice could make better spectacles. Octavia's already low opinion of the local glass singers' guild dropped even further.

"I'm Scholar Alex, studying at the College of Commerce." She winked at Octavia. "And it's all right, Brother Gustav. This woman is with me. I'll vouch for her."

"Glass singing is an art, Scholar Alex, not ..."

"Of course it's a business," Octavia jumped in. "How can we afford to buy supplies if we don't make a profit?"

The receptionist looked down his nose at them. "Go on then. Mind how you handle the scrolls. They are difficult to replace."

"Oh really ..." Octavia breathed out to calm herself.

"Come on," Alex jerked her head toward the shelves, "before he changes his mind." The student led the way through a swinging gate into the main part of the library. She moved easily down the carpeted aisles despite her wasted leg. "The scrolls on glass singing are over here. What do you want with them?"

"I'm looking for any information they have on healing mirrors, especially healing mirrors that turn *mortolo* in the making process," Octavia said. "And thank you for helping me. Why did you?"

"Why not?" Alex pushed her spectacles back into place. "He's such a stuffed shirt, old Brother Gustav. I enjoy tweaking his nose when I can. But my goodness, why do you want to learn about *mortolo* mirrors? I'm not sure they'll have anything on those in the regular library. Any works on that subject are probably in the esoteric section. You have to be a senior scholar with special permission to look at those."

"Oh, I hadn't thought that they might be restricted."

"Well, here are the regular works, anyway." Alex pointed out how the hand-written scrolls and flat printed books were organized according to language and then alphabetically by author or place of origin. Octavia ran down the listings of authors.

"What's your interest?" Alex asked.

"Well, my family are glass singers …"

"Oh really …" The scholar gave Octavia a pointed look.

Octavia sighed. "I've read all these. They're just the standard works. I don't suppose you have access to the restricted section?"

Alex regarded her with a less than friendly expression.

"I'm sorry," Octavia said, "have I upset you in some way?"

"I may be from out of town, sweetheart, but I'm not stupid," the student snapped. "We've all heard the song."

"What? What song?"

Alex just shook her head, shoved her spectacles into place and hurried off. Octavia heard her muttering "how could I be so stupid?"

"No, really, I honestly don't know what song you're talking about," Octavia called after her, but the woman kept going.

Fine. I can't even meet someone without putting my foot in it.

She sighed and ran through the list again to see if she'd missed anything. She hadn't.

"You've lost your escort." Brother Gustav appeared unexpectedly from behind a pillar. Octavia squeaked in surprise. "I'm afraid you will have to leave."

"I don't suppose you could show me what you have on glass singing in the esoteric section, could you?"

"Only the most senior scholars are allowed to peruse those works," Brother Gustav said as he herded her towards the exit. The man's tones were as oily as his hair.

"Your list of works on glass singing is quite small. Does no one here study the craft?"

"The glass singers are a closed guild and do not care to share their secrets with the world."

Well, that was certainly true. Octavia had another thought.

"Are you aware of any songs about glass singing? Something that might upset people?"

They had reached the exit. Brother Gustav cocked his head to one side as if considering. "No, not at all. But I don't spend much time in the public houses, either. Good-bye."

The River Rat and the Glass Princess

Fortunately, it was still a beautiful day outside. A coolish breeze cleared the air of the usual urban scents of horse manure and cooking. She hurried down the main street towards the river and the Elephant's Head. To her surprise Mischa and Tamisin were already there, smiling at each other over a jug of wine.

"Have you eaten?" Octavia asked. "I'm starving."

"Not much," Mischa said. "Some bread and cheese. The stew they're serving here smells wonderful. I wouldn't mind trying a bowl or two of that."

"Or three," Tamisin giggled. The pair disappeared into another round of kissing.

Octavia rolled her eyes and turned away to signal a waitress. "Money first," the hefty woman wearing a yellow apron growled. "The lovebirds haven't paid for their wine yet." Octavia handed her several silver coins. The waitress's expression cleared and she hurried off to speak to the next table.

Octavia looked around. The restaurant was as busy as you might expect on a festival day. A small band performed in one corner. Their tunes were more restrained than the lively dance music playing in the streets. A woman began singing a wistful ballad. The audience murmured its appreciation and the level of conversation dropped.

Many of the other patrons were townsfolk. Traveling merchants and their staff made up most of the rest of the crowd. A gaggle of students in the robes of their colleges clustered around a table on the other side of the room. Their food arrived during a break in the singing. Octavia gave an internal sigh of relief when Mischa and Tamisin turned their attentions from each other to the stew.

"Why is that woman staring at us," Tamisin asked half-way through the meal.

Octavia's Journey   *by Lynette Hill*

Octavia looked up. Scholar Alex had joined the university group. The students now whispered together and stared at them.

Mischa frowned. "What's their problem? Are they prejudiced against Khelani or something?"

"That woman in the black spectacles," Octavia said, "The one with the crutch. I met her at the library. Something I said upset her."

"What did you say?" Mischa glared back at the scholars. Alex now spoke to the waitress with the yellow apron and handed her money. The large woman nodded and went over to the musicians.

"I honestly don't know. She helped me find the works on glass singing and asked why I was interested. When I said my family were glass singers she got angry and walked off. She said she wasn't stupid, that she'd heard the song. Do you know what she was talking about?"

"Oh no," Mischa said. Tamisin just looked confused.

"What?" Octavia asked. "Do you know what she meant?"

"Did your parents never tell you? You've really never heard it?"

"Tell me what? What song, Mischa?"

"She's coming over here," Tamisin warned. "She looks drunk."

"Hello." Alex beamed brightly at everyone around the table. She wobbled on her crutch and pushed her black-framed spectacles back up on her nose. "You said you didn't know what song I was talking about. I thought you might like to hear it." She pushed her way onto the bench next to Octavia.

"It's a great song," the scholar added. "I really like it."

An older man with bushy eyebrows and a mischievous expression changed places with the singer. The woman sat down with the band and picked up a viola. The musicians began a much livelier tune. The crowd cheered and clapped in time to the music. Several people jumped up to dance. Tamisin smiled as well but stopped when Mischa glared at her.

"Oh. It's *The River Rat and the Glass Princess*," Tamisin said. "I like it. It's really popular." She leaned towards Octavia to be heard over the music. "I'm surprised you haven't heard it before."

"See." Alex nodded excessively. "She likes it too. Let's get some more wine." The scholar waved to the waitress with the yellow apron and mimed drinking out of a bottle.

Mischa stood up. "Let's go. We don't have to put up with this."

But by now Octavia was truly curious. At least this was one mystery she could solve. She kept her seat and Mischa reluctantly sat back down. The singer enthusiastically belted out the verses in an attractive baritone. He changed his voice to indicate each of the different characters, as if telling a story.

The song lyrics began something like this:

A young river rat toiled with all his might
He worked in the day, he worked all night
He did nothing but work until he caught sight
Of the world's most beautiful princess.

"It's a love song," Octavia said. "What's wrong with that?"

"Wait until you hear the rest of it."

The student's wine arrived. She offered the bottle around. Octavia declined, feeling the need for a clear head. Mischa grabbed it and downed a good amount before Alex snatched it back again.

"Oi! Leave some for the rest of us." She finished the bottle with one gulp and slammed it down on the table.

"Shhhh," Octavia hissed. "I can't hear the song."

It told the story of a lonely rat. He fell in love with a beautiful singing princess who lived in a glass tower atop a high mountain. Day after day he heard the princess sing. Finally, the besotted rat determined to meet her. He made friends with the castle cook, who told him about a secret tunnel that led to the princess' suite.

Octavia looked at Mischa.

"All right, I get it. Father's the river rat and Mother's the glass princess. Is that right? And Alma's the cook. I just can't believe someone wrote a song about them."

"Wait a minute," Tamisin gasped. "This song is about *your* parents?" She blushed. "Oh no. Mischa's right. We should go."

"Yeah, right," Alex snorted. She reached for the wine bottle again and was disappointed to find it empty. She looked around without

Octavia's Journey   *by Lynette Hill*

success for the waitress.

Mischa nodded unhappily. He opened his hands in supplication. "Now can we go?"

"Shhhhh," Alex shoved her spectacles back into place. "We're just getting to the good bit."

The rat followed the tunnel, charmed the princess and began a passionate affair. Several bawdy verses followed. Then the lovers were discovered by the princess's father, the evil sorcerer Fortis Verre.

"What?" Octavia gasped. "Grandfather isn't a sorcerer. He's not evil. I can't believe they named him outright."

Alex snickered.

"It just gets worse from here," Mischa warned, but Octavia was determined to hear the rest. The unhappy rat was lured into a trap by a bit of cheese. There he was given the choice of leaving his love behind forever or allowing Fortis Verre to fling him to his death from the tower. The rat chose to live and left the sobbing princess behind.

"Grandfather would never … Father would never …"

"You really shouldn't take it too seriously," Mischa said.

But the song wasn't finished. The evil sorcerer discovered that his daughter was already pregnant by the rat. In a rage, Fortis Verre flung his own daughter from the tower. She was saved only because she landed in the softest mud on the riverbank. She sank up to her neck in filth. Other rats pulled her to safety and took her to her lost love.

Then the rat revealed his true colors. He was nothing more than a common gold-digger after all. Alas this realization came too late for his lover. Octavia listened in outrage to *The Princess's Lament*. It lasted several verses and detailed all that the princess had lost, the beauty she gave up for love, the ugliness that now surrounded her. The music and lyrics were heart-breaking and beautiful.

"My father is not a gold-digger," Octavia hissed at Alex. "My mother loves her life on the river." The laughing scholar took a second look at Octavia's angry expression and lost her mocking smile.

All seemed lost to the princess until her daughter was born. The child was born singing, with such a strong and beautiful voice that even the sorcerer could hear her from atop his tower. The sorcerer's heart melted. Fortis Verre sent for the rat and his daughter and begged them to forgive him. But the evil rat displayed his true nature. He demanded that Fortis Verre buy back his grandchild.

"What? What are they saying? My father never …"

"You aren't serious." Alex was beginning looked worried. "It's just a song … a fairy tale. What are you getting so upset for?"

"My father didn't sell me to anyone," Octavia all but shouted at her. "He loves me. He loves all of his children. He loves my mother. She chose to live with him on the river. It was her choice and she is very happy about it. And Grandfather didn't banish her. Ever."

"Your father… wait, no, it's just a song." Clutching her spectacles protectively, Alex scooted back away from her.

"Can we go now?" Mischa jumped up from the table.

"Yes, please." Tamisin stood up as well.

"But who wrote that horrible song?" Other diners were beginning to look over at them.

"I have no idea. It's been around forever," Mischa grabbed Octavia's arm and pushed her towards the front door. Tamisin grabbed Octavia's other arm, to make sure she continued towards the door. "Actually, there are several versions. Some are worse than this one. I'm surprised you've never heard it before."

"But who would write such a song about Mother and Father? How did our family's relationships become everyone's business? Why would anyone else even care about their marriage?"

"You can't be serious." Alex wobbled after them on her crutch. "That song is a fairy tale. It's not about you …"

"Yes it is!" Both Mischa and Octavia turned and shouted at her. "And my father did not sell us," Octavia added. "He's not greedy. He's not a gold-digger. My grandfather is not a sorcerer. He's not evil!" The scholar stumbled back away from them.

"Have Mother and Father heard it?" Octavia asked Mischa.

"Yes, of course they have. It's pretty popular."

"What do they do when they hear it?"

"Aunty Melody just laughs," Mischa said. "But Uncle Paul, he gets really angry. So they always leave once it begins."

Octavia's Journey   by Lynette Hill

"How can Mother possibly laugh about it?"

"Aunty Melody says that when she was a little girl she always dreamed of being a princess in a fairy tale. And now she is."

They had not quite reached the outskirts of the Khelani neighborhood surrounding the river docks when two girls ran up.

"Are you Singer Octavia?" the older girl asked.

Octavia nodded.

The younger one handed her a bunch of yellow flowers, then stared shyly at her feet. "You saved our little brother," she all but whispered. "Thank you."

"Yes," the older girl added. "Your parents said you don't want people to make a big fuss but our family is really grateful. We just wanted to let you know. Your cure saved our brother and a lot of other people in Clan Feni. Thank you."

"I'm really glad it helped," Octavia said. They all stood around awkwardly for a moment, then the girls nodded and dashed off.

"Um …"

Octavia turned to see Alex standing behind them, leaning heavily on her crutch.

"You should go now," Mischa told her.

"Mischa! Octavia! What are you doing here? Not done with the festival already, are you? I told you two to have fun." They found Father, slightly tipsy and in the company of some other Khelani men already back at the raft. "And hello Tamisin. I hope you are well."

"Hello Trader Breydon. I am, thank you."

After some polite chit-chat, the other men left. Mischa escorted Tamisin back to her raft.

"Father…" Octavia said, uncertain now how to ask about it. "In town … we heard a song.…"

He sighed. *"The River Rat and the Glass Princess?"*

"Yes, Father."

"I'll make tea," Father said. "Then tell me what happened."

He fussed about with fire and kettle for a bit. Octavia realized that he was stalling. Eventually, however, they settled under the raft's shelter, cups in hand with nothing left to do but talk.

"I don't know what others have told you about how your mother and I met," Father said. "But I want you to know that whatever our faults, whatever our differences, I love your mother very much and I believe she feels the same about me."

"I know that you do," Octavia said. "And Mother loves you just as much. No one who knows you could doubt that. But that song ..."

Father grimaced. "Yes. That song. Among the Khelani, Octavia, love and marriage are fairly simple. A boy and a girl meet, they decide that they like each other, they spend time together. It works out or it doesn't. Eventually they find someone to share a raft with or children come along or you know. Life happens." He shrugged. "That's how it's supposed to work anyway, among the river people. For some reason townspeople always need to complicate everything." He sighed. For a moment he looked almost as old as Grandfather.

"Anyway, I first saw your mother at the Midsummer Festival in Albermarle all those years ago. Verre House put on its usual demonstration in the market square. I watched in amazement from the crowd as your mother sang some birds into form. I knew, at that moment, that she was the woman for me. Of course, I also knew that it was a doomed love. She could never love me back. Even if she did, well, it was impossible for such a prominent townswoman to become involved with a river rat like me."

"Father! But you took her a cup of tea after she sang and the two of you talked for hours. That's how Mother tells it, anyway. She says it was love at first sight. You're not a gold-digger. You didn't sell us or abandon Mother. Grandfather might not be happy about your marriage but he isn't a sorcerer. Who would write such a song?"

"Perhaps you should wait until you've heard the whole story before you decide who the hero is, and who the villain."

Octavia couldn't read his expression. Father looked tired, worried ... why? Nothing about that vile song could be true.

"Despite everything," Father continued, "I couldn't stay away. I kept finding excuses to go to Albermarle, and to visit Verre House. I kept knocking on the gate and asking for contracts. I would sit outside for hours, just hoping for a glimpse of your mother."

"How romantic."

"I suppose. Perhaps that's what I thought at the time. At any rate, Alma did her best to shoo me away. It was Alma who told me that your mother was being courted by Alfonso, the prince of Kenifra. So you see, sweetie, you might have been born a princess if I hadn't come along and gotten in the way."

"Father, you won Mother over a prince?" Octavia gasped. "Wow. And don't be silly. With a different father I wouldn't be me. But wait." She reviewed her mental map of the world.

"The prince of Kenifra? Kenifra is just a city in Malmesbury, isn't it? It's a big, wealthy city, granted, but it doesn't have a prince. It doesn't even have a port."

"Kenifra used to be a princedom," Father said. "It fell on hard times during the reign of the prince's grandfather. The last prince, Prince Alfonso, believed that marrying Melody would create strong ties between Kenifra and the glass singers' guild. He hoped that this would draw business to the princedom and so better the fortunes of its people. He thought this would improve his own hold on power."

"All that, from a marriage?" Octavia considered this. "Do you think it might have worked?"

"Perhaps. It was a step in the right direction. But it is also possible that the princedom was simply too weak by then to be saved. Your mother's refusal of Alfonso was not the last straw, but it didn't help. Within a year of our marriage he was murdered by members of his own court. The rulers of Malmesbury were distant relatives of the prince. They decided that their claim to Kenifra was as good as anyone's and took over in the chaos that followed."

"Oh my," Octavia said. "I hardly know what to think. If Mother had married the prince, Father, it doesn't sound like I would have been a princess. It sounds more like I might not have been born at all. But that dreadful song ... who wrote it?"

"I suspect the song was the prince's revenge for your mother's rejection. I heard it for the first time just before he was murdered."

"You think the prince wrote the song?"

"I think he may have commissioned it. Or one of his officials, anyway. It is, unfortunately for us, a catchy tune and very popular."

"Wow, Father. I've never heard it in Albermarle."

"No," Father laughed. "Your grandparents' influence is enough that we don't have to listen to it there. Your grandmother threatened to personally skin alive anyone heard singing it within the city limits. I imagine any Verre House staff member who mentioned it would have been instantly dismissed."

"Is that why Grandfather was so against your marriage? Because of the prince?"

"I believe that he would have tried to stop our union regardless. Octavia …"

"Hello you two." It was Mother, returning with a tired and fretful Cadie. "You look quite serious. Did something happen?"

"They encountered our favorite song," Father said. "Octavia had never heard it before."

"Oh dear. Which version?"

"It wasn't very nice, but Mischa says he's heard worse."

Mother put Cadie down next to Father. The toddler grabbed his shoulder for balance. "Some are worse than others," Mother agreed. "Some are actually quite clever. I'm sorry we didn't prepare you for that. I haven't heard it in a while. I hoped it would die out."

"Someone requested it," Octavia said. "Everyone seemed to know it. But we were just talking about how you and Father got together. Father says you were courted by a prince."

Mother rolled her eyes.

"Not really. He courted my father and the guild. He craved their business, not me. It wasn't a flattering experience."

"But Grandfather wanted you to marry the prince?"

Little Cadie tumbled over and put her small hand atop Father's. Father grinned and tweaked her nose. Cadie giggled and reached out to be picked up. Father obliged and started pacing the length of the raft, jiggling her as he walked.

"You mustn't think ill of your grandfather," Mother said. "He is human, after all, even if he rarely admits it. The marriage would have added to the prestige of Verre House and the Guild of Glass Singers."

"And you would have been a princess?"

"Your mother IS a princess," Father said. "She's my princess." He made silly faces at Cadie. The little girl frowned a moment, then stuck her tongue out at him.

"Gilded bars still make a prison, sweetheart," Mother said. "The prince didn't care about me as a person. We never met, before or after. The prince simply wanted better trade with Albermarle. The guild and Albermarle's leaders all supported the idea, of course."

"Oh my. What did you do?"

"I was deeply conflicted," Mother said. "I was a dutiful daughter who felt that she had always let her father down. I am a competent glass singer, but only competent. I don't have the soaring talent that your grandfather wanted; that you have. Sorry." Mother winced, but Octavia just shrugged. Maybe she was getting used to the pain. She also wanted to know the rest of her parents' story.

"For a time I thought that by marrying the prince I could make it up to my father for having merely average talent."

"But you did marry Father. Did you run away? And why haven't I heard this story before? Why didn't you tell me?"

"Yes, we eloped." Mother broke into the most brilliant smile. "But there were consequences, as there are with every choice. Perhaps we haven't told you about this because we wanted to protect you from them. That song is one. There are others. Some quite painful."

"What did Grandfather do? And Grandmother, was she against the marriage as well? I mean, you're all friends now. More or less."

"Time is a great healer. And more recently we have all worked very hard to get along. It wasn't always that way. At first, your grandfather tried to ban Paul from Albermarle. He threatened to have him beaten by the city guard. Fortunately, your father had the sense to make friends with Alma."

"Yes, so he said."

"For a time I thought I might never return to Verre House, or speak to my parents again. I wondered if I had made a terrible mistake. But life on the river ... well, I learned a few things. The Khelana River and its people taught me that nothing is ever final. There's always another bend in the river. You will always find another verse in the song; another chapter to the story. Always, the waters flow on."

"Mother, you've left a few chapters out of your story, I think. You and Grandfather made your peace. How did you manage that?"

Mother smiled. "Well, you helped with that."

"Me?"

"When you were born, I sent word to Alma. She and your grandmother hatched the most devious plot to bring you and me and your grandfather face to face one afternoon in Albermarle's market. You wailed a great wail at that first meeting. Your grandfather could not help but hear the power of your voice."

"And now that power is gone."

"No, sweetheart," Mother said. "You may sing the glass again, you may not, but you have your voice. Perhaps you just have to use it in a different way. At any rate, your cry got through to your grandfather in a way that my words never could. He loved you at first sight. He could hardly bear to let you go, from that first moment."

Octavia sighed. "Will he still love me, if I never sing again?"

"Oh, Octavia. Of course he still loves you. That's why he is so upset." Mother said. "I thought that once, that he did not care for me because I did not sing as he wished. He is a hard man, in his way. Or he was. Life has dealt him a number of blows. His heart has softened. He weeps now because he feels responsible for your loss."

"You're just saying that, to make me feel better," Octavia muttered. "You haven't seen the way he looks at me. The way Grandfather doesn't look at me, actually. His expression ...."

"He truly is a fool, if he cannot love you without your song. But he does love you, Octavia. That is why he cannot bear to look at you. He feels so incredibly guilty for your loss. He blames himself. If he had not fallen, or waited so long to make the mirror; if he had been more firm in his refusal to make it ...."

"Oh please. Even I know that regret is pointless. The question now is not what we did then, but what to do now. The past is done."

"Well, listen to my wise daughter," Mother said, her eyes bright.

Octavia's Journey   by Lynette Hill

"I will pass your words on to your grandfather in my next letter. Perhaps he will listen."

A curse on this house

  The day before the tests, Halfnote opened the visitor's gate to a giant. The man, his dust-covered traveler's cloak wrapped tightly around him, pushed past her without a word. Dried mud flaked off his worn boots as he strode up the path to Verre House.
  The giant stood wide-legged in the foyer and bellowed.
  "Boy! Git yer things. We're going home."
  Dan, apparently fore-warned, staggered out of the visitors' chambers dragging a heavy canvas bag. His face, though less swollen, still showed the black-and-blue mark of the hammer. Alma, drying her hands on her apron, hurried out of the kitchen.
  "Mr. Connor, come have some tea and cake. Master Verre would like to speak to you before..."
  "I've naught to say to 'im," the giant said. He spat on the newly cleaned floor and stalked out. "I declare a curse on this house, and all those within it." His son stumbled after him.
  "Bye, Dan," Laiertes called. "Good luck."
  "You aren't serious," Halfnote said. "After what he did?"
  "He hates farming," Laiertes said. "And his father's a hard man. He's in for a rough time."
  Good, Halfnote thought but decided not to say aloud.
  Alma hurried over with a broom to clean away the mud and spit from Dan's father. She sprinkled a hefty amount of salt onto it "to absorb the filth" she told Halfnote, then briskly swept it all out the front door.
  "A curse on this house indeed," she said indignantly. "As if he could. As if we haven't survived every other malevolence that has come our way. This house was founded by dragons, it was, and nothing that fool farmer can do will hurt us."
  Curse deflected, she had Halfnote mop the floor with lemon-

scented water. "A little extra cleansing never hurt."

The Lochsa Rapids

They reached the rapids the day after they left Vara Nasim.
"That was quick," Mischa observed. Father just shrugged.
"The river runs as it chooses."
Father decided to avoid the rapids altogether. He hired a wagon and two men to take their cargo by road on to the docks in the lower river. He also found a young family of Clan Breydon who needed to deliver a cargo upstream. To them he gave the raft in exchange for unspecified future favors. Octavia marveled at the way Father relinquished the sturdy craft on a promise and a handshake.

"What if you never see those people again?" she murmured to Mother. They walked now at a leisurely pace behind the wagon carrying their goods. The wide gravel path paralleled the river. The afternoon sun still shone from somewhere behind the trees, but nightfall wasn't far off. Octavia wondered where they would sleep.

Mother smiled. "I used to wonder the same thing. Now I know not to worry about it. If we don't receive payment from them, specifically, our needs will be met later by some cousin or other."

"What if you forget a promise to someone?" Octavia asked, still disturbed by the informality of it all. "Or what if you don't have a raft to give them or their relative the next time you meet?"

"It's only a raft. Those are traded at need between clan members. We don't have to keep track. If the contract was for something more valuable, then of course we make a record."

"How? You carry almost no paper."

"That woven band your father wears around his right bicep," Mother said. "See the colored beads? Each records a specific agreement of future payment of some kind."

They cleared the high point above the rapids and headed down the much steeper path toward the market town also called Lochsa. Here the waters of the Khelana slowed down, deepened and spread out. This made room for much larger cargo ships and ...

"Aunty Lily!" Mischa cheered. Docked at the far end of the riverside market and proudly flying the banner of Clan Breydon floated the strangest boat Octavia had ever seen. It was not a raft. It sported a keel and stern as if it meant to go to sea. A proper cabin straddled the wide upper deck. Strangest of all, however, were the wooden wheels set amidships. These looked like water wheels for a mill, with one set on each side of the boat.

"When I am older I will have such a craft," Mischa announced. "Two people can turn the paddles with their arms or legs and take it upstream twice as fast as any boat can ride the current down. It has sails too. Aunty Lily says she has taken it into the open sea. Maybe we could even sail to Samoya in it."

"Is that Father's older sister?" Octavia struggled to remember if she'd met Aunt Lily. She had a vague memory of being introduced to a slender woman of about her own height at her singer's celebration. The problem for Octavia was that she had met quite a few new people on that amazing night.

"That's right," Mother said. "Now, while your father and Mischa deal with the cargo, you and I will go up to the aviary to get our messages. Perhaps we'll get a chance to meet the Birdman himself. I think you'll find him quite interesting."

Octavia craned her neck trying to see the aviary. She couldn't quite make it out. The cliff leaned out over the river, blocking view of the building or buildings. They would have to take a lift up to reach it. The Birdman and his family maintained a network of messenger bird posts stretching from Haverley in the north to Samoya in the south. Albermarle's aviary stood on the cliff face just a few doors down from Verre House. In the morning, when the wind was right, you could hear the pigeons cooing excitedly as they were fed. And, Octavia wrinkled her nose, smell the ammonia stink of their droppings.

"Where is the Birdman from? Not Samoya, surely."

"No one is quite sure and he never quite says. I do believe his old home was far to the east, across the deserts. He came here as a young

Octavia's Journey   *by Lynette Hill*

man. I believe he arrived alone, banished from his home for some political offense. Two wives and some children joined him later, traveling separately for safety. Some say he was heir to a throne and banished by the successful claimant, though that may just be a story. Anyway, he brought the art of the messenger birds with him," Mother said. "Do not be surprised by what you see there. The Birdman's people have a different view of matrimony."

"What do you mean, 'a different view'?" Octavia considered the rumors she'd heard. Could any of those lurid tales actually be true?

"Well, how shall I put this? They do not confine themselves necessarily to one spouse. They see no shame in multiple couplings, so long as any children that result are cared for. A man may take several wives, as the Birdman has. Women may take more than one husband, or share a man between them without a formal marriage. How they work it out between themselves I confess I do not understand."

"I thought those were just silly stories. What about those among them who love only their own gender, or both?"

"No one interferes with love, but I don't believe this absolves them from the duty they feel to bring new children into the world. It is a complex culture. It does explain how they managed to create a widespread network in such a short time. Every relay post is run by a child of the Birdman or another relative. Forty years ago there were no aviaries. Now they are everywhere and we are all grateful for them."

They'd climbed steadily since leaving the riverbank. Now they stopped outside a hut at the foot of the cliff. Mother knocked on the door. A young man dressed in a blue and white uniform popped out and bowed to Mother. The man's unrestrained and naturally kinky red hair blew wildly in the afternoon breeze. He escorted them onto a nicely decorated platform, reminiscent of the lifts that carried people and cargo between Albermarle and Kerguelen Lake. It was, of course, much smaller than Albermarle's great lifts but worked on the same principle. Mother took firm hold of Caddie as they rose. Octavia leaned over the banister to take in the view. The rapids strung out along the river for several miles. The waters foamed around and through a maze of giant boulders. No wonder everyone avoided them.

Once at the aviary there was no more chance to talk. A smiling young woman met them at the door. She introduced herself as Tanya and showed them into a large and elegantly decorated waiting room. Tanya had the same long, red, kinky hair as the lift attendant but she kept hers in check with a brilliant blue scarf. A pleasant scent, something Octavia couldn't quite identify, filled the air. Tanya led them to comfortable seats beside a table of polished wood. She made a fuss over Cadie while another attendant brought hot tea and cinnamon cakes.

After hearing so many lurid tales and Mother's comments about 'different views of matrimony' Octavia felt slightly disappointed. She hadn't expected such an atmosphere of restrained elegance and, well, normality. After all those days on the raft she particularly enjoyed the plush comfort of her upholstered chair. Most of the staff did share a family resemblance but that was hardly unusual.

Mother sorted through bits of parchment with the help of a reading glass. Octavia wondered how anyone could write in the tiny, curving print used for the messages. She watched the other customers while keeping one eye on Cadie's wanderings. Octavia made a game of it, considering each individual and trying to guess where they'd come from, where they were going and their trade.

Most were townies of one sort or another: craft makers or traders. There were no Khelani, she noted. All right, no *other* Khelani. The robes and amulets of the makers made them an easy read. Most crafts centered in a particular area, so she could guess even their origins and likely destinations with confidence. There was perhaps one party of minor royalty sequestered in the far corner. Everyone in that group wore loose-fitting silk trousers and long tunics. The gold trim on their purple and blue clothing indicated high status. Could they be Ephthalids this far to the west? One, a young man with sharp grey eyes, looked up and caught her staring. Octavia looked quickly away.

Embarrassed, she busied herself by chasing Cadie. The little girl, tottering on unsteady legs, wandered over to inspect another table. She grabbed for balance and pulled down a piece of parchment.

"I'm so sorry," Octavia said automatically to the table's lone occupant. She retrieved the parchment and handed it back.

"It's all right. I like children." The female voice surprised Octavia. The woman wore a rather frayed student's robe in the blue color of the University of Vara Nasim. Her short hair was unadorned and her hands spotted with ink. She looked down at Octavia through spectacles of such poor quality that Octavia's hands positively itched to replace them.

"Oh," Octavia gasped.

"What are you doing here?" Alex the scholar demanded. She flushed a deep red.

"I might ask *you* that," Octavia snapped. "We're here to collect our messages, what do you think? What are you doing?"

"The same. Look, I'm really sorry … "

"I'm glad to hear it." Octavia stood up. She grabbed Cadie's hand and turned to leave.

"Octavia," Mother hurried up. "A message from..."

"Ah, Mother." Octavia turned back to the woman. "Here is my mother Melodia Verre Breydon, the glass princess of Albermarle. Mother, this is Alex, a scholar of the University of Vara Nasim. Alex thinks that you are a fairy tale and I'm a liar. Come to dinner with us," Octavia told Alex, "and I'll introduce you to my father, the gold-digging river rat as well."

"Octavia, stop it," Mother said. "I seriously doubt that this poor girl is responsible for that ridiculous song. Why would anyone believe it might contain a nugget of truth?"

"Madame," Alex said, writhing with embarrassment, "I can only apologize. I am genuinely sorry. I had no idea …"

"No, of course you didn't. For the vast majority of people in this world that song is nothing more than a popular bit of doggerel. My daughter is being unkind."

"What? Me?"

"Yes. Grab Cadie before she upsets the scholar's messages."

Cadie, holding onto the table leg for support, reached up for another piece of parchment. Octavia bent down to pick the toddler up. Alex leaned over to grab the parchment. Their heads banged together. Octavia fell back, overbalanced by Cadie's weight. The toddler landed heavily on Octavia's stomach, knocking out her breath. Alex bounced back the other way. Her spectacles flew up into the air. Alex held her forehead and swore. The spectacles dropped onto the edge of the hard wood table. The wooden frames cracked. The lenses shattered into a thousand pieces.

"My glasses," Alex gasped.

"Oh dear," Mother snatched Cadie up out of harm's way.

"What horrible workmanship." Octavia managed to stand up, also holding her head. "I can't believe the guild would allow it. Why on earth did you buy such cheap spectacles?"

"So I'm not a rich glass singer." Alex sounded near tears.

"No, don't try to pick up the glass," Mother told Alex. Mother's eyes lingered a moment on the scholar's frayed collar. One of the staff hurried up, a boy with the same red kinky hair and blue scarf as Tanya; Mother sent him off for a broom. "I don't suppose you have another pair," Mother said. The scholar shook her head.

"It's all right," Alex muttered. "There's nothing in my messages but bad news anyway. I'd rather not read them again."

"Don't worry. At least, don't worry about your spectacles. We'll replace them."

Alex blinked. "Look, it's been a bad day. Don't tease me."

"I wouldn't dream of it. We are, after all, glass singers. We'll make you some new spectacles that won't break."

"Mother," Octavia gasped. "You know I can't."

"No, dear." Mother sounded a bit irritated. "But I can. Please do come to dinner with us," she told Alex. "Yes, you will meet my husband, the Khelani trader Paul of Clan Breydon. You will also enjoy a decent meal, friendly companions and then I will make you some new glasses to replace these."

Alex looked as if she didn't quite know whether to laugh or cry. Octavia bit back the rude comment that popped into her head and struggled with her own mixed emotions. Truth to tell, she'd wanted to replace those awful spectacles from the moment she'd first seen them. And Octavia had forgotten that Mother was a competent singer in her own right. That realization shamed her more than anything.

Octavia's Journey   *by Lynette Hill*

Tested

The oppressive feeling built up through the night. You couldn't say that test day dawned, exactly, but it did begin. Heavy, low-hanging clouds created a dim, gray atmosphere. The clouds darkened and began to grumble. Just before breakfast, Robbie looked out the kitchen window at the impending storm.

"Will it flood, do you think?" he asked.

"There's been no warning," Alma said. "The glasses normally cry out if there's to be flood or fire. This rain will be welcome, after the dry summer."

The three judges dashed from their carriage just before the first heavy drops fell. They had barely settled in Master Verre's office when the deluge struck. Master Verre hurried to greet them.

"Welcome. We appreciate your help in this delicate matter."

"And what matter is that?" asked the youngest looking judge.

"Ah, Master Rimsky. We were expecting Madame Berry."

"Yes, she asked me to step in at the last minute. She was called away by a family emergency, I believe. Of course I'm always happy to help out. I understand that we are to test two of your staff today?"

Halfnote, standing to one side after delivering a tray of cakes, narrowed her eyes. Something about Master Rimsky's accent sounded familiar. In fact, she thought, it sounded very much like Dan's. Master Rimsky's voice was better trained, of course, and more cultured. Still... And in the shape of his face Master Rimsky bore a close resemblance to Dan's father. Hadn't Galliard said something about Dan claiming to have distant relatives who also sang the glass?

Oh no ...

"Halfnote," Master Verre said, "Please tell Robert to meet us in the smaller creation room."

Alma gave Robbie a hug and last bit of fussing before allowing him to go meet the judges. Robbie headed out of the kitchen, Halfnote thought, like a boy on the way to his own execution.

All pretense at work stopped. The other apprentices gathered around the kitchen table, ignoring their cups of tea as they *listened*.

Octavia's Journey   *by Lynette Hill*

"If only the thunder would go away," Halfnote said. The storm must have been right overhead. Lightening flickered insistently through the windows. Non-stop thunder shook the ground.

"They're underground," Laiertes pointed out. "Robbie and the judges. I almost never notice storms in the making rooms."

"When have we had a storm this bad?" Marissa asked. "It rains all the time here, sure, but this is as noisy a storm as any I've heard."

"The glasses haven't warned of anything," Laiertes said.

"The vibrations from the making room do feel really good," Galliard observed. "I think he's going to be all right."

The thunder eased off just as the singing ended. A long quiet spell followed, punctured only by the sound of steady rain. It was nearly lunch time, but neither Alma nor anyone else moved from the table. Finally, the door to the smaller creation room opened. Robbie came into the kitchen, silent tears rolling down his cheeks.

Raised voices emanated from the making room. "This isn't a singer's test," the older judge's voice rang out.

"No. It's an entry test and after two years of training and practice the boy can't even pass that." That was Master Rimsky talking, Halfnote realized. Again she heard the similarity between his accent and Dan's. "I simply can't believe that you of all people, Master Verre, could support such an unqualified candidate."

"Master Rimsky, you are unkind," the female judge, Madame Donatello, weighed in. Halfnote's heart rose in hope. "The boy is unsuitable, yes, but considering his history …"

"We cannot let sentiment cloud our judgment in these matters," Master Rimsky continued. "We have a duty to the guild…"

Someone closed the making room door, cutting off the voices. Robbie, weeping audibly now, buried his face in Alma's ample bosom. Halfnote sat down beside him, too disappointed to think. It felt so unjust. He'd worked so hard.

"I thought Robbie did well enough," Marissa said. Laiertes and Galliard just nodded.

Could that judge really be Dan's relative? Halfnote wondered. Did Master Rimsky fail Robbie on purpose? If Grandpa couldn't prevent that, what could she do about it?

Alma put out cheese and bread for lunch. Hardly anyone ate anything. Even the arrival of old friends like Ted and Martin barely lightened the mood. Lorraine and Phyllis hurried immediately up to Sylvia's room. The senior singer hadn't been seen since breakfast.

While entry to a singer's test was limited to those who had already passed it, anyone with an interest could attend a junior master or master's test. More confident and flamboyant candidates had been known to face their judges in the market square in the hopes of jump-starting their reputations.

"I can't believe she changed her test piece at the last minute," Ted told Frank through mouthfuls of the venison pastry Alma set before him. "Her eagle fountain is amazing. She made feathers with individual barbs. That's more impressive than repairing some old doll."

"That 'old doll' is a work of the original singers," Frank said. "It's part of a structure built into all of the outer walls of this building. Let me show you. I promise you've never seen anything like it. The whole thing is amazing." The boys all clattered down the steps to the lower basement.

"It's time," Master Verre announced. Marissa dashed up the stairs to call Sylvia. Everyone, including many local glass singers and a number of top clients gathered in the main creation room. As Sylvia had no living relatives, Lorraine and Martin stood in as her family.

With Frank acting as dragon, Sylvia demonstrated the various techniques needed to create her test piece. "Working with a mere singer as dragon increases the perception of her mastery. And it will count in Frank's favor when he tests," Marissa whispered to Laiertes.

Sylvia's tones and technique were flawless, though clearly powered by an over-abundance in nervous energy. Halfnote knew, and she could see this knowledge mirrored in the expressions of the other witnesses, that Sylvia had done very well indeed.

"Your techniques are most impressive," Master Rimsky said before anyone else could speak. "And it is a very pretty doll. As it happens, musical instruments are my specialty. The layering of colors, the clear structural virtues, the inner tube work, all of these are very nice for a mere copy. I have but one question. Does it work?"

"I beg your pardon," Sylvia asked in faint tones.

"This piece is part of a much larger installation," Master Verre explained. "Sylvia created it to repair damage to the apprentice's challenge, which is worked into the walls of this building."

"Then how do we know whether this is a successful piece?" Master Rimsky asked, "while it stands alone and silent? Can you return the doll to its proper place?"

"Of course I can," Sylvia said. "That's easily done."

After a quick discussion between Sylvia, the judges and Master Verre, it was agreed that they and a few witnesses would adjourn to the lowest basement to watch Sylvia install the piece. The space was too small to allow the entire audience. Everyone else would wait in the reception hall, feasting on the extensive buffet provided by Alma.

"She can attach it," Halfnote breathed, "but only Robbie can make it work."

"Hsssht," Galliard replied. "Hopefully that will be enough."

"Galliard and Marissa, help Frank set up a brazier in the basement next to the last line of the apprentice challenge," Sylvia commanded. "Halfnote, Laiertes, we'll need proper lighting. Get some of the pillar candles, like the ones we used in the sick rooms."

Everyone rushed to their assigned tasks. When Halfnote and Laiertes took their candles to the lower basement, they found that no one had swept up the remains of the smashed tile.

"I'll get a broom," Halfnote said. For speed and to avoid the others already coming down the stairs, she jumped into the dumbwaiter. She pulled herself swiftly up to the kitchen. There a red-eyed Robbie and Alma sat together, consoling each other.

"What's happening?" Alma asked.

"I need a broom," Halfnote said. "The judges say Sylvia must install the figurine, to see if it actually works. No one's swept up in the lower basement." She snatched up the closest broom and dust pan and jumped back into the dumbwaiter.

"But ..." Robbie looked up.

"I know, I know," Halfnote said. She could hear the judges

talking as they headed for the basement. "Sorry, I've got to go." She dropped as swiftly as she dared. She swept up the crushed tile even as the judges cautiously made their way down the slippery steps. Halfnote hopped back into the dumbwaiter with her broom and full dustpan. Even with the sliding door shut she could see through a gap.

Frank lit the brazier. He placed a lamp with a reflective backing that focused the light into the dark gap left by the broken piece.

Sylvia showed the judges the lines of figurines and explained how the challenge worked. With great care and Frank's able assistance as dragon, she sang up the necessary spirals of tubing. She cooled the tubing slightly with her tones. The new piping needed to remain warm and flexible enough to attach to the tubes already in place. With great care she installed the figurine back into its rightful niche.

The judges crowded around to inspect.

"Magnificent," the oldest judge, Master Gibb, said in his raspy voice. "I know of no one who could do a better job."

"Pretty yes," Madame Donatello acknowledged. She glanced at Master Rimsky, "But we still don't know if it works."

"Indeed. Will you show us, please?" Master Rimsky asked.

Sylvia's dark eyes widened in panic.

"I ..."

"The structure is keyed to one person," Master Verre said. "As Sylvia has repaired the piece properly only that person can make it work." "The malicious destruction of this figurine prevented him from completing the challenge."

"So, Singer Sylvia, you admit you cannot make your piece work," Master Rimsky smirked. "That's hardly a sign of mastery. Any competent singer can make a doll, even one with a variety of colors. But a master? Her piece must do the task it was created for. Really, Verre, I had no idea that standards here had fallen quite so low. I shall have no choice but to make a report of these failings to the council."

"Your conclusions are premature," Master Verre said. "The piece has yet to be tested."

"Our candidate admits she cannot make it work."

"Indeed. The structure is keyed to one person. If she recreated the piece correctly, then only this person can activate it."

"What, you mean that pathetic tongue-tied little boy you forced us to listen to earlier?"

"I thought he sang well enough," old Master Gibb rasped, "for an apprentice of two years' experience."

"Then bring him down," Master Rimsky jeered. "Let him complete this challenge for us."

"Indeed," Master Verre murmured. "He is already here."

Movement on the stairs drew everyone's attention. Without a word to anyone, Robbie walked over to the last line of tiles.

"A moment, Robert," Master Verre said. He turned to the three judges. "Before he sings, I need your word on this. If Robert Dinaldo completes the challenge, it means he can sing at the required level. It also means that Sylvia has properly repaired this ancient work. Both have passed. Robert Dinaldo is once again an apprentice in the Guild of Glass Singers. And Sylvia Klein a junior master."

"And when he fails?" Master Rimsky didn't try to hide his delight. "Then both fail? Miss Klein, do you accept this? Is this fair? Simply make your piece sing and I will declare you a junior master on the spot. Surely my companion judges will agree to this."

"Of course," Madame Donatello murmured. Master Gibb frowned but said nothing.

Sylvia paled and closed her eyes.

"Miss Klein," Master Rimsky all but whispered. "Can you make your piece sing?"

"No," she said. "I cannot. Only Robbie can do that."

"Then let the boy perform for us one more time," old Master Gibb declared. "Both candidates pass or fail on the results. Yes, Master Verre, you have my word on it."

"This is highly irregular." Madame Donatello looked closely at Sylvia's unhappy expression. "Still, if Miss Klein agrees to it ..." Sylvia nodded. "Well, then, yes, I give you my word as well, Master Verre. If the boy completes this ... challenge, both pass. And I will declare to the guild that Sylvia Klein has demonstrated full mastery. If she can truly repair a work of the ancients, then she is no junior. She is a master of her trade."

"Yes. It shall be as Madame Donatello says. I will stand witness to this as well," Master Gibb rasped.

"I can't believe my ears," Master Rimsky laughed. "The boy has already left us half-deaf with his strangled warbling."

"Enough, Master Rimsky," Madame Donatello snapped. "Do you agree to this test or not?"

"Oh, yes. Boy, please, carry on. Show us what you can do."

"And if he makes Sylvia's piece sing, you agree that both pass," Master Verre insisted. "We have your solemn word on it in front of all these witnesses?"

"Oh yes." Master Rimsky gestured lazily. "My word on it. I'll stand with my fellow judges and declare Miss Klein a full master."

"Very well. Robert? Are you ready?" Master Verre asked.

Robbie nodded and stepped up to the broken line of tiles. Master Rimsky started to speak but Madame Donatello silenced him.

"Give the boy his chance."

A long silence followed. Halfnote could see Robbie's chest move as he used the breathing exercises Master Verre had taught him. When he opened his mouth to sing, Rimsky gave a loud sneeze.

Robbie's undisturbed tenor filled the room. He began with the simple scales of the very first line. He sang from memory, Halfnote realized. The first lines were behind him, lost in the shadows. Note by note, with rising confidence, he sang each line of the challenge.

Up until then, Halfnote always thought that the most exciting moment of her life was when she watched Octavia pass her singer's test. Or perhaps it was in the tunnels with Papa and Robbie; when she realized she could use the counter clockwise swirl to protect Octavia from the *mortolo*. But then she watched Robbie complete the apprentice challenge. He was not a master, nor even particularly gifted, but he hit every note spot on with absolute assurance.

His voice soared and reverberated off the walls of the natural chamber as he reached the very last note. He held it for a full minute before stopping. The echoes of his song finally faded away.

Nothing happened. For the space of 12 heartbeats everyone

stood in silence. Rimsky's smirk widened in triumph and he opened his mouth to speak.

A sudden hissing filled the walls. It sounded, Halfnote thought in alarm, as if they were suddenly surrounded by an army of snakes. Or as if a great wind swirled around them. Or as if Verre House itself were taking an enormous breath.

The last line of tiles flipped over to reveal their figurines. In pride of place, at the end, stood Sylvia's renewed work. Every piece of finished glass in Verre House burst into song. The glasses performed the now-forgotten First Song learned by humans from the dragons. To the wonderment of everyone in Verre House, the glass performed in triumphant chorus *The Dragon's Lullaby*.

Peacock tile in the east

Mischa's eyes widened in shock when he saw the crippled scholar walking up with Octavia and Mother.

"Lily," Mother called out as they boarded her boat. "We've brought a guest for dinner."

"Wonderful." Aunt Lily came out to greet them. "Cookie prides himself on always preparing too much. I hope you're hungry."

Aunt Lily was the slender woman Octavia remembered. Unusually for a Khelani woman she wore her waist-length black hair straight and unbound. She greeted Octavia with delight, but embarrassingly believed that Alex was Octavia's friend.

"What's that girl doing here?" Mischa hissed when they had a moment alone. She rolled her eyes.

"Her spectacles broke. Mother's going to make new ones."

"I can't believe it," Mischa said. "I didn't realize she was a con artist. Your mother's usually pretty good at spotting a fraud. What's her name again?"

"Alex. She's here for dinner. Mother insists that we treat her kindly. She says the stupid song is not Alex's fault."

And, Octavia realized, in all the excitement they had forgotten about the message. She made a mental note to ask her mother later that evening. Over a dinner as plentiful and delicious as Aunt Lily promised, Alex told them a bit about her life.

"My home country, Tan Sikar, lies just on the edge of the great desert. My family farms spices like eelbezar and jinjelan. Those are about the only plants that can grow there. With my bad leg I wasn't much use on a farm, but I do have a brain. My father realized that I was good at sorting things. I worked with him in the evenings, preparing the spices for sale.

"Our priest did his best to teach the local children how to read and write. Many people considered this a waste of time. I wasn't much use anyway, so I spent more time than most in his classes.

"My people are trapped," Alex said. "If my father could sell his harvest directly at almost any market on the river just once, he'd be set for life. But to reach any of these markets he first has to get past the desert bandits, then find the hard coin to pay the road toll. Then he would have to buy a seller's license from the market guilds. And pay rent on a space. All of this costs more than what merchants will pay in Tan Sikar for a year's harvest. The traders may bribe the bandits but they pay no toll or license fee. They grow fat on the harvests of Tan Sikar while my people struggle just on the edge of starvation."

Mischa rolled his eyes. "Told you," he whispered. "Con artist. She'll be asking for money or offering an impossible deal next."

"How did you end up at the university?" Mother asked.

"Pere Budian, our *dukun*, the priest, he convinced my father that I deserved a proper education. He arranged a scholarship from Vara Nasim's temple. I think Pere Budian hopes I will replace him as priest. But I am more concerned about helping my people find a better life in the here and now than with what comes after we die.

"The first year I studied history and economics and the philosophy of the seven shadows of Mon Terre. I received excellent grades and the praise of my professors, but nothing they taught showed me how to change the fate of my people.

"This year I'm studying mathematics, astrology and business

practices. I spend all of my free time in the marketplace, watching the traders. I want to understand how things are valued. I want to find a product that isn't controlled by a guild; something my people can sell for hard currency to improve their lives. Then they can pay to import more food; perhaps even spare some coin for teachers and healers and so ease their burdens."

"That's a most ambitious goal," Father said. "Tan Sikar is a month's journey across the desert from Ansia. And another month from the largest markets in Tulum. The real block is in getting your product to the most profitable market."

"That is a problem," Alex said, "but the real block is the costs imposed on my people by the merchants. They set the bandits and the toll barons on anyone who tries to sell their own harvest. And the guilds are in it with the traders. How do the Khelani do it?"

"We transport the goods," Aunt Lily said. "We don't sell anything directly."

"But Khelani are found in every market, selling everything."

"May I be excused?" Mischa asked. "I told Harper I would help him work on the paddle mechanisms tonight."

"Oh, me too," Octavia said. "I'd like to see how it works."

They hurried off out of the dining room.

"That was just an excuse to get out of there." Mischa led the way towards the stern.

"Yes, exactly."

They found two of Aunt Lily's crewmen, Harper and Bill, relaxing next to one of the boat's paddle mechanisms. They played some sort of betting game with clay tiles by the light of a glass oil lamp. Octavia blinked and kept her focus away from the lamp.

"Sorry, Mischa," Harper said. "It's too dark to work on the gears at night. Can't see what we're doing, even with the lamp."

"What's the game?" Octavia asked. "I've never seen tiles like that before."

"Tong-mak," Bill said. "It' quite relaxing."

"Bill thinks you can use it to tell the future." Harper added with a teasing grin.

"Me da says that," Bill protested. "I know it' jost a game."

"Unless you get the peacock tile in the east." Harper winked at Octavia. "Mmmm, unlucky that. On a moon dark night, anyway. Good thing our moon's full this evening."

"Ah coorse it' unlooky," Bill protested. "Upset the whool bahlance, that dooes."

"Can you teach us how to play?" Octavia asked.

"Ah coorse. Set yoorself doon here. We'll give ya a go."

They were well into the intricacies of chows and pungs when Harper suddenly punched Bill's shoulder and jumped up. Bill stood as well, rubbing his shoulder.

"Good evening, Madame Breydon." Harper bowed.

"Hello, Harper," Mother said. "Could you get the portable fire stand out of storage for me, and some coal? I'll need it on the forward deck. Octavia, we need sand. I'll give you the money to go buy some. Mischa, you know the market. Will you take Octavia around the stalls? As quickly as possible, please. I don't want to be at this all night."

Octavia hurried after Mischa down the path toward the markets. Light from large oil lamps hanging off poles the size of tree trunks illuminated their path. Octavia kept her eyes on the path. Despite her experience at the festival, she still felt as if she had gained a measure of control over her problem. The monster roared out at her from any piece of sung glass, but she knew it had its limits. She could bear it, at least for a while.

"Octavia," Mischa said. "Are you angry with your mother for singing new spectacles for that scholar girl?"

"What? No. Truthfully, I wanted to make new glasses for her from the first time I saw the old ones. I still can't believe the guild in this area allows such poor quality."

"Why are you so quiet? You haven't said anything since your mother told us to buy sand."

"It's just, I think ... I think this is the first time I've ever had the chance to see my mother sing the glass. Does she sing often?"

"From time to time. She makes gifts for people, needed items, stuff like that. She enjoys it. She says she likes to stay in practice."

"I never knew. I mean, she came to my test and wore the dragon's head but I didn't think she still sang. I thought she gave it all up when she married Father."

"Not at all. It's just... well, your grandfather ..."

"What?"

"Nothing. I'm sorry. I shouldn't say anything."

"Go on. I'm tired of feeling ignorant about my family."

"It's just I never see him smile ..."

"What? He smiles all the time."

"Only when you and Halfnote are around. The rest of the time, when it's just us, I mean, just your parents or other people, he never smiles. He just looks grim."

"So what does that have to do with Mother singing?"

"I just get the impression that she doesn't enjoy singing or much else when he's around. It's like she's always waiting for him to correct her. On the river your mother is almost always happy and relaxed. In town she's all right. On the way to Verre House she is usually tense."

"But we're there," Octavia protested. "She's always glad to see me and Halfnote. Grandfather is strict, yes, but he just wants everyone to do their best."

Mischa shrugged. "Here we are." He looked relieved at the chance to change the subject. "What kind of sand do you need?"

On the way back Mischa asked another difficult question.

"Will it bother you when your mother sings the glass?"

"Yes," Octavia said with a sigh. "I'll have to leave. That's so disappointing. Open air singing is a skill all its own. You have to curve the sound waves yourself. In a making chamber the walls do it for you. Mother's a better singer than she admits."

Harper and Bill had the portable fire stand set up on the forward deck when Octavia and Mischa returned. A banked fire glowed red under the making dish. They found everyone waiting for them on the deck. Octavia handed Mother the sack of sand.

"Is this what you wanted?"

Mother ran a few grains through her fingers.

"Perfect. But I knew it would be."

"Can I see?" Alex asked. She looked at the grains with a mystified expression. "Where does this sand come from?"

"I didn't think to ask," Octavia said. "It's very fine, though, and white, so it's from a coral beach. Probably an island on the western edge of Samoya or in that area, don't you think?"

Mother nodded.

"Oh." Alex looked disappointed.

"But we use different sands for different products," Mother told Alex. "Some things require heavy sands, or crushed quartz or even a mixture of sands. The sand in your area will have its own weight, its own unique origins. It's definitely worth investigation."

"Now." Mother looked at Octavia. "I'm ready to begin."

"I'll take a walk," Octavia said hurriedly. "I wish I could stay and watch. I've never seen you sing the glass before, Mother."

"Never?" Mother looked startled by this news.

"Anyway, I'm off."

"Mischa, go with her," Mother said.

"Why is she leaving?" Alex asked.

Mischa ran to catch up as Octavia hurried down the gangplank back onto the shore.

"Mischa, I need to be alone right now. I need to think."

Octavia all but ran up the path in her hurry to get away from Aunt Lilly's boat. She followed the walkway back up to the cliffs, near the lift to the aviary. She was too lost in her own thoughts to realize that Mischa followed at a cautious distance.

She found a quiet spot overlooking the river. From here, she could see the full display of the Lochsa Rapids illuminated by the full moon and lights from the aviary above.

I didn't know my mother still sang the glass. Now I can't even listen to her when she does.

That hurt more than the thought of never singing again.

Octavia noticed an enormous whirlpool about a third of the way into the rapids. If she turned her head just so she could position the reflection of the full moon so that it filled the whirlpool.

"And why would I want to do that?" she asked herself.

The whirlpool's foaming turmoil, turned silver by the glittering moonlight, took various strange forms. At one point it almost seemed to form a face and stare back at her. She looked away.

The wind picked up. It blew from the north, making it that much more difficult for her mother's voice to reach her. She felt cold. The full moon hung just above the eastern treetops. It still had a way to go in its nightly journey. The silver orb's reflection filled the disturbed waters below. The whirlpool took the form of a face again. Octavia found herself staring into its eyes. She tried to look away and could not.

Then, as if she could do nothing else, she dove into the river.

Torn between Aunty Melody's command to accompany Octavia and his cousin's request for privacy, Mischa decided to let her go on alone. When she seemed no longer aware of him, he followed quietly behind. She didn't go far. She climbed the cliff to a quiet spot overlooking the rapids and stopped. She leaned against a banister and stood there for some time.

Mischa sat on a convenient rock in a shadowed corner of the path to wait. Fortunately, he'd thought to pull on a thick shirt before leaving the boat. Octavia had no such protection against the cool night breeze, but she didn't seem to notice.

Mischa considered the stars above. He understood wanting to think things through. Octavia's life at Verre House had always puzzled him. He didn't comprehend how Uncle Paul and Aunty Melody could stand to divide up their family. On the other hand, everyone seemed happy with the arrangement. Well, everyone except Uncle Paul.

The rising moon filled the sky. A night bird called. Octavia still stood, looking out across the river. Mischa's eyes closed. He dropped into a light doze. He dreamed of his family in the days before the flood. They were docked at Tondo, his brothers jumping on and off the raft. His mother cheerfully scolded them when they splashed cold water into the sleeping area. She looked at Mischa, her expression serious.

"Something's wrong."

Mischa woke with a start. He glanced up at the moon but it had barely moved. The breeze blew coldly against his cheek. He stood and stretched. It was such a quiet evening. No one else had come this way. He glanced at the overlook and blinked. Octavia wasn't there.

"Octavia?" He hurried to the place where she'd been standing. She really wasn't there. He stared down at the river.

No. Of course not.

Mischa ran up the path, calling her name.

In the presence of the Queen

Light flickered against her eyelids. Octavia took a deep breath, as if she'd just come up from under water. She reached out with one hand to orient herself. She found rough stone wall. It felt like natural rock, curving and uncut, similar to the walls in one of Verre House's lowest basements. Torches set into the wall snapped and flickered, creating restless shadows in the corners. Octavia had the sense of being underground, but fresh air must be coming from somewhere. As her eyes adjusted to the dim light she made out a number of hooded figures standing around the edge of the room. She heard a low chanting and assumed they were the source.

"Where am I?" Octavia asked, her voice unsteady. "What is this place? I don't understand."

A tiny, grey-haired woman in glittering robes stepped into the center of the room. A taller woman stood behind her. Their clothing identified them as Samoyans; as rich and powerful Samoyans.

"Please calm yourself, my dear," the older woman said, her low voice cultured and well-modulated. "You are quite safe. You were brought here on my orders."

"You ... brought me here? But I fell into the river ..."

"You were called to me by the craft of my singers." The tiny woman indicated the hooded figures with the flick of a bejeweled finger. "We used the powers of full moon and whirlpool to create the portal that brought you here. It was a difficult rite," she added with a satisfied

Octavia's Journey   *by Lynette Hill*

expression.

    The last thing Octavia remembered was the shock of cold water when she jumped into the river. She clutched at her skirts. Her clothing and all of the rest of her felt completely dry.

    "Who are you? Why have you brought me here?"

    "My dear, I am Bhima Suresha Niliya Anula of Samoya," the tiny woman said, "grandmother to King Negarawan. I am also great-grandmother to the Intan Negarawan, whom I believe you met during his recent visit to your fair city. I brought you here because, alas, the Kingdom of Samoya desperately needs your help again."

    "How can I be in Samoya? It takes three months to sail to Samoya from Tulum and I am at the Lochsa Rapids, three weeks north of Tulum."

    "My dear, I will endeavor to explain. You have been brought here for my purposes, by the art of my magi and the power of my living mirror. There is so much more to the power of glass and mirrors than you have been told. Of course you doubt me, girl, how could you not? But you won't for long. You will see for yourself that I speak truly. Clara, don't dawdle. Bring refreshments for our guest."

    The taller, more plainly dressed woman gestured. A maid, a straight-backed middle-aged woman, appeared with a large silver tray. She placed it on the low oak table in front of Octavia. The tray held a variety of honey cakes and dried fruits. Another servant arrived with a silver tea service. She hurried to pour out hot drinks for both the Queen and Octavia.

    "Please." Queen Anula picked up her own porcelain cup. "Sit. Eat. Drink. You have much yet to do this evening."

    Octavia barely knew how to respond. She took the offered seat and drink. Sipping the hot liquid, she discovered it was a cinnamon-based tea, a Samoyan delicacy rarely available in Albermarle.

    "Now, listen closely, Queen Anula said. "No, no, finish your cake and tea. You need your strength. You must deliver a message for me. The journey will not take long, but it requires nerve and courage. Of course it is impertinent of me to ask for your assistance, again, after you saved us from the plague. Even so, your ability is unique. Only you can help me.

"In exchange, all of your amazing talent will be restored."

Octavia took a calming breath. It didn't help. The heavy scents, the flickering torchlight, her sudden jump from Khelana riverside to Queen's quarters (in Samoya? Really?), left her dizzy and uncertain.

Perhaps I'm dreaming. All my talents restored? How?

She glanced at the poker-faced woman who stood behind the Queen's right shoulder. Something about the set of Clara's jaw ... Octavia blinked and smiled uncertainly.

"I don't understand. What do you need me to do?"

"Time is short," the Queen said. "Too short I fear for a full explanation. We have only until the moon sets to complete our task. The matter is this: many years ago, a confused young woman made a terrible mistake. I need you to take her a message. By passing through the mirror on the wall there, you will be able to go back in time to speak to her."

"You want me to enter the mirror ..." *And go back in time?*

"Yes. It is the only way. You will help yourself while also righting a great wrong. Previously you fell into a mirror and came out reversed. That is why everything goes wrong when you try to sing the glass. To correct the problem you must enter a mirror again. When you come out of it you will be reversed back into your old self."

"I ... reversed?"

"If you look at the mirror, what do you see?" Octavia glanced at the place where the Queen pointed and then cringed back. There was the source of the energies that made her feel so off-balance. Her pearl pendant warmed the cleft of her neck. The roiling energies retreated a bit and her nausea eased a little.

"You have a healing mirror, a broken healing mirror here?"

"Not a healing mirror, no. There would have been no need for my great-grandson to visit your fair city if this were a healing mirror. This one is meant for scrying, for seeing things at a distance. And it is not broken, merely cooperative."

"I've never heard of such a thing. It sounds like a telescope."

"Child, that you of all people should remain so ignorant ..." Queen Anula looked truly outraged, "that is a tragedy. Once, the *Peili potencia* were common. Anyone of note had one. The *potencia* were used for communication, for healing, yes, and even for divination. Some mirrors became storehouses of knowledge. Fearful, narrow-minded people suppressed all knowledge of these mirrors. Or tried to, anyway. It has taken me a lifetime to discover the little that I know."

"If the healing mirror was an example of a *potencia,* well, I can only say that their fears seem justified," Octavia said.

"Pah! Their timidity causes the very disasters they seek to avoid. If they retained the knowledge of how to control the living glass ... but never mind. It is an old argument. My mirror was meant for seeing at a distance. When my great-grandson traveled to Albermarle and my heart feared for his safety, I used this glass to know that he was well."

Octavia's eyebrows rose.

"To see that your child is safe; do you believe this is evil?"

"No, of course not, your Majesty."

"But I digress. My mirror is mature. It is well trained."

"Trained?"

"Yes. My glass is well fed. Perhaps in time I will show you how to feed a mirror of power. But, to the point. When you look into a mirror the image you see there is reversed.

"When you fell into the mirror the first time, and returned, you came out as a reflection of yourself. That is why you cannot sing the glass anymore. You have not lost your voice or your talent. But those best attributes of yourself have been inverted to become your worst."

"My best gifts are now my worst ..."

But what of the monster?

"Child, you are not stupid! When you look into a mirror, right is left and left is right."

"But ... but ... up and down are still the same."

"An interesting observation. Yes ... still. You fell into an unformed mirror and absorbed the core of its soul. You are inverted."

"It sounds as if you are saying that what I need to do now is sing backwards."

The Queen laughed, a false tinny sound. Octavia cringed.

"Can you sing backwards? That would make an interesting

experiment. But I believe my solution is more practical."

"So, if I pass through the mirror again I will be restored?"

"Yes. All of your talent will be returned to you."

A small noise, a drawn-in breath. Clara's stone visage cracked, then recovered. Octavia glanced at the maid, then back at the Queen. She fought down a rising sense of nausea.

Go back inside the mirror? Was the Queen mad? This wasn't a dream. It was a nightmare.

"But if I enter this mirror, won't that taint it? Won't your mirror then become *mortolo?*"

"No child. This mirror is solid, mature, finished. Tame, if you will. It is quite ancient. It is old even by the lifespans of a living mirror. It has quite a strong will of its own and cannot be tainted."

"A living mirror. How can a mirror live?"

"Asks the granddaughter of Fortis Verre," Queen Anula sneered. "These are the things you should have learned while still supping your mother's milk. When you return home, ask your grandfather why he insists that you remain ignorant of the knowledge that should be your birth right. Ask him how the glasses of Verre House are able to scream their warnings in times of trouble."

Octavia pretended to take a sip of tea, buying time to think.

"If I enter the mirror," she asked, "how far into it must I go? You said you need me to deliver a message? To whom? How would I find them? And how would I find my way out again?"

"My singers are well trained and highly experienced. Their song will carry you to your destination and back again. Of course I understand if you are frightened at the thought of re-entering a mirror. Just remember that this journey will bring you out whole in the end. It is what you must do, if you wish to sing the glass again."

Octavia swallowed. Hope fought with the rising howl of her inner turmoil. Did the monster within understand and fear its demise? If the Queen spoke the truth ... Octavia glanced at Clara again. The woman stood immobile behind her mistress, shoulders straight, spine erect, hands clasped, eyes boring a hole in the opposite wall. She appeared the very picture of the perfect servant.

Octavia's Journey   *by Lynette Hill*

Why do I get the feeling that she wants to tell me something?
"It would be a great challenge, to enter another mirror. But what is the journey you speak of? What is the message?"

"Thank you my dear. I knew you would do it."

"Wait, I haven't agreed," Octavia said, but the Queen didn't appear to notice.

"You will enter the mirror." Queen Anula certainly knew how to use command tones, Octavia thought. "You will walk directly down the corridor that you find there. It is possible that you will see or hear things that don't really exist. These will merely be reflections of your thoughts and fears. Ignore them. You will see round openings in the walls. Ignore these as well until you reach the end of the corridor. There you will find the door to a nursery.

"It is the royal nursery of Samoya, a few generations back. A wet nurse cares for two infant boys. The message is for her. If there is anyone else in the room wait until they leave before entering.

"You will tell her," the Queen continued, "and make certain that she agrees before you leave: she must not switch the babies."

"I will tell her not to switch the babies," Octavia repeated obediently, "but, your Majesty, why would she switch them and why would she listen to me, a stranger?"

Queen Anula smiled. "You will be a stranger who, from her point of view, has stepped out of a mirror to give her an urgent message from the great beyond."

"How will I know if I am speaking to the right person?"

"It is in the nature of the mirror and the songs of my singers to take you to the right time and place and person. The mirror cannot do otherwise. The matter is complex. Now …"

"But how do I convince the nurse, when I am uncertain whether this is the right thing to do?"

The Queen stopped and visibly reined in her impatience. "The wet nurse Davina looks after a king's son. The other child is her own. This happened many, many years ago. All involved are my own relatives. Davina's son was quite ill but as a mere maid she could not afford a physician. So, desperate to save her son's life, Davina switched the

Octavia's Journey   *by Lynette Hill*

babies. She dressed her son in the prince's clothing and the prince in her own son's cotton swaddling.

"Even with the best care the royal physicians could provide, the impostor lived only two more years. When the king died a few months after his false son, Samoya was left without a clear heir. The country fell into a devastating civil war. The dreadful consequences of that war linger to this day. In the meantime, the true prince lived to manhood, even fighting as a common soldier in the war.

"Surely you understand, my girl. If the babies had not been switched, if the healthy prince had remained in his rightful place, a horrible war could have been averted. So many terrible wrongs could have been avoided; so many lives saved. That is why you must convince Davina that she must not switch the children. There are so many more lives at stake than just that of her child.

"It will be as if you stopped the plague before it began."

"By all the dragons," Octavia gasped. "The plague. If we can use your mirror to visit the past, then we can go back and stop the plague as well. Thousands would be saved. Queen Anula ..."

"No, by all the gods, no." Was it Octavia's imagination or had the Queen actually turned green with horror? "Alas, no. Stopping the plague is the one thing you cannot do."

"I don't understand."

"No, of course you don't. And there is so little time to explain." The Queen looked genuinely distressed. Much of what she said to Octavia earlier sounded false, but now her tones rang true.

"If you, Octavia, stop the plague by passing through the living mirror, this would create a never-ending loop in time. Think of it as an action that would create the greatest *mortolo* that ever lived.

"The plague is the event that brought you to me. If there is no plague, you will never attempt to make the healing mirror and fall into the *mortolo*. Thus, I would have no reason to bring you here. Then you would not stop the plague before it began. And so it would occur. You would come to me and stop it and yet again it would not happen. Do you understand, child?"

"I ... I think so ..."

"The more people caught up in the loop the stronger it becomes. Consider all who are affected by the plague: all of Samoya, all the citizens of Albermarle and every land in-between. Consider the strength of a loop encompassing so many lives. We would create a *mortolo* likely strong enough to destroy the whole world."

Octavia felt cold all over. "But ... won't stopping the nurse from switching the babies, won't that create the same kind of loop?"

"No, not if *you* are the agent of change. You had nothing to do with the events surrounding the nurse maid. You speak to the nurse, you leave, events change or not but you carry on forward to your future. You still move through time in a straight line, so all is well. It is the looping back that must be avoided. Oh, how I look forward to sharing my knowledge with you, when this is done."

Octavia nodded. "Indeed, Your Majesty, I am anxious to learn all that you can teach me"

The Queen's smile revealed a mixture of triumph and genuine relief. Octavia glanced at Clara. She remained the very image of the obedient servant; inscrutable. And yet...

"Time is running out." The Queen's command tones called Octavia back to attention. "I cannot answer every question. The energies of tide and moon will not again be right for this ceremony until late next year. There is no time to lose. We have only until the moon sets. We have already dawdled too long."

She gestured. The robed figures, their faces hidden by large hoods, suddenly advanced. Their low chanting filled the room. Strong arms caught Octavia from behind. They carried her forward toward the ornately framed mirror that filled one wall.

As the chanting rose in volume so did Octavia's terror. A gray whirling mass filled all of her senses. It tore at her clothes and hair like a whirlwind, all too like the *Hygeia mortolo*.

"No! Wait! I'm not ready."

Queen Anula grabbed Octavia's arm. Her nails dug into Octavia's flesh until they drew blood.

"Singer Octavia. We can wait no longer. You must deliver the message and return before the moon sets. If you remain inside the mirror after that, you will be trapped within forever."

Octavia took a breath and wrenched free of the strong hands that held her. She took another breath. Before they could grab her again she stepped into the mirror of her own free will.

Inside the looking glass

Warm glass whirled around her in a slow-motion splash as she moved through the surface. Once inside, she found herself in a cool, still place, standing on an opaque path. The mirror's silver surface solidified behind her. Octavia released her breath.

The monster howled and exploded within her.

No! Oh no!

She clutched her head, overwhelmed. The curved, opaque walls of the mirror reflected the monster's raging chaos. It exploded out of its trunk but remained trapped within the golden net woven by the mothers of Tondo. The monster screamed and wept and flung itself against the energetic strands without regard for the way they burned its flesh. The scent of burnt glass singed her nostrils. Still the creature struggled for its freedom. For the first time, Octavia felt sorry for it.

In its place I would fight as well. If only there was a way to let it go. But where could such a creature live without harming others?

To free a *mortolo* .... Unthinkable. Worse, she had brought the monster into a mirror. What had she been thinking? What if it broke loose? What if this mirror became contaminated?

The Queen said that wouldn't happen. But the Queen doesn't know about the monster. She thinks I am merely reversed.

The creature's distress disturbed her. Instinctively she hummed the calming song. The clear tones bounced against the curved walls of the corridor and returned to her, flawless. The monster still fought, but she relaxed. Within the mirror, at least, she could sing again.

The calming tones continued to reverberate instead of dying off as they normally would. As she listened, Octavia realized that the notes were changing into a different tune altogether.

The picture displayed in the walls changed as well.

As if from a great distance she saw a large red and gold dragon winging its way toward her; actually, towards the monster. The dragon's cruel mouth moved as it sang. This, then, was the source of the new music. The silver light of the dragon song wrapped itself around the monster's whirling chaos. The *mortolo* stopped struggling. It solidified into the form of a gray, dragon-like beast. The beast reached out towards the silver light of the dragon's song with its horrible claws, much like a curious toddler trying to catch soap bubbles. The beast, much calmer now, sat back on its haunches and stared at the dragon through the holes in the golden net.

The dragon, still singing, swooped down and caught the net in its jaws. It flew up, carrying the net and the monster within it. The monster fell against the strands underneath its body and howled as they scorched its skin. The dragon returned the net and its captive to the ground (the floor? Where were they, exactly?) From its nostrils the dragon blew a healing mist over the monster. The scorch marks on its skin vanished. The monster calmed again, though it whimpered occasionally. The *mortolo* looked over at Octavia with great sad, black eyes. The eyes reminded her disturbingly of Cadie. The monster shook itself, turned three times on itself as a dog might and fell asleep. The dragon looked at her as well, then vanished.

Octavia woke to find her cheek pressed against a cool, white surface. Not white, she realized, merely opaque. Glass. She sat up and looked around. She was inside a long tunnel; a round glass corridor stretched away in front of her. Did it curve? She couldn't see the other end. She looked behind. At the end of the corridor she saw a clear, round window the size of the mirror. Queen Anula glared through it. The Queen shouted but Octavia couldn't hear her. How long had she lain unconscious? She remembered the Queen's warning. She had until moonset to complete her journey. Octavia waved to the Queen and scrambled to her feet.

After hurrying down the corridor a few minutes, Octavia stopped

Octavia's Journey   *by Lynette Hill*

to get her bearings. Her headache and nausea had vanished. Even her heart beat out a calmer rhythm. She felt good. She felt better than she had in a very long time; since she had fallen into the healing mirror, certainly. So the Queen had been right about that part anyway. Perhaps Octavia's fears had been just that. Fear.

She put a hand on the curved, cloudy wall. It felt smooth and cool. She closed her eyes and took a calming breath, then realized she didn't need it. And what of her monster? She took a moment to listen. She felt the pounding of her own heart, the whoosh-whoosh of blood through her veins. The corridor seemed infinitely quiet and peaceful. She felt infinitely quiet and peaceful.

Octavia tried a calling note. Her tone was perfect. The sound flowed out and reverberated against the walls, filling the corridor and rebounding back to her in overwhelming sound. A calming note returned so calming that it nearly knocked her out. Octavia squeaked out the fire chant that Mother and Halfnote always called the 'wake up song.' Mother used it when she needed to wake reluctant sleepers. Glass singers used it to light tinder to spark a new heating fire.

The tones resonated in her glassy chamber just as the calming tones did. Though she'd barely voiced the notes, they bounded out against the curved walls and strengthened. Heat and excitement replaced the calm of a moment ago.

"Stop!" Octavia instinctively shouted in the deadening tone. Miraculously, everything did. She stood in the cool, calm place she'd found when she first stepped into the corridor. What a place to sing the glass, if you could just control the heat and tones.

"Enough," she said aloud. "I promised the Queen." Her words bounded down the corridor, echoing eerily off as if flowing into a great distance. She began walking. Her path curved slightly, so she could not see too far ahead. Her leather slippers slapped against the glass floor, which felt a bit slippery underfoot. The sounds and echoes of her footsteps fluttered around like birdcalls.

The passage looked just as the Queen described. Circular windows notched the opaque walls. She resolutely ignored these. *Walk briskly down to the royal nursery, deliver the message, return. All shall be well. All will be well and all manner of things are well again.* How many years ago had Alma taught her that little charm to ward off nervousness?

Sandrigal

How much time was left? The moon had risen high enough to be seen above the far bank of the river when she fell into its reflection. That meant it still had more than half its night's journey left. How long had she and Queen Anula talked? More importantly how long had she lain senseless after entering the mirror? And how far did this corridor stretch, anyway?

She asked that last question aloud.

"At this pace you will reach the royal nursery in a few moments," a well-polished baritone voice announced.

Octavia all but jumped out of her skin. She whirled around in search of the source of the voice, but saw no one.

"Hello?" she called.

"Hello," the voice replied. It sounded male and nearby. "I'm sorry if I startled you, but you did ask a question."

"Where are you? Who are you?" Octavia demanded.

"I surround you," the voice said. "You currently stand within my abode. I am the entity which inhabits this mirror. My name is Sandrigal. It is my nature to answer questions."

"Well, the Queen did warn me about hallucinations."

"I am NOT a hallucination. May I ask you a question?"

"Go ahead," Octavia said warily.

"Why do you obey the Queen? You are not her subject."

"Shouldn't I help if I can? She said that if I enter the mirror and return, my talent will be restored. And that by delivering a message I can stop a terrible war. Did she lie?"

A moment of silence passed, then another. Octavia began to wonder if she really had imagined the whole conversation.

Octavia's Journey *by Lynette Hill*

"It is only right that I tell you," Sandrigal said finally, "that I am bound by her power not to contradict my mistress. However, in this case I can tell you truly that the Queen does believe your message will stop Samoya's civil war."

"Then why not?" Octavia knew she sounded defensive. "If she's helping me, surely I owe her something in return."

"You owe Queen Anula? For what? Kidnapping you? She owes you, for saving the life of her great-grandson as well as the lives of thousands of her subjects from the plague."

"And now I can save thousands more by stopping a war."

"You *may* be able to save thousands. Seeking change is always risky. If events play out in the way that the Queen believes they will, then the war *might* be averted."

"*Might* be averted? You said she did not lie."

"No, but it is possible that she is mistaken. My mistress believes that the civil war occurred because Samoya lacked a strong and healthy heir. To a degree she is correct. On the other hand, those who seek to take power for themselves will exist no matter who sits on the throne."

"All right. I just wish we had a way to help the poor nurse and her son." Octavia continued walking. "It seems horrible to ask a mother to let her child die. Is there nothing else we can do?"

"As the Queen said, even with the best care the nurse's child only lived another two years."

"If only we could give the nurse's son a true cure. You said it is your nature to answer questions. Can you answer health questions?"

"That is not one of my functions. I am not a healing mirror. If I were, you would not be here."

"Oh, of course. I'm not thinking. The Queen called you a scrying mirror. Does that mean what I think it does? You spy on people? How does that work?"

"Scrying is just one of my functions. How it works … hmm, the most accurate answer is rather long and technical. A number of conditions must be satisfied for scrying to take place. A connection must be made between myself and the subject under scrutiny; also between my mistress and the subject. I must be instructed by my mistress to keep watch. And in order for me to stop scrying, she must remember to order me to stop."

"What sort of connection? How do you make it?"

"There are several methods. A connection can be created by presenting me with an object of value to the subject or through a strong emotion held by one or more of the parties involved."

"I see. Do you spy only or do you have other talents?"

"Well, as you will note, when properly tuned and directed I can take a person from one place to another, even to a different time."

"Yes." Octavia's mind burned with possibilities. "Another time. How is that even possible?"

"Actually, it's not that different from scrying. A connection must be made. In this case, the connection already existed."

"What connection?"

"I hung on the wall of that nursery for many years. I am the party that told my current mistress that the babies were switched."

"Interesting. Sandrigal, can you see the future?"

"Sometimes, but not always."

"Could you take me to the future?"

"Under certain circumstances I could take you to a possible future, if the right connection was made. Going to the future is much more complicated than going to the past."

"How?"

"The past has happened. That energy is set. Unless someone decides to go back in time to change it, of course. The future, on the other hand, is quite fluid. The future is the result of all the decisions people make. As people make their choices the future changes to one degree or another. A few moments are set in stone and easy to see, but most are in a state of change most of the time."

"Are there other mirrors of power still in existence?"

"Mmmm … at least one other."

"Is it a healing mirror?"

"As it happens, yes."

"Can you talk to it?"

"Under certain circumstances. But why would I want to?"

"To ask it for a cure for the nurse's son."

"Ha! You are most determined, Singer Octavia. I do like that about you. But it's not that simple. The healing mirror has to see the child in order to provide the cure, if one does exist."

"If ...?"

"Not every illness can be healed with a simple herb. You were lucky in that, with the most recent plague."

Octavia's heart skipped a beat. To have come back from the *mortolo* with no cure ...

"I thought healing mirrors could heal anything."

"That, alas, is a myth. And are you certain that healing the boy is a good idea?"

"What? Why wouldn't it be?"

"The maid might still prefer to make her son king."

"So? If he grows up strong and well-educated, Samoya has a healthy heir and war is at least possibly averted. If the heir is properly nurtured and trained, does parentage really matter so much?"

"Oooh, don't let my mistress hear you say that. Tell me, Singer Octavia, heir apparent to Verre House of Glass Singers and daughter of Clan Breydon, would you be so gifted with different parents? Suppose you had been switched at birth with another Khelani child. Even with the same training, could she have sung so well?"

Octavia considered this. "Actually, the Khelani are quite a musical people in their own right. She might very well have excelled under Grandfather's tutelage."

"As well as you?"

"My gift ... is more than my voice. I still have my voice. I have great knowledge, but my gift is more than knowledge. Lorraine, Sylvia ... their voices are just as fine and they know more. My gift ... the thing that has been taken from me ... the reason everything goes wrong every time I try to sing the glass ... it is the place of peace within me. That's what I lost. I had a still point within, an inner balance.

"I had a confidence of action; actually, more than confidence, for anyone can be confidently wrong. I had a knowing that I could, no matter what, achieve my goal. I just knew that I could."

"You just knew that you could."

"Yes. If she had that sense, this mythical other girl, then yes, she could be as good as me. So there's my question for you, Sandrigal. How do I get that back?"

"How did you get it in the first place?"

"Perhaps Mother or Grandfather gave it to me. They were always so certain that I was born to sing. I never questioned it. I never, until this happened, considered any other life. I lived to sing the glass. If I do not sing, what do I do with the rest of my life?"

Sandrigal did not respond for a moment. Octavia remembered the look on Clara's face and her own sense that the Queen's attendant wanted to tell her something.

What am I missing?

"Sandrigal," she asked, "If I convince Davina not to switch the babies, or if we heal her child, will that make any difference? Even if we stop the war, will the Queen get what she really wants?"

"That is not a question I can answer. And you still aren't asking the right question."

"So what is the right question? Can you take me back to the beginning of the plague after all, so that I can give them the cure?"

"Better, but the answer alas, is no. The connection to your destination was irrevocably set by Melampus before you arrived in Samoya. Neither you nor I can change it. And the Queen spoke truly. If *you* used *me* to go back in time to stop the plague, we would likely create such a loop in time that it would destroy everything in existence."

"But warning the nurse not to switch babies, won't that also create a loop?"

"Not if *you* do it, no. As the Queen said, your path through time remains one-directional. You and therefore the rest of us will be safe from that fate. However, you might want to consider more conventional perils. How does this action affect Albermarle and the Khelani? How does it affect you? As I said before, a prince is a pawn. There will always be those who seek to use him to their own ends."

"Will healing the boy or stopping the war harm Albermarle or the Khelani or even Samoya?"

"Not ... directly, no. Not that I can see, anyway. Stopping the war makes the future less clear. It's hard to say what will happen."

"So how does stopping the war or healing the boy hurt me?"

"It changes events. There's always an element of risk in that. Better the demon you know, and all that. If the war occurs, well, I can see what happens next. Peace is so much less clear. Many small decisions by the masses cloud the outcomes of everything."

"You prefer certainty to peace? I've seen what happens when the wise become overcautious."

"And I have seen the consequences of daring too much."

"This argument is pointless," Octavia said. "Any choice I make now will be followed by many other decisions by many other people. Each will change the future in some way. Isn't that what you said?"

"Yes. Thank you for actually listening. But the real question you need to ask Octavia, is how does saving the boy affect you?"

"Me? How could saving a child in the past affect me? You just said it wouldn't create a loop."

Release the monster

Octavia stood at the end of the corridor. Through the clear portal she saw a young woman dressed in red and gold bending over a crib. Another crib sat nearby. The room was large and well-appointed. The wide windows revealed blue sky and bright sunshine. The woman picked up a child and began nursing him. She walked around the room swaying her hips a little to rock the child. Her lips moved. Octavia could not hear but believed the woman sang. She was surprised at how closely the woman resembled the Queen's maid, Clara.

"Well Sandrigal, here is the boy. Can you ask the healing mirror for a cure for him?"

"At the moment, I cannot."

"Because the healing mirror cannot see the boy or because you cannot speak to the mirror?"

"Clearly, Octavia, your gift is more than your voice. I do admire both your determination and your attention to detail." Sandrigal sounded amused, but also ... what?

He wants something.

"How far are you willing to go, really, to save this child you don't know? Even if he lives a long and healthy life he will die long before you are born; before your grandfather is born. It is the same with all these thousands of other lives you want to save. Samoya's despair is but a distant cry to Albermarle. What will you give me in exchange for the life of this child?"

I knew it! "You want to bargain for a life? For an infant's life? How completely disgusting."

"There is another life I wish to save. You carry the healing mirror within you. Free her, and I swear that we will do all we can to help you save the boy. A life for a life, Octavia. Surely that is as fair a trade as anyone can make."

Octavia stood very still, her mind whirling. Distantly she noted that in the midst of her emotional turmoil, the monster still slept.

"Free the *mortolo*? Inside a mirror of power? Are you mad? Then you will be monstrous. Or are you *mortolo* already?"

"Espeja is no monster and neither am I."

"Espeja?"

"Listen, Octavia. I am Sandrigal, a mirror of power. I am not the first *Peili potencia* but I do carry the remains of the first within me. I am not the oldest *potencia* ever but I am the oldest currently in existence. I was created before Mother Piasa ever sat on her perch. I am not the last of my kind but only just. Those who fear the *potencia* have all but destroyed us. I survive only through diligent service to my Queen. As she told you, fearful people seek to wipe my kind off the face of the earth; even the knowledge of my kind. The descendants of those who in boldness created us now out of fear seek to destroy us.

"Espeja, the glass infant you carry within you, is a child of my people. I wish to save her, as you would save the nursemaid's boy. Please, I beg you, give her to me and whatever you ask that is within my power to give is yours." Sandrigal's resonant baritone echoed through

Octavia's Journey   *by Lynette Hill*

the corridor.

"The chaos within me? That's no child."

"A being new to this world, driven by hunger and fear; unable to communicate its needs except by screaming? Of course it's a child. Have you never encountered a human infant? Espeja is no monster. And she stopped being a *mortolo* when you exited her glass shell. It is the human who taints the mirror, not the other way around. Espeja is merely a baby, hungry, confused and afraid."

Octavia scarcely knew how to respond to this. A baby? The demanding, raging energy within that had all but destroyed her; the monster that had engulfed her, that was a baby?

"A human infant doesn't try to devour all those around it."

"A human infant is brought into the world by its own kind and, unless something goes horribly wrong, almost immediately receives love and food from its mother. Espeja, like most living glass, was brought into existence by strangers who did not understand the nature of the new being they created.

"*Potencia* eat energy. A hungry adult of our kind will always seek out light. Sunlight, moonlight, candle light, lamp light. Moonlight reflected off an active sea is a particular favorite of mine. In a pinch, though, we can sustain ourselves on anything that generates heat. What does an infant know? Only that she hungers. So, starving and lacking guidance of any kind, driven from her own glass shell, Espeja instinctively sought out the closest source of living heat she could find. You, in other words."

"So, essentially, you're saying that I'm pregnant?" Oh, she didn't like that thought at all.

"No, you merely have a visitor. You are Espeja's host. She is a guest in your house as you are currently a guest in mine."

Well, that certainly *sounded* better.

"If I release ... if I release Espeja, what will become of her?"

"I will raise her according to the ways of our kind."

"Your kind. Living glass."

"Yes. *Potencia.*"

"I'd never heard of *potencia* before meeting the Queen."

And that is all but unforgivable.

Octavia snatched one question from the many that whirled through her startled brain.

"If ... if it's the human that taints the mirror, then why aren't you monstrous with me within you? Queen Anula assured me that that couldn't happen, but I don't think she knew about Espeja."

"Actually, the Queen does know of Espeja. But she was correct when she told you that I could not be tainted. I am quite ancient, intelligent and well settled in my form. You are within me, but still separate. It is the new born glass, still unformed that is in danger of becoming *mortolo*."

The Queen knows ... but Sandrigal said she didn't lie ...

"But, but, Grandfather said some healing mirrors were made *mortolo* later, after they had been formed. They were broken ..."

"No, that is not correct. I don't mean to be rude, my dear, but your grandfather doesn't know everything. In some things, in fact, he is woefully ignorant. Although, those who fear the *potencia* have deliberately obscured some knowledge so it may not be entirely his fault. At any rate, only molten glass, unsettled and newborn, can be made *mortolo*. You yourself know how difficult it is to break sung glass."

"Sandrigal, Queen Anula said that you are quite ancient, even by the standards of *potencia*. How old are you?"

"Older even than Mother Piasa, if she still lived."

"So you were not made by glass singers?"

"Not the sort of glass singers that you know."

"What other kind are there?"

"Today there are no others. Those who made me are long gone. They were sorcerers, more interested in power than glass. I was meant to be a tool, nothing more. Like the glass singers of today, my makers did not understand the nature of ... well, most things."

"Glass singers are not sorcerers."

"I suppose that depends on your definition of sorcery."

Octavia decided not to be drawn into that argument.

"If I release Espeja do you swear she will not try to take me over? I will be safe from her?"

"Yes. By all creation, I swear it. By everything that matters."

Octavia remembered her dream: the dragon singing, the monster taking form and falling asleep. Even with a clear shape the *mortolo* did not look childlike. She thought of Mother Piasa, desperate to feed her two sons. To save them she had put their lives into the hands of her most hated enemies.

How did you make a decision like that? How did the dragon Piasa know that she could trust the human Bartholomew?

"Please, Octavia, release the child to me. I will look after her as you would an infant of your own kind. As Verre House cares for little Robbie; as your parents foster Mischa."

"Mirror, you know entirely too much about my family."

"I have watched you most of your life. If you release Espi she will tell you the cure for the maid's son, if one exists. And consider this: you cannot sing the glass so long as she remains within you."

Octavia looked again through the clear portal. The nurse picked up the other infant. Snot and tears covered his face. Octavia could not hear any sounds from the room, but it certainly looked as if the infant cried. Loudly. The woman bared a breast and tried to suckle the child. After a few moments of squirming the child accepted her nipple.

Octavia thought again of her dream: the singing dragon, the monster's response. Release a *mortolo* into a mirror... Madness.

"I know what a *mortolo* does with its freedom, Sandrigal."

"A *potencia* is *mortolo* only as long as it is tainted by human will. Once free, it is a *potencia* again and not a monster. Espi is a healing mirror once more."

"I did taint the mirror by falling into it," Octavia mused. "That's what Grandfather said. The unformed mirror is deliberately created with a strong appetite, so that it will draw in all the elements necessary to make it a healing mirror. No one ever considered what happened to the mirror once I left it. The shell was destroyed, but not its spirit? Is that right Sandrigal? I carry the mirror's spirit."

"Yes."

"How can I trust you, Sandrigal?"

"You must. And quickly. You're running out of time."

"Espi is no longer *mortolo*. She's a healing mirror again."
"Yes."
"Can she lie?"
"You helped make her, Singer. How true is your work?"

Octavia's head ached. Had she truly considered all of the necessary elements required for the making of this piece?

"As you pointed out, Sandrigal, I don't really need a cure for the boy. From my point of view, he's already dead. What I need is a cure for is Espi and myself."

She sat on the floor and hummed the calming tones.

"What are you doing?" Sandrigal asked, clearly perplexed.

"Coming to terms with my monster." An image of the *mortolo* appeared in the walls. The beast sat up. It was still enclosed in the golden net. It looked at her with its sad, familiar eyes.

"Hello Espi," Octavia said.

It raised a claw as if in greeting.

"Sandrigal tells me that you've turned back into a healing mirror. You may think it's wrong of me, but I still need to ask you for a cure. I need to know what to do with you. How do I cure you, Espi? How do I cure me? How do I free you without harming anyone else? More than anything, I'd like to sing the glass again. Is there a way I can do that? And if you know, is there a cure for the wet nurse's son? Can or should we help her boy?"

A series of images appeared on the wall next to Espi. The first showed the gray beast free of the golden net and flying off with the red and gold dragon. The second showed Verre House shining atop the great escarpment above Lake Kerguelen. The third image showed the wet nurse brewing tea; a pile of candied herbs lay nearby.

"Right," Octavia said. She sang the calming notes again, to stop her own trembling. They didn't help. The next step terrified her.

Unbidden a fourth image appeared in the walls: the moon over Lochsa Rapids, nearing the western horizon. Time was running out.

"Mother Piasa, watch over me," Octavia whispered. She closed her eyes and placed her pearl against the image of the net. She imagined the strands flowing back into her pendant. For a moment, nothing happened. She called to mind the memory of the mothers of Tondo and their strange humming. The golden net vanished into the river pearl.

Octavia's Journey   *by Lynette Hill*

The gray beast stood unbound before her.

Espi stepped out into the corridor. Octavia held her breath. The beast nodded, crouched and flung herself into the air. She merged effortlessly with the ceiling. Octavia watched as the gray beast grew smaller and smaller and eventually vanished.

"Thank you," Sandrigal said, his voice rich with relief.

Octavia laughed. "Espi is free. And so am I. Praise be."

"You are not free yet," Sandrigal warned. "We need to get you home before the moon sets."

"How long do I have?"

"About half an hour. A little more. Fortunately, it's a very clear night. No clouds to obscure the light."

"Can you take me back to Lochsa? My parents will be frantic."

"Alas, no. There's no portal there now that the moon does not peer directly into the whirlpool. I will return you to Verre House."

"You truly have a connection there?"

"In a house of glass singers? In Verre House of Glass Singers? It would be more surprising if I didn't. Come along, now."

"Half an hour. Sandrigal, can you tell the wet nurse about the cure for her son?"

"Only if she asks me. Which I admit seems highly unlikely."

"I thought so. There's just enough time for me to tell her …"

"Octavia, no there isn't. We have minutes."

"Then stop wasting them by arguing. I won't be a moment."

"Wait. All right, if you insist, the child the nurse now holds is the crown prince. He is as healthy as any child can be. Although, hmmmm … Espi suggests that you can teach this lullaby to the nurse, to help ease the boys to sleep."

Sandrigal hummed a few notes in a textured baritone. Octavia felt a tingle up her spine. No mere lullaby this!

"That's a dragon song."

"Indeed. I wondered if you would recognize it. It is, the scrolls say, the lullaby Mother Piasa sang to her own rambunctious boys."

Octavia gasped. "I thought that song lost to the ages."

"Perhaps in your day. But the first villagers of Albermarle heard it almost nightly from the dragon herself, and sang it often to their own children. Such a song could never truly be lost. In the right circumstances I imagine the rocks of Piasa's Perch themselves could sing it back to you. Shall I sing it again for you?"

"Yes, please."

He sang it over and again Octavia felt the thrill of power up her spine. It was a simple round, easily sung by one or many. Octavia nodded along and then joined in.

"And for the ailing son?"

"Yes. His is a respiratory problem. He must drink three times a day a strong tea made from the herb called *Elecampane*. She may know it as 'horse heal.' If his coughing becomes too frequent, she might let him suck on a small candy made by a reputable herbalist from horehound. The wet nurse knows her business. She will know when the treatment has had its effect, and when to stop it."

"Thank you, Sandrigal," Octavia said. She turned and stepped through the portal into the nursery before her nerves could stop her. The maid turned and nearly dropped her baby in shock.

"Who are you? Where have you come from?"

"That is unimportant. I have a message for you."

"What message?"

"First, your son is ill. I know how to cure his ailment. You must make a strong *elecampane* tea for him, three times a day. If he coughs too much, let him suck on candied horehound."

"By all the gods. How do you know this? Who are you?"

"Time is short. Do you remember the name of the tea?"

"Yes, yes, *elecampane* tea and candied horehound."

"Excellent. There is one more thing. Here is a lullaby you can sing to your charges, to calm them into sleep." Octavia paused, but the maid gestured for her to continue.

Octavia took a breath and felt suddenly nervous. Outside the mirror, was she truly free? She sang. Her voice quavered at first but nothing terrible happened. Her confidence returned.

The music left its mark on everyone in the room. Octavia's anxiety vanished. The babies fussing in the background fell silent. And the nurse's bewildered expression relaxed into simple surprise.

"What a lovely song," she said. "Please, sing it again."

Octavia repeated the notes and the nurse joined in. They sang several rounds. The wet nurse even began to sing the counterpoints. Both laughed when the song came to its natural end.

"That's wonderful," the nurse maid said. "Thank you for sharing it with me. I will do as you say. But, truly, where have you come from? Who has sent you to me?"

"I'm sorry," Octavia said. She regretted not being able to explain. "I cannot stay. I must return home before the magic ends."

Trapped

Loud footfalls sounded in the hall outside the nursery. Octavia waved goodbye and stepped back into the mirror. From inside she saw the nanny staring after her, then turning quickly to courtesy to the regal looking women who entered the room. Octavia retreated, in case the room's occupants could still see her.

"That went well," Octavia said aloud.

Sandrigal did not answer. Octavia looked around and realized that the corridor had changed significantly in her short absence. It was much darker. The air tasted stale, as in a room that has been closed off for a long time. The walls, previously smooth and cool, now felt rougher and brittle, like very old glass.

"Sandrigal? Sandrigal! Where are you? What's happened?"

There was no response.

Oh no. I'm too late.

She turned back to the portal. The glass there had thickened and become opaque as well. She could see a bit of movement from outside; dark shapes against the white of the glass. It thickened as she watched. Clearly she could not leave that way.

Well, at least I can see.

She ran down the corridor back towards the Queen's quarters.

Octavia's Journey   *by Lynette Hill*

The corridor ended abruptly. The way back had closed completely.

"Sandrigal!" Octavia shouted, pounding on the walls. "Sandrigal! Please! Help me!"

She could see the walls closing in. *Oh help.*

It seemed impossible to breathe. She tried to sing Sandrigal's lullaby, but her throat closed. She collapsed in a terrible coughing fit. It seemed as if all of the air had left the shrinking chamber. Hands pressed against the crumbling, brittle glass wall, she managed to whisper the notes. Nothing appeared to change, but she felt better. She sang again, a little louder. A cool breath of air brushed her cheek. She took a deep breath and her aching lungs sucked in all the air she could hold. She sang again and the walls stopped closing in.

"Sandrigal! Are you there? Can you hear me?"

Some of the air seemed to leave the chamber. Panicked, she sang the notes again, over and over, as loud as she could. Suddenly the whole chamber shook and expanded. Air rushed in, almost as if the chamber were taking a large breath.

"Sandrigal?" she called cautiously.

A moaning filled the air. The floor and walls trembled.

"Who's that? Who's there?" a querulous voice demanded. It sounded like Sandrigal, but different somehow. He sounded drugged, or as if just waking up after a long sleep.

"It's me, Octavia. We just spoke a few moments ago. The Queen, your mistress, gave me a message for Davina, the nursemaid. I left you to speak to her just a moment ago and now I'm back."

Sandrigal groaned and the chamber walls trembled again.

"Are you all right? Have you taken ill?"

"Octavia," Sandrigal said, his voice doubtful. "I don't know anyone named Octavia."

"Now, really!" Octavia smacked the wall in frustration. "I brought you Espi, the glass child. You took me to the royal nursery at the command of your mistress, Queen Anula. You promised to take me safely home to Verre House in Albermarle."

"My master was never a queen. And he has been dead all these years. No one took his place."

"What? But it was Anula who sent me through you, no more than an hour ago! Here, look at this." She held up the river pearl. "Remember this? I freed Espi with it. And then you taught me the dragon lullaby." She sang the notes again.

The whole chamber trembled in response. A click sounded in the wall. A small hole appeared. On a whim she took off the necklace and put the pearl into the hole. It fit perfectly.

The chamber shuddered again. Sandrigal gasped.

"Ah," he said, his voice clearing. "Now I remember. Anula sent you through time to speak to the nursemaid. In speaking to the maid you changed the Queen's future. And so by consequence, mine."

"I gave Davina Espi's cure for her son. And taught her the lullaby. But what changed? I didn't mention switching the babies."

"Please, sing the lullaby again."

Octavia did so. Her voice resonated off the walls, which trembled again in response.

"That is not the music that I need." Sandrigal sounded stronger. "That is a song which encourages a healing sleep. I have slept long enough. I need something to help me wake up."

Sandrigal sang out suddenly, in the wonderful textured baritone that Octavia remembered. The hair on her arms stood up in response to the bouncy, energetic tune. She trembled with excitement.

"Wow. Another dragon song."

"Indeed." Sandrigal sounded more like his old self. "Now, my dear Octavia, I do remember. I did warn you that changing the past is risky. It is difficult to anticipate how every detail will play out."

"Am I too late? Has the moon set?"

"Not yet. But the events you inspired by speaking to the nurse changed things beyond all recognition."

"But I didn't say anything about switching the babies. I just gave her the cure for her son and the lullaby you taught me. Have we created a loop in time after all?"

"No, not a loop. But the nurse's son, both boys actually, lived out the full measure of their lives. The civil war was averted. Things changed. The crown prince who visited Albermarle was the direct descendant of the true prince. The maid did not switch the babies. The Intan Negarawan owes you his throne, though he does not know it."

"But what happened to Queen Anula?"

"Oh yes. The woman who sent you on your way ... I cannot say what has happened to her. I am still looking, but ... hmmm, I simply don't know. As there was no civil war the noble houses of Samoya remained intact. This gave the Samoyan nobility of Anula's generation many more choices in marriage. It appears that her parents married different people and had other children. This raises all sorts of interesting possibilities, but I don't know what happened to our Anula. The woman who married the Intan's great-grandfather is quite a different person. She is a devout follower of Samoya's pantheon of folk gods. She has no interest in magic or other esoteric matters."

"So where are you, Sandrigal? Are you safe?"

"Yes. So long as no one delves too deeply into a particular store room in Samoya's royal palace. I am tucked away among a great deal of other unused furniture."

"And Espi?"

"Safely stored away as well."

"Sandrigal, what would have happened if we just let the m ... Espi go? If she had gotten loose in the forest?"

"Without some sort of physical shell to hold her together, some home to anchor to, she would have disintegrated and died."

"Oh."

"But you would have been free of her."

"Oh. Did Mother Lara know this?"

"I cannot say with any certainty what Mother Lara might know and what she doesn't. The Khelani have been remarkably successful in keeping their knowledge a secret from me. It is only recently, through your parents' influence, as a matter of fact, that the Khelani have begun to use mirrors and glass. Previously they just looked in the river to see their reflection."

"Is this good or bad, the Khelani taking up with glass?"

"Well, it does change things."

Octavia shook her head. Yes, but was it a good change or a bad one? No doubt Sandrigal would say that that depended on the person and the circumstances. *Fine.*

"Do you have enough light? Are you hungry?"

"We are well enough, Octavia. Thank you. Serves me right, you should say. I warned you of the consequences of changing events, but I did not consider the consequences to myself. Albermarle is far enough away to be relatively unaffected, but I live in the heart of the palace of Samoya. Well, never mind. It's time we got you home, Octavia."

"You did try to warn me," Octavia said ruefully. "I didn't realize that the changes could be so far reaching. Or that they might keep me from getting home. Sandrigal, am I trapped here forever?"

"Trapped inside a mirror? Singer Octavia, heir to the House of Verre, only known survivor of a *Hygeia mortolo*? How could you possibly think such a thing? But we must act quickly. Where shall I send you? Back to where Queen Anula found you?"

"Yes. To Lochsa, near the aviary. I was taken from above the rapids through the whirlpool. My parents are there on a boat owned by my Aunt Lily. They will be quite upset if I just vanish. And how would I explain turning up at Verre House? My grandfather ... is completely opposed to mirror magic. He'll be quite upset as well."

"Yes, I imagine Luciano's grandson would have reservations. Alas, the Birdman's house is safe from me. He does not hold with mirrors, so we have no connection there. No way to enter. The moon is no longer in a position to reflect on the river as it did earlier."

"What does the Birdman have against mirrors?"

"We're the competition, *dahling*. When people communicated through glass portals they had no need of winged messengers. If we ever made a comeback, the Birdman would lose his livelihood."

"Ah. But people still send coded messages by light signals. Across great distances. In some ways those are faster than birds."

"Yes, but those messages have no privacy. Any code created by a human intelligence can almost certainly be broken by another knowledgeable human. At any rate, we will have to return you to Verre House. And that will be a bit tricky. Do you mind arriving there a little earlier than when you left the Queen?"

"I guess not."

"Excellent. This way, please. And quickly."

A corridor opened. Octavia ran down it. In moments she reached a portal looking into her grandfather's empty office. A bit of gray daylight filtered in through a window. Was it raining?

"I do not know if we will speak again, Singer Octavia, but please, do keep this with you." Octavia looked up and just managed to catch the necklace of glass beads as it dropped from the ceiling. She put it around her neck, then placed a hand against the cool wall.

"Thank you, Sandrigal. Thank you for everything. I am so very pleased to have met you."

"And I you. Now quickly. You must go."

Octavia stepped into her grandfather's office. She turned around to look at Sandrigal but saw only bare wall. Now how had the mirror managed that?

Suddenly, every bit of finished glass in Verre House sang out.

~~#~~

Dear Reader,

    I hope you enjoyed this story of Halfnote, Octavia and the other glass singers of Verre House as much as I enjoyed writing it. I do appreciate your support.
    You can, if you like, leave a review to let others know how much you enjoyed the book.

    Visit **www.facebook.com/halfnotesong** anytime to find out what's new with the glass singers of Albermarle.

ABOUT THE AUTHOR

Lynette Hill is an American writer who lives in middle England with Ruth, her partner, and Badger, their cat.

As a print journalist in Oklahoma she watched elephant races and delved into the secrets of professional magicians.

On the web she covered amateur sports and recreation as a 'Going Out Guru' for the Washingtonpost.com's Entertainment Guide in Washington D.C.

As a freelance writer she explained whale hunts and the mechanics of flying squirrels for the Washington Post newspaper, and other publications.

When not writing she enjoys hiking, music and live theater. She is taking advantage of her time in England to explore places made famous through folklore and mythology.

She has climbed the coastline around King Arthur's castle Tintagel in Cornwall and visited his apparent burial place in Glastonbury. She knows where to buy a magic wand in London and has made a wish inside the Uffington White Horse in Oxfordshire.

Her adventures and the *Glass Singers'* series continue.

Halfnote's Song is her first novel.

Octavia's Journey is the second.

Publication of *Prelude,* the third novel in the *Glass Singers* series, is planned for the summer of 2016.

Printed in Germany
by Amazon Distribution
GmbH, Leipzig